After The Light, After The Love.

S C Richmond

Other Titles by S C Richmond

The Alex Price Series

The Community – Alex Price, Book 1

Pictures of Deceit – Alex Price, Book 2

Others

In The Spotlight and Other Stories

After The Light, After The Love.

By

S C Richmond

ISBN   9781787231641

CompletelyNovel.com

Chapter One

Alex was wide awake and in organizing mode, early, there was so much that needed to be done today. First of all, she thought, I need coffee, it was her mantra, she knew she would never get started in the right frame of mind without it. Her mind swept over everything that needed doing. All the wedding clothes for Matt, Lily and herself were ironed and laid out on the bed in the spare room, ready to step into. Lily had been asked to be a bridesmaid, although, she kept insisting that she's the flower girl, not a bridesmaid. Alex smiled to herself thinking that she must have been watching far too many Disney movies, even at her age her mum still treated her like a princess. It was no great surprise that no one wanted Lily to grow up after what she had been through in her young life and it seemed that Lily was only too happy to oblige.

Once Alex had finished her coffee, she threw on her jeans and a t-shirt and drove across town to Angie's house. She had to deliver the bridesmaid's dress to Lily, it had been left with her so that Lily didn't keep trying it on and possibly have an accident in it, no one wanted any last minute dramas. Her Mum, Summer, was already there, with Lily's adoptive parents, Angie and Steve. Lily was getting increasingly excited about the day ahead, she had her hair in rags to create her perfect ringlets, she was taking all the attention she was getting in her stride and loving every minute of it. Alex stayed long enough for Lily to show her how she would have to walk later and her well-practiced actions of the scattering of the rose petals; she was a very excited young lady.

An hour later Alex returned home and pulled up on the drive outside her house, hoping that Matt would be up and about by now, there was so much to do today she could do with his help. She needed to ring her Nan and make sure everything was going well there, nothing today was going to be left to chance; this day had been too long in the making. As she got out of her car the postman came walking up to her, smiling. "Morning Alex, you've got a big day on your hands, how's the bride feeling?"

"Morning Mike, I haven't spoken to her yet but I'll bet she's nervous. I'm going to ring her now."

"Tell her good luck. I'll see you at the wedding, can't wait to see the cake that everyone's talking about." He smiled as he handed her the days post and carried on along the road.

Alex loved this town, everyone seemed to be so incredibly happy for her Nan and many people from the town would be attending the wedding later. She flicked through the post, just one for her, the rest were for Matt. She walked into the kitchen, threw the post on the table and headed for the percolator, there was no sign of him, it seemed he was still sleeping. She felt tired already and the day had barely begun.

She poured him a mug of coffee, took it into the bedroom and woke him up. He smiled sleepily and made a grab for her, trying to pull her back to bed but she was too quick for him, smiling, she left him to wake up. Alex returned to the kitchen, sat down and pulled out the envelope addressed to her. The paper was expensive and the logo on the top of it made her heartbeat increase a little, why would 'The Chronicle' be writing to her? She read on, they had seen her story about Michael Masters and had looked into her work, they also mentioned the underground tunnel discovery and her book about the community, they liked her work. They were offering her a job! A well-established national newspaper wanted her; could this day get any better?

She heard the floorboards creak above her, Matt was finally moving around upstairs. She slipped the letter back into its envelope and slid it into her bag, today was about her Nan and Jack. It would keep until tomorrow and she didn't know how Matt would feel about it, he probably wouldn't be as pleased as she was. She was experiencing a rush of excitement, but would have to keep it under wraps until the day was over, she still had a lot to do, but this was turning out to be a very good day indeed.

She picked up the phone and rang her Nan to be certain there was nothing else she needed, but Mary had everything under control. Alex was beginning to wonder who was the most nervous, her or her Nan.

Chapter Two

Jack had never felt so nervous or as proud as he watched his bride walk towards the well, where he was patiently waiting for her. More than fifty years had passed and now finally, he had to wait just a few moments longer. He had no idea how she had made any of this happen, at the tunnel of all places, but their wedding day was turning out to be the most perfect of days, even the weather was obliging. It was being held in the place he had spent fifty years of his life after he had lost her, so long ago, yet the memories still seemed fresh. The tunnel had been the place where he had felt safe and kept his mind away from the pain of his former life, it had turned out to be his life's project.

He looked around and saw the bunting and the balloons swaying gently in the warm breeze as his Mary walked towards him on the arm of her son in law, Paul, Alex's Dad. She slowly drew closer, now she was almost beside him, this was the moment he had hoped for since he was seventeen and they had first met. Beyond her there were almost a hundred guests watching as she reached his side and smiled up at him. The guests were instantly forgotten.

The well head was decorated with flowers and was acting as an altar for them to exchange their vows, his mind flipped back to the times he had sat here with his back to this well wall, thinking about her, wondering where she was and if she was happy. Had it not been for his family and their pompous outlook, their lives could have been very different. He looked up at his bride, she was beautiful in ivory and peach and he told her so. At her feet were deep red rose petals that had been scattered by Lily who was standing to the side to her, proudly holding the small basket now devoid of rose petals. The rings had been placed on the well lid in front of an empty bottle of 'Chance' perfume, which had always been his reminder of Mary when they couldn't be together. She had given it to him as a gift when she was a girl, to remember her by and since that day it had never been far from him. Mary reached into a small cloth bag she had draped over her wrist and pulled out a brand new, full bottle of 'Chance' and placed it next to the empty one, she looked up at Jack smiling softly. It was to signify the new stage of their lives together. He smiled in return, picking up the bottle and spraying a little onto her throat. He inhaled deeply and gently touched her face. It was turning into an incredible day.

Watching them you would have been forgiven for thinking that they were in the first flush of love, regardless of their age, but everyone present knew that this had been a relationship that was a lifetime in the making. A real life fairy tale.

For all of the trimmings that this wedding had, the ceremony itself, performed by a local registrar was simple and meaningful, carefully chosen words that meant the world to them. The moment arrived for Jack to place the ring on Mary's finger and it was all he could do not to cry with sheer joy. He need not have worried, there were plenty of guests who were already doing that for him. For Jack, at that moment they were the only two people in the world, no one else mattered. The registrar pronounced them man and wife. He leant forward taking Mary's face in his hands and tenderly kissed his new wife, suddenly he was startled by the applause from behind them, bringing him back to the realization that there were almost a hundred pairs of eyes watching them. He looked around to take in the sea of faces and he could feel the happiness and love that was radiating from them. He felt like the luckiest man in the world.

Chapter Three

After the ceremony the guests started to move off towards the refreshment marquee, everyone had been catered for today, there was so much food Alex couldn't believe even this amount of people could eat it all. There was a bouncy castle for the children and they had all made a bee line for it, everyone was having fun. Mary had made sure the day would be perfect not just for her but for all of their guests. Jack and Mary stayed by the well for a while just holding each other, it didn't look like they would ever let go of each other again. Alex smiled as she watched them, it made a touching scene. Jack wasn't her Grandfather but he was the next best thing and she loved him dearly, she silently wished them all the happiness in the world before she headed off to take a look at the triquetra cake that Mary had baked for the wedding.

It was displayed on a large table, waiting for the bride and groom to turn up to show it off, it was in the shape of a triquetra with a heart woven through it. Designing it had taken her Nan almost a year and there had been many sleepless nights over colours, flavours and the size it needed to be. It was perfect, a chocolate heart with a lemon triquetra and it was decorated with homemade sugar flowers and butterflies. Alex had never seen such a beautiful cake or such a large one, there would be more than enough for everyone. She walked back to the entrance of the marquee and looked around at the amount of people who were attending the wedding; there were many familiar faces, she had grown up with most of them. She watched, as they moved off into their own huddles, chatting and laughing, everyone seemed to be enjoying the day. She watched as Summer and Mark fussed over Lily, who was loving all of the attention, Mel was talking with a man who Alex had been told was a new arrival at the tunnel, they looked like they were getting on well, to the side of them was a group of ladies who were laughing raucously. She was just sorry that her Uncle Christopher hadn't been able to make it over from New Zealand but at least she had plenty of photographs to send him of the day. She felt an arm around her waist, the familiar touch of Matt, she leant back into him and continued people watching. There were probably five or six people in total here that she didn't know, a young couple who she should introduce herself to as she'd never seen them before and a couple of men who seemed to be milling around a group of people from the tunnel. She had heard from Mark that there were some new faces in the tunnel community, she really should visit more often, then she would have got to know them. Matt leaned in and kissed the top of her head. "It's all gone so well."

"It has, and look at them, they look so happy, so right together." Alex pointed over to the well, where her Nan and Jack were still hand in hand talking and smiling.

"I hope our day will be as good." Matt said.

"Well... Inspector Jones, are you proposing?" Alex asked playfully.

"Hmmm, I don't know... We'll have to wait and see who catches the bouquet won't we?" He walked off smiling to himself, to join some of his friends and get a drink. Alex felt a ripple of happiness run through her, she really had got lucky meeting Matt, she still had to pinch herself at times.

Whilst Matt was occupied with his friends Alex went to chat with her Mum and Dad, it was a rare occasion to find them in the same place at the same time, her Dad worked away so much with his company they were rarely seen out together. She heard the sound of a gong ring out across the field and everyone started making their way to the area where the cake would be cut and speeches given. It seemed a real shame to divide it up, it was so beautiful, but that was exactly what they did after a lot of photos had been taken of it and its admirers. The happy couple brandished what appeared to be a small sword to cut it and more photographs were taken. Lily filled her basket up with pieces of cake and distributed it out to all of the guests, eating a piece herself as she went but still playing her part perfectly.

Mary walked around to the front of the marquee ushering everyone outside, the bouquet was about to be thrown, she pulled a rose from the hand tied flowers and handed it to Jack, she would keep just one flower for herself to go in her memory box. Once everyone was outside the tent she turned around and launched the flowers over her head. They went skyward then plunged down into the huddle that was waiting with their arms outstretched. Summer stood looking surprised with the flowers in her hands whilst the crowd around her started applauding.

It had been a wonderful day, even the weather had been beautiful. People started drifting off to the marquee where the entertainment would be put on for the evening, Alex was looking forward to letting her hair down. As the light started to go out of the day a few of the younger families started to leave and new people turned up bearing gifts and offering their congratulations. There was just one more surprise waiting to be sprung on the couple. As a wedding gift, Alex and Matt had booked three nights in a romantic, cliff top hotel in Cornwall with a chauffeur driven limousine to take them. As if by magic the car, a top of the range Mercedes drove onto the scrubland and the couple were bundled in amidst hugs and kisses with everyone around whilst the chauffeur patiently held the door open for them. Their cases had already been packed and put into the car without their knowledge, Alex had done it whilst her Nan was fussing over last minute details to the cake. Everyone gathered around, cheering and waving them off, watching the car until it was out of sight and then went back to the serious business of enjoying themselves.

The day lost its light quickly and the whole field began to sparkle with fairy lights and flood lights. Most of the family groups with young children had left already and those who had stayed were in the marquee dancing to the old time DJ, it seemed it had all gone well and everyone was having a good time. Alex heaved a sigh of relief and sat in a chair outside watching the sun go down, listening to the hum of the music coming from the disco tent, with a well-earned glass of wine. Summer and Mark walked towards her. "Great day Alex, have you seen Lily?" Mark asked.

"She was with you last time I saw her, she'll be around somewhere, she's been brilliant today, a proper princess." Alex yawned. Matt wrapped his arm around her as she started to unwind.

"She has, hasn't she." Summer smiled proudly. "If you see her, will you keep her here, with you, we're going to look for her, it's time we got her home."

"Of course we will."

Chapter Four

It was less than an hour later when all hell had broken loose. Lily was missing. Summer was almost hysterical, Mark, Angie and Steve were all trying to console her, whilst all of the remaining wedding guests were scouring the field looking for Lily. The police arrived and made a bee line for Matt who was already coordinating a search of the area. She couldn't be too far away, she had been seen about an hour ago by the well, Matt had called the station just to be on the safe side as the area to cover included a large nature reserve and if she was hurt somewhere he wanted her found quickly. A group of women were searching the tunnel whilst most of the men were checking all over the field and out into the nature reserve. It seemed no one had seen anything suspicious and now the police had turned up they would start questioning the guests in depth. There was nothing else that any of them could do except for keep looking and answer the police's questions.

Alex was beginning to feel panic rising up within herself, Matt had gone into full on police mode and was organizing everyone. Everything possible was being done. There was a police officer with Summer trying to calm her down and get Lily's details, the young woman was having trouble getting anything other than tears out of Summer. Luckily Angie was on hand and able to answer all of the officer's questions.

There was a shout from the garden area beyond the tunnel entrance, several people went running in that direction. Everyone around stopped and held their breath, hoping she was okay. There were two police officers holding up a small wicker basket in the beam of a searchlight, the same one that Lily had been carrying the petals and later the cake in. There was a moment of silence whilst everyone took in what this could mean.

Alex stopped and looked at the basket just as everyone else close by did, she could feel the blood pumping faster around her body as the anxiety set in. It was almost a symbol of the worst thing that could possibly have happened. An eerie silence fell over the group as they absorbed the knowledge that Lily really had disappeared, this may not just be an accident.

After the initial shock started to wear off, it spurred everyone on to look harder and move faster, everyone including Summer who was now scouring the tunnel, shouting and screaming Lily's name, hoping to find that she was sleeping in someone's room because she must have been so tired, but there was no sign of her, Finally, Summer leant against a wall, slid down it and cried, she had lost Lily once she couldn't go through it again.

The music had stopped and the floodlights were being used for different reasons now, there were no longer any thoughts of the wedding celebrations. Alex was relieved that her Nan and Jack had already left for their honeymoon. She would hate them to remember their day like this, they would be shattered by the news, but there was no need to tell them, yet, with any luck Lily would be found safe and well any second now.

Chapter Five

He had kept her company on the dance floor, teaching her the steps to some of the old party songs from his youth, like YMCA and Agadoo. She was a nice kid, sweet looking too, with her pretty ringlets and she really seemed to be enjoying herself. She was of the age where she didn't want to dance with the other kids, she thought she was too grown up, but still wanted to get out there, enjoy herself and mess around to the music. He still liked to have a laugh too even if he was old enough to be her father, and some.

He hadn't expected to have enjoyed the wedding as much as he had, but everyone had accepted him and included him in all of the celebrations. Also since he'd been here no one had asked him any awkward questions or tried to pry into his reasons for wanting to be at the tunnel. When he had arrived he had told them he didn't want to talk about his reasons and they had respected that. He was beginning to understand why people enjoyed living here and on the whole why they were reluctant to leave the community.

Tom knew he needed to do something soon, the longer he stayed here the more he was getting to know and, unfortunately, to like, the other people around him, if he started getting sentimental he wouldn't be able to go through with doing anything against them. In all fairness, he really only wanted to get at one person, Jack, but everyone in the community seemed to look up to him and thought he really was something special, Jack was the founder and the driving force behind the community. He knew Jack's wedding day would be the best time to make the maximum impact. Nobody wants their wedding day ruined, but as the day went on there seemed to be virtually no opportunities to create any problems. It was all going smoothly and then before he had any real chances, that annoying granddaughter of Mary's had gone and sprung a surprise honeymoon on the couple and they had been whisked away. Tom had lost his opportunity, he had gone and found the bar and got himself a drink. He stood at the end of the makeshift bar, gazing over at the other guests and tried to decide whether he should now do nothing and wait until Jack came back, or up the stakes and do something that they would never forget and if so, what? As he stood brooding over the question, he had spotted Lily passing around the last of the cake from her little wicker basket, it sparked an idea in his mind. Yes, he could really hurt them even whilst they weren't here. He finished his drink, now feeling much better having made a decision. He noticed his hand as he placed his glass down, no wedding ring, it still surprised him when he became aware that it wasn't there, it was safely stored in his pocket but he missed wearing it, he always felt naked without it. His thoughts turned to his wife and family, they were waiting for him at home. They had no idea what he was doing or where he was, but his wife had understood that he needed to work out all of the hatred that he carried around with him and he could only work it out for himself. She had let him go with her blessing. He knew she'd be horrified if she had any idea of what he was about to do, he was horrified himself, but it was time to even the score. This would hurt Jack and everyone associated with him. It would rock them to their cores.

He had approached Lily and after he had shown her how to dance to the YMCA they had laughed so hard that there were tears in both of their eyes. He was exhausted at the end of it and sweat was running freely down his face, there was no longer any defined hair line there to stop it. He wasn't as young as he used to be and more than a little out of condition, he went and got her a drink, dancing and laughing was thirsty work. Tom remembered showing his own daughter the same dance when she was younger than Lily, it was always fun, especially when she had then in turn tried to teach her Granddad, who would always get it wrong. Tom had always been under the impression that he had messed it up on purpose just to get a laugh.

They were still laughing as they left the disco tent but no heads turned their way. He had checked. Once they got outside he was surprised by how fast the daylight had diminished and the fairy lights around the tents were sparkling in a myriad of colours, everywhere looked so pretty and dark.

Chapter Six

Matt sat down heavily behind his desk and put his head in his hands. The reason he never had any clutter in his office was so that there was nothing to look at to distract him from his work. Alex had always asked him why there were no photographs or personal stuff there but today he really wished there was something to offer a distraction. When he closed his eyes all he could see was an image of Summer's distraught face, he didn't know how any of the family were coping, Summer had had to be sedated to calm her down. He was determined to find Lily, he would not let whoever had her get away with this. He just prayed that she was okay, the investigation was going into its second day and that was never a good sign with a thirteen year old girl, they should have found her by now. They had looked everywhere they could think of; she hadn't fallen in a ditch or gone to sleep under a bundle of bed clothes and coats in the tunnel. Every hedge, field, building and tunnel had been thoroughly searched with a fine tooth comb and they had come up with nothing more than her flower basket. He felt like he could cry himself, but he had to be strong and find the answers, they were all relying on him.

The strongest lead they had was that one of the new guys from the tunnel, Tom, hadn't been seen since the previous night but that could be nothing, he had helped them search for Lily when they had first started looking for her and he had spoken to Summer, he had been around at the time it had happened. Knowing some of the characters that gravitated towards the tunnel Matt thought that Tom could just have been freaked out by the amount of police that there were around the community at that time. He didn't think it necessarily had anything to do with Lily's disappearance but no one knew much about Tom, so that raised some questions. Apparently he had come down from the North, having fallen foul of an unloving spouse and family. A regular tale for many of the people living in the tunnel, most of them found a happy outcome there though. Matt needed to find out where he was and why he had chosen now to leave. He would need to go and see Mark for that information and that was the last person he wanted any favours from. He often wondered why they couldn't get along, Alex had always said that they were too much alike, maybe she was right, although, he thought it was more likely to be because it was always Mark that Alex went to for information and help instead of him.

He sat up straight; sitting here with his head in his hands wasn't going to help him find Lily. He needed to get moving, every minute counted, especially at this time in the investigation. He would first of all go and see how the team who were still scouring the nature reserve were getting on. He got up grabbed his coat and headed for the door. He would take a leaf out of Alex's book, swallow his pride and go and ask Mark if he could help him find Tom or at least help him to get some information, he was sure Mark would already be looking.

First he would need to run the gauntlet of the national press, who would be waiting outside the police station for someone to speak to them. He launched himself through the double doors with his head down and didn't look up until he reached his car, no one had tried to stop him, nor were there any shouts asking for a statement. He looked around, nothing, no press. He got into his car thinking he'd never understand the media, last year a middle aged businessman disappears and the media were all over it, now a teenage girl and there wasn't a journalist in sight.

Chapter Seven

Tom looked around at the small room, it was grim in the pale, washed out light of dawn, there wasn't much furniture but still the room seemed cramped. There was a small lamp in the corner of the room but he hadn't bothered to switch it on. A table holding a few old shop catalogues with two almost matching chairs at one side of the room, by the side of that a small cooker and fridge and on the opposite wall a small threadbare settee that doubled as a bed. On it was a bundle of blankets that was in fact Lily, she was wrapped up in the blankets to keep her warm and she was fast asleep. He marvelled at how she could sleep after what had happened, even with the sleeping pill he had slipped into her drink.

He hadn't had a wink of sleep, he was too wound up with wondering what he was going to do next, he hadn't thought it through at all. It had all happened on an impulse, he had taken her to hurt the people around her but now he was beginning to regret his actions, it had seemed like a good idea at the time. What was he meant to do now? He felt sorry for Lily she was a nice kid and she'd done nothing wrong but at least he had been right about one thing, this was going to hurt everyone more than anything else he could have thought up. All of those smug people who were living in the tunnel, who all thought that Jack was something special would be racking their brains to try and remember every little bit of information he had told them, trying to work out how and where to find him. His biggest problem now was the police, he had no idea what to do next or where he could go, having this old flat as a bolt hole was a blessing for him. He hadn't known how things would go at the tunnel or even if he would have wanted to stay there, so he had rented this place, it was cheap and far enough away from town that no one would think of looking here, he was glad he had kept on renting it.

Whilst he tried to think through his options he watched the bundle of blankets move steadily in rhythm with Lily's breathing and the movements that dreams create. He sighed … What had he done. He wished now more than ever that he had a cool head like his father, he would have known the best thing to do next. Instead he had inherited his mother's quick temper and devil may care attitude. With that thought Tom fell into a fitful doze, uncomfortably scrunched up on a hard wooden chair, his fleeting dreams just confirmed that he really hadn't thought this through, he opened his eyes and looked at his watch, he had managed to get all of twenty minutes disturbed sleep. Thoughts began to close in on each previous thought and his mind started to spiral out of control.

Lily was still sleeping, he watched her but nothing had changed, however much he tried, he wished that none of this had ever happened. He couldn't change it now, tears spilled down his cheeks. He consciously took a few deep breaths and tried to calm his mind. He raised himself out of the chair, stretched and got himself a glass of water from the tap, he took his pack of sleeping pills out of his pocket he couldn't use these now, he may need them to keep Lily quiet he had no idea how she would react when she woke up. He put them under the sink, hidden behind a bottle of disinfectant and alongside an old mobile phone that he had put there for emergencies. He started to think through his options, finding there were very few. He couldn't hurt Lily but he couldn't take her back either. He'd done it now and he needed to make it work for him, he just hoped that Jack was being racked with worry and his honeymoon had been ruined. He would have to stay here until he could come up with a better plan, he couldn't leave yet, he needed more time to think. Every police officer in the county would be on the lookout for Lily, if he stayed here at least he was well away from Charmsbury. The other people who lived here in the rooms of the shared house were the type of people who wouldn't take much notice of him anyway, if they did ask any questions he would tell them that Lily was his daughter, who was staying with him whilst her mother got on with her life with her new boyfriend. That should stop them asking too many awkward questions. He thought that it may work for a while, as long as she didn't make too much of a disturbance, at least it would give him some time to think about what his next step should be. With the beginnings of a plan forming in his mind he finally drifted off to sleep.

Chapter Eight

Alex was sitting in front of her computer absently tapping away at the keyboard, barely thinking about what she was writing, her mind was a million miles from the keyboard. She had asked her editor, Charlie, if she could work from home this week whilst everyone was looking for Lily. He had readily agreed, he knew what Lily meant to her and added that there was no pressure for her to do any work if she didn't want to. But she did want to, she wanted to find Lily and get her home safely, she wanted the world to be looking for Lily. Mark had agreed to come and talk to her, helping to construct an article, Alex hoped he would bring Summer with him because she wanted to write the most powerful story she had ever written, she wanted Lily back where she belonged. Matt had mentioned that one of the guys from the tunnel had gone missing too, she hoped that Mark would be able to throw some light on that.

She opened the door to Mark and was shocked at the sight of him, he looked like he hadn't slept or eaten for a month, there were deep dark rings around his eyes and his hair was unkempt. Next to him was Summer, looking small and frightened, he had his arm around her so tightly it almost appeared that he was holding her upright, Alex ushered them into the house. Mark had managed to talk Summer into seeing Alex, explaining that a direct story about Lily from her mum would pull at the heart strings of the readers and hopefully lodge the story in their minds. Alex would need to talk to Angie and Steve too as

Lily's adoptive parents. Mark knew Alex had written the initial story about Lily going missing but he thought a follow up with words from her mum might carry some weight. Alex agreed with him but she knew that this was going to be a difficult story to write especially as they were all such close friends.

They sat around the kitchen table, Summer was hunched over, her dark hair falling over her face, she seemed to be just looking at her hands in her lap, she wasn't talking, Alex wondered if she was still sedated. Mark was quite the opposite, he was psyched up and talking freely. To look at them you'd think they were on drugs, Summer may be, but Mark was just trying to make sure that everything that could be done, was done.

He was justifiably angry that Tom had disappeared not leaving any trace but couldn't believe that this was done by him, Mark thought he had seemed like a gentle kind of man who had fallen on hard times, that was why the community had agreed to help him. They never seemed to be too far off the mark when it came to new dwellers, they certainly didn't take just anyone in, it was always discussed amongst the community members and if anyone felt uneasy about someone new they didn't get in, it was simple but effective. They had also taken in another man, Jez along with his girlfriend Lou, they had been sleeping rough for a few months on the streets of Bournemouth. They were leaving too but they had done their best to organize search parties around the area, they had also explained that having the eyes of the public on the tunnel was making them feel uncomfortable. They didn't want the people they had got away from to find them and potentially bring trouble to the community. They didn't know exactly where Tom had come from apart from North, he said little about his predicament to them and the rules of the community meant that no one ever tried too hard to find out, he was accepted and welcomed just the same as anyone else would have been. The only thing they did know was that he had family problems. They were leaving the community but they weren't running so much as moving on, there was no suspicion falling on them.

Alex's phone buzzed on the table, she picked it up and glanced at the screen, it was her Nan, she didn't want to answer it just yet. They had decided not to tell the happy couple about Lily's disappearance until they returned from their honeymoon but Alex was finding it increasingly difficult, she knew her Nan would want to know, but no one wanted to ruin their honeymoon and there was nothing they could achieve from Cornwall that wasn't already being done here. She just hoped and prayed that they hadn't picked up any newspapers whilst they were away, she was sure that they would leave messages if they had got wind of what was going on in Charmsbury. Alex wouldn't have been surprised to see them on her doorstep either. She clicked the disconnect button. No message pinged through, she was certain they hadn't heard, yet.

She looked up, Mark and Summer were watching her. "Nan." She said by way of explanation. "I haven't told her yet." They both nodded but no expression passed across their faces, they had much more to worry about. "Mark have you checked your computer, is there anything that could give us a lead at all, however tenuous?"

"I wish I had something, anything at all would be a start. I suppose the only thing that was flagged up was that a couple of young girls went missing last year in Somerset, there are no reports of them having turned up, they seem to have been forgotten, what I mean is, I couldn't find out anything else about them." Mark looked towards Summer wishing he'd never mentioned that in front of her. Alex made a mental note to chase that story up, now he'd mentioned it she had some vague recollection of a story about missing girls. Missing people in Charmsbury was a regular occurrence, maybe that's why no one took much notice of the story.

"Summer, is there anything you want to say that I can put in an article for the paper?" So far she had said nothing. She raised her head and looked Alex in the eye.

"I want my baby back, that's all. I just want her home and safe. I want to hold her and never let her go." That started the tears again. Within moments they were all crying and hugging each other.

It was all getting to be far too much for Summer, Mark decided it would be best to take her home and let her get some rest, if he could talk her into it. Eventually she gave in but first she said in a low, unusually menacing tone. "If I find them I'll kill them, if they harm my baby in any way."

Alex knew she would have to pull out all of the stops with her story and get this noticed, if she could pull at the heartstrings they might get a better reception from the public. She picked her phone up and rang Matt. "Any news?"

"Nothing yet, are you okay?" He was concerned about her, he knew how much she loved Lily.

"I was talking to Mark, he mentioned two girls that went missing last year, can you check that out and see if they were found? You never know there may be a connection."

"I remember that, it wasn't in Charmsbury though, but I'll look into it and get back to you. You just relax today, please Alex, we're doing everything we can." He tried to comfort her.

"I can't relax Matt, this is Lily. I need to write a story that will make people sit up and take notice, I'll be at home if you need me." She disconnected the call, she knew he was trying to reassure her but it hadn't helped.

Alex turned on the computer and started tapping away at the keyboard but her head was thinking about the other girls that had gone missing, could there be a link, could someone unknown to any of them have mingled with the guests and taken Lily without anyone noticing. She didn't think so but there was always a chance. She closed down her story and went to the internet to start looking for news on the missing girls from last year. As she started trying to trace the stories there were more appearing, she worked on the internet for a few hours and found that all in all there were seven cases that seemed not to have been solved within a one hundred and fifty mile radius of Charmsbury. She was shocked, she couldn't ask Mark to start looking into this for her, it would be far too distressing for him, he loved Lily like she was his own. No, she would have to do this herself. First, she needed to get this story written carefully and poignantly, she needed to make people sit up and listen and she needed to speak to Steve and Angie, they must be going through the same hell as Summer was. She picked up her phone and rang them, Steve spoke to her for a couple of minutes but he was busy looking after Angie who he said was in a really bad state, Alex promised to go and see her soon, she explained to Steve about the story she was writing and he gave his blessing.

It took her the best part of the day to write the article between all the tears she had shed, as soon as she finished and was happy with it she sent it off to Charlie with a footnote, asking that he didn't change a word of the article.

A thought crossed her mind, she reached into her bag and drew out the envelope that held the job offer in London, she definitely couldn't go now, she couldn't possibly leave all of this going on to take up a new job, she would have to turn it down. She shrugged, easy come, easy go, she thought as she scrunched up the paper and threw it across the room into the kitchen bin. "Shot." She said as it landed exactly where it was meant to, directly on top of the bin but there was no pleasure in it today.

She went back to the computer and tried to get more information on the girls that had gone missing, she needed to find out if Lily fitted into the same type of groups as these girls, certainly they had all been young teenagers but she needed more detailed information. She hoped that Matt would come home with some information that could help her.

Chapter Nine

It was a little chilly in the farmhouse this morning and Cathy knew she would need to get the fires going before June got up. She set about cleaning the grate out, she hadn't thought that anyone still heated their house this way but it was certainly cosy once the fire got going. By the evening the house would get so hot that they would need to open the windows to let some fresh air in and there was all the hot water they could use. At this time in the morning her hands were cold but she never felt quite as cold as she had when she had been living on the streets. She had run away from her home a year ago following an argument with her mum's new boyfriend, who was far too handy with his fists and had a nasty temper. Regardless of the tough times, living on the street had been easier to cope with than living in the same house as an angry, hate filled man. Then there was being here, taking care of June, which was much better than being on the street.

It was nice here, June was kind to her, there was plenty of food and she was nearly always warm and clean, she even had her own room. The days were long and there was a lot of work for her to do but she was happy and June told her that she was the best help she had ever had. She smiled to herself as her hands instinctively continued to clean out the grate and start to build a new fire, her mind reached back to the time when she hadn't been so lucky. She had been sleeping in the doorway of a furniture store, as places for the homeless to sleep went, it was one of the better spots, she had always had to get there early, before anyone else took her pitch. It was dry and sheltered from the wind, if she got there early enough there would be a warm draught that seeped out from under the door, she had grabbed warmth wherever she could.

One morning when she woke up there had been a man sitting next to her, she was nervous and immediately pulled herself up into a ball, she squeezed herself tight into the doorway but he hadn't tried to touch her nor did he say anything sleazy, he was just watching her, smiling. She thought he must one of the do-gooders that sometimes stopped by, he hadn't got anything with him though and normally the do-gooders arrived armed with plastic cups of steaming coffee, cakes and leaflets. Sometimes they were religious and wanted to point out the error of her ways to her, whilst easing their consciences with hot liquid and a couple of quid. She was one of the lucky ones that so far had not succumbed to taking drugs or drinking alcohol, so if she got any money she would hide it away under her many layers of clothes, then if she was ever really hungry or needed a bed for the night she could afford to go to a local hostel. When she had been in big cities she had got more money but there was the constant threat of being beaten up or robbed or sometimes worse, simply ignored. City dwellers were far too busy to notice if anyone needed help but they were faster to toss a coin at you to ease their conscience. When she moved to a smaller town it wasn't long before a few regular people would stop by for a chat and just to check that she was okay and buy her a coffee or some food. This man was new to her though, she hadn't seen him around before, she was always cautious around new faces. He waited for her to settle again and then started to talk to her and offered her a hot breakfast at a local café, he had said she looked like she needed a good meal, she was far too thin. He had seemed harmless so she decided to go, he was a normal enough looking bloke, dark hair thinning on top, a little overweight and he seemed genuinely interested in why she lived the way she did. They ate and talked, all the while she was alert and trying to work out his angle, there must be an ulterior motive, she was far from stupid and was just waiting to see what he wanted. She didn't mind, she could wait, the breakfast was good and the coffee hot, it was the warmest she had been in days.

He said his name was Shaun, he was married to June and had been for twenty years, it turned out his wife was ill and she needed a lot of looking after but he didn't mind, he loved her more than anything else in his life. Cathy liked him, he didn't appear to be after anything from her it seemed like he just needed someone to talk to and she knew how that could feel, she let him talk and unusually she listened, she pushed her untidy blonde hair behind her ears and made sure he knew that she was interested in what he was saying. It turned out his wife suffered from something called COPD, he explained, it meant she had trouble breathing and got tired very easily from just doing the things most people took for granted, sometimes just eating a meal could be difficult for her. He openly talked about his wife and she noticed the tears in his eyes when he talked of her illness. It seemed he didn't know how long she could go on for. Cathy had emptied her mug of coffee, feeling quite content with a full stomach, the warmth of her surroundings and the low hum of the radio in the background. Shaun kept talking. "…and I just want the best for her, I love her so much but I don't know how best to help her." He blinked away a tear and looked at Cathy who was now running her finger around the rim of her mug. He noticed immediately that her mug was empty. "I'll get you another." With that he went up to the counter to order more coffee. When he returned he said. "Could you help?"

"What could I do? I don't know anything about her illness and I'm no nurse." Here it comes she thought, I'd been right all along, he wants something from me, she sat back from her fresh mug of steaming coffee and waited.

"You could just help out around the house, I could pay you a little." He pleaded.

"I suppose I could help for a while, after all I don't have anything else to do." She smiled at him; the money would mean she could sleep in a bed most nights. It made his offer almost impossible to refuse.

"Why don't you come and meet her now and see how you get on." His attitude had changed to happy now. Cathy was nervous but felt sure that Shaun was harmless and was being genuine after everything he had told her. They left the café and he drove her to meet June.

Cathy heard a noise behind her, it brought her back into the moment and back to what she was doing. Today will be a good day for June, Cathy thought, she had managed to get herself out of bed and downstairs, the noise she could hear was the sound of June's walking frame against the floorboards. She didn't always need the frame but it did make getting around much more comfortable for her. "Good morning." Cathy said as the lounge door swung open, June smiled. She didn't speak much as she didn't want to waste her precious breath talking if she didn't need to, Cathy was used to that now, in the beginning it had been strange. She finished cleaning the grate out and started a fire for the new day, Shaun had already left for work so they were alone in the house at least until the afternoon. She went into the kitchen to make a start on June's breakfast.

31

Chapter Ten

Matt had come home looking tired and somehow older, gone was the lopsided grin and instead there were frown lines etched across his forehead. Alex was still sitting in front of her computer doing research into the missing girls and scouring social media for news of Lily, with no results. Matt sat down next to her and started to tell her everything he knew about the missing girls from the surrounding areas. One of the girls Alex had read about had turned up at home shortly after she had been reported missing, Matt suggested that maybe it was just that the newspaper hadn't published a follow up on her. There were always kids that went missing but most of them turned up at home within a day or two, when they realized it wasn't any fun being out of their comfort zones, being cold, hungry and worst of all alone. There were however six teenage girls across the region that were actively being looked for after going missing from their homes, all of them in their early to mid teenage years. As so often happened the individual forces hadn't got together and seen the similarities in the cases, so it wasn't until Matt had flagged it up that they started putting the cases together and linking them up. Alex scribbled away in her notebook as Matt gave her as much information as he knew or at least as much as he was allowed to share. There wasn't a lot of specific information, Alex knew he wouldn't be able to tell her everything but there was enough that she could delve deeper into the newspaper archives and the internet to try and fill in the gaps. She knew Matt always tried his best to share stories with her but there was never too much detail, she couldn't run the risk of him losing his job, it was difficult for a police officer and a journalist to live together without crossing the lines, more so now that it was a personal case as he would be under close observation. Matt sat next to her and watched her work, continually tapping away at the keyboard. She looked up from her computer noticing how tired he looked. "Can we eat now?" He asked.

"Sorry. Yes of course." She had been immersed in thoughts of finding Lily. She got up and walked into the kitchen shouting back. "Nothing at all on Lily yet then?"

"No… But at least we don't have a body." Matt immediately cringed, he hadn't meant to say it the way it had sounded, it was just the way he would have talked at work. "What I mean is, that's good news, we've combed the nature reserve and there's nothing there." He hastily added.

"So, no news is good news then." She retorted from the kitchen but he still caught the hurt in her voice. He walked through to the kitchen and wrapped his arms around her. "I'm sorry but at this stage, it is good news, at least we don't think she's dead." He held Alex as she cried.

"I'm going to the tunnel." She announced once she had dried her eyes. "Someone's got to know something."

"Not now sweetheart, eat something and get some rest."

"How can I, we have to find her Matt, she's somewhere out there, alone and scared." The tears threatened her eyes again.

"It's dark now and there are police out looking for her, try and get some rest and we can go in the morning." He wasn't cajoling, he was telling her, she could hear the edge to his voice.

"No, we, can't go, they're more likely to talk freely if I go on my own."

"You're right, but please wait until tomorrow." He had to concede that she would be better off on her own. It seemed he had finally got through to her though. Together they made some food and sat down to eat, although both of them now only felt like picking at their food.

As soon as they had finished eating they put the television on and Alex curled up and fell into an exhausted sleep in Matt's arms.

Chapter Eleven

The restaurant was beautiful, candles and flowers on the pristine tables and tiny sparkling fairy lights draped around the walls. The art was spectacular and softly lit with spotlights, some of the paintings that adorned the walls looked like they could be worth a fortune. There was a roaring fire at the far end of the room and they had been given the best table in the house, right beside the ornate fireplace. Jack pulled out the chair for his new wife to be seated. The food here was reputed to be some of the finest in Cornwall and this was another gift from Alex and Matt, they had been so spoilt and Mary couldn't believe her luck at how happy she was, she looked across the perfectly laid table to her husband and smiled.

"This is perfect isn't it, they've really spoilt us." She cooed. Jack instantly returned the smile, he couldn't believe this had happened either, after more than fifty years he had waited for this and now they had been married for a whole day and he couldn't be happier.

The restaurant staff knew the story, Alex had told them the couple's history in some detail and they did everything within their power to make the couple as welcome, relaxed and spoilt as possible. This morning they had arranged for the couple to have breakfast in bed, so they could relax and enjoy their day in their own time, knowing they would have a day of being pampered ahead of them by all of the staff at the hotel. It seemed everyone had been touched by their love affair.

The couple chatted about how beautiful everything was and how happy they were as they enjoyed their starters of mini crab pots, and they re-lived their wedding day in some detail throughout the main course. "I tried to ring Alex earlier but I couldn't get much reception, I got through once but there was no answer, I hope they managed to get everything tidied up after we left. I hope everyone enjoyed themselves" She mused.

"I'm sure Alex had it all sorted out, I'm quite enjoying being somewhere where all I have to do is relax, with nothing to think about except for you. I'm just glad we didn't have to do the clearing up after the party." Jack said, smiling at her. "Why don't you use the land line if you really want to get hold of her." He added.

"No, I'm happy with just you for company, it really is beautiful around here isn't it and it's like there's no one in the world that matters except for us." They enjoyed their three course meal and each other's company, then moved to a leather couch beside a smaller open fire in the bar and finished the night off with a large brandy before retiring to bed. The perfect end to the perfect day.

The following morning they had got up and been treated to a full Cornish breakfast, the breakfast room which overlooked the sea offered a spectacular view, Mary made a mental note to bring the camera to breakfast with them tomorrow, for today they could just enjoy the view and the sunshine reflecting off the waves. Jack had been tempted to pick up the day's newspapers but Mary had insisted that today was just theirs, the world could wait a couple more days, he gave in to her knowing she was right, he didn't need to let the world in just yet. They had spent the previous day walking across the cliff tops, holding hands and watching the birds swoop over the sea, it had been idyllic. They hadn't wanted a honeymoon but now they were pleased that Alex and Matt had organized this for them, they couldn't have wished for a nicer more peaceful break.

They planned to have foot massages today and to go down into the town for lunch, they were only here until Tuesday and wanted to make the most of it, Mary also wanted to go and do some shopping. She planned to buy something special for Alex and Lily as a thank you for everything they had done for the wedding. Jack didn't care what Mary had planned, he just couldn't stop smiling.

Chapter Twelve

Lily opened her eyes, she was in a room she didn't recognise, it was cold and she pulled the blankets closer around her. Her head felt cloudy as if she hadn't really woken up at all, maybe it was a dream. She didn't know this room at all and as she tried to find something familiar, some of the memories of the previous evening started to come back to her, slowly at first but enough so she had an idea of what was going on, if not why. She had been at the party dancing with Tom, he was funny. She smiled. They had gone for a walk and she had been telling him about some of the things that happened in the tunnel and about how Jack had founded it. Then suddenly out of nowhere he had grabbed her and she had dropped her basket, he wouldn't let her go back for it, he had made her run. She had felt tired, really tired and she couldn't remember anything else.

She peered out from under the blankets again and took in the room around her, she'd never seen this room before, from what she could see it looked small, a table, a chair and what looked like a small kitchen area and it was cold. A new memory surfaced for a moment, a struggle, she was trying to hit Tom, trying to scratch at his eyes. She looked around again from under the blanket, she didn't want to give away that she was awake, her head was clearing fast now, leaving just a dull thud behind, she wondered if she'd hit her head. She tried to keep still, she saw Tom by the sink, he had his back to her, he put something down and leant into the cupboard underneath the sink, he stood up and turned around, looking at her but not seeing her underneath the blankets. He looked worried and like he might have been crying. Good, she thought, I hope he feels really bad. She watched and studied him for a short while; she had left quite a scratch down the side of his face. She couldn't work out why he would want to have brought her here, wherever here was, or what he was trying to achieve.

If she wanted to get any answers she knew she would have to come out from under the blanket, but she felt safer here for now, at least until she got used to her surroundings. She looked around again, she was sure she could find her way out of here and get home, first, she thought she would need to get him to trust her, then the rest should be easy. All she wanted was to be at home with her family but she was smart enough to know that if she just tried to run it might not end well, she had no idea what Tom was thinking or why he was doing this to her. Her mind turned back to the fight between them, he had seemed nice enough at the party but he wasn't really, he had tricked her. Her head thudded and she was aware that he was watching her, she stretched and emerged from under the blankets, he was watching her carefully, as she knew he would be. "Hello." She said quietly and uncertainly. Tom smiled, not a warm smile but a cold, routine one but at least he acknowledged her. "Hi, want a drink?" Was all he said.

"Yes, water." She requested, he seemed relieved for some reason and went and pulled a glass of water and handed it to her.

"How are you feeling?"

"Where am I?" She didn't want polite conversation, she wanted to understand what was happening.

"Don't worry about that." He replied as he walked away from her and towards the kitchen area, returning almost immediately with a pot of yoghurt and a spoon, he placed it on a small table close to her. She ignored it for a moment and just looked at Tom but now the thought of food had been put before her she realised that she was really hungry, she had been too excited to eat much yesterday except for the cake, her stomach rumbled. She grabbed the pot and ate.

Once she had eaten he guided her to the bathroom which was outside the room, he stayed very close to her, she couldn't run, he was blocking her way. The bathroom was at the end of a grubby hall and where the windows would have once been there were boards nailed across the space, the only light came from the bare bulb above her head. She was grateful to be able to clean herself up at least, even if it was the dirtiest bathroom she had ever been in, she grimaced at the old dry, cracked bar of soap with an unknown persons hair stuck in it. She opened the door and Tom was waiting right outside for her, it didn't seem that he was going to let her out of his sight for even a moment.

"Feel better?" He asked.

"No, I want to go home now."

"No, we have to stay here for a while."

"Why?" She asked trying to sound as innocent as she could. He didn't reply, he just guided her back towards the room holding her firmly by the top of her arm. He opened a can of something fizzy and eventually handed her a glass of lemonade. Lily watched as he fussed around the room, bagging up some rubbish and wiping down the sink, she drank her drink, it was cold and sweet, kind of nice. She saw him getting a bag out of a drawer and taking something that looked like it might be a phone out from under the sink. She yawned, how could she be tired, she'd only been awake for about half an hour? Her head felt heavy and all she wanted to do was curl up underneath the blankets again where it was warm and comfortable, maybe this is just a dream after all she thought, I'll wake up in my own bed and everything will be fine. Just before her eyes closed she looked up to see Tom standing over her, watching. "Sleep well." He whispered. Lily's eyes closed and she slept.

Somewhere in the fog of sleep she thought she heard voices but she was too sleepy to understand anything that was being said.

Chapter Thirteen

Alex was getting nowhere with finding Lily or any of the other missing girls. How was it possible for six girls to just disappear? It seemed as if they had just fallen off the edge of the world with no trace. They had to be somewhere and she was determined to find them.

Mark had phoned first thing this morning with the latest update on Summer, she had had no sleep again and had spent most of the night walking around the area of the tunnel, the last place anyone had seen Lily, she had been trying to find clues. Finally exhausted and tearful it was one of the women from the tunnel that had brought her home. Mark was worried about her every bit as much as he was worried about Lily, he thought this would tip her completely over the edge. They had to find Lily. Alex was frantically doing her best and didn't know what else she could tell him, Matt was out at all hours questioning people and chasing what had so far been dead end leads, all he kept telling her was the one thing she couldn't pass on to Mark and Summer 'At least there's no body – that's the good news.' Alex couldn't bring herself to repeat those words to the people who were hurting the most. She sat on the edge of her bed and cried, for Lily, for Summer and for herself.

So far she had put out stories in the newspaper and Charlie had contacted her to let her know that the national newspapers had picked her story up, she was starting to get a reputation in the world of journalism, little did he know, that she had a job offer from one of the top national newspapers. He had also helped by putting the story all over the internet. She could only think of one more thing to do now and that was to get out onto the street and speak to people, she could only hope that someone would recognise Lily from a photograph. Matt and many other police officers had been out asking questions but there were plenty of people that may talk to her but not to someone in a uniform, she could only hope.

Her first stop would be a local print company and get them to make her some flyers, she could hand them around and stick them on lamp posts, she just felt like she needed to be doing something, she needed to be proactive. Lily was out there somewhere and someone must know where, she needed that information. She walked into the bright, colourful office of the printers and met with the manager, Rob, she explained what she wanted, Rob listened to her and gave her a few ideas of his own, he couldn't have been more helpful. He tapped away on his computer and came up with a flyer that was simple and eye catching. Alex had an idea, Rob pushed the computer towards her and she took a few minutes to crop and download adding a strip of photographs of the other missing girls below the large picture of Lily. It was the latest photograph she had, Lily was dressed up and happy playing her part as a flower girl. She wiped away a single tear. Rob took over again and pointed her in the direction of a coffee shop across the road. Telling her it wouldn't take long to get this done.

Whilst she waited she checked all of her social media sites and scanned the internet for any news, she came up empty. She phoned Matt. "Any news?" Was all she said when he picked up her call.

"Nothing yet sweetheart. How are you feeling?" He was concerned.

"Terrible, what can I do Matt?"

"Nothing, we're doing everything we can, there're just no leads at the moment, it's as if she was abducted by aliens. There will be something soon, we can't find Tom either so we're thinking that they're together." He sounded as sad as she felt. "We can't even check our files for him, we don't know if Tom's his real name or where he comes from, no one new fitting his description has come onto the missing persons register. We're stuck."

Alex went on to tell him of her plan with the flyers and Matt agreed that it might be a good idea, she thought that he would have agreed to her doing anything at the moment just to keep her positive, she loved him for that.

Just as she hung up from Matt, her phone rang, it was Mel, she immediately felt bad that she hadn't spoken to her yet. Their friendship had just been getting back on track before this had happened and she could have kicked herself for not thinking about contacting her. Mel would be trying to keep her sister Angie calm, everyone thought about Summer but Angie had been a wonderful adoptive mum to Lily since the time when she had been left at the hospital for the staff to take care of as a baby. Lily had been lucky to end up with such a caring family and one that gladly opened its arms to include Summer back into Lily's life. This was turning into a nightmare. She answered the phone, Mel was in a state, understandably, it took Alex a few minutes to calm her down, she explained to Mel what she was planning to do and told her how much everyone was helping, promising to keep in touch as much as she could. Alex listened whilst Mel cried then she could hear another call coming through. She reluctantly said her goodbyes to Mel and picked up a call from Rob, the flyers were being printed now and would be ready in ten minutes. She drained her coffee cup and returned to the printers.

She walked back slowly, knowing that she had a long day ahead of her. Rob approached the counter as soon as she walked through the door and he presented her with a box of a thousand flyers, he had a nice smile Alex thought absently as he handed them to her. She reached for her bag, he waved his hand. "These are free, good luck with your search and let me know if you need more."

"You can't…"

"Yes I can and if you need anything else, please just ring."

"Thank you." She managed to reply, she noticed to the side of Rob there was already one of the flyers pinned up on the wall, she took his hand. "Really, thank you Rob".

She walked around the town centre for the rest of the morning handing out leaflets, pinning then to notice boards and tree trunks. Every time someone took one they would look at the pictures and shake their heads, no one it seemed had seen Lily anywhere. Alex started to target the shops but again people just shook their heads, although most of them took leaflets to put up in their windows. It was beginning to feel hopeless, she decided she would need to go and see the homeless community, that had not been a successful tactic in the past, in fact it had scared her but this time it wasn't just a story, this was Lily so she would need to face up to her little meaningless fears. She went into a café for coffee and whilst she waited she got chatting to the cashier and showed her the flyer. Her eyes widened and she pushed a loose strand of dark unruly hair behind her ear. "Her." She pointed, but not at Lily, it was one of the girls along the bottom of the flyer. "She was in here a few weeks ago with an older guy."

"Are you sure?" Alex asked.

"Yeah she's been on the streets round here for a while, she used to sleep in the doorway of the furniture shop down the road, that's how I recognised her when she came in."

"What about the guy?"

"I don't remember much, he was older than her with dark hair, a bit thin on top and carrying a few pounds, I can't tell you much else, just another customer. He bought her breakfast and then I didn't take much notice of them. I just remember thinking that it was nice of him to feed the poor girl."

"Any idea where I might find her now?" Alex mentally had her fingers crossed.

"She used to sleep in the furniture shop doorway but I haven't seen her for a while, I have to walk past everyday on my way to work. Why, what's she done?"

"Nothing." Alex pushed the flyer back towards her hoping she might read it now. "I'm just trying to track down some missing girls, she went missing from her home a year ago." Alex wondered if this was just a genuine missing person, it didn't sound suspicious, she was okay and had been seen. It was time to tell Matt that one of the girls was accounted for and alive, certainly up until about three weeks ago.

"I hope you find her, sorry I can't help more." She turned away from Alex and carried on with whatever it was she had been doing before she had been disturbed.

Alex picked up her coffee, leaving the flyer on the counter and chose a table outside so she could ring Matt without anyone listening in to her conversation; she wanted to tell him about girl number six on the flyer - Cathy. He picked up the phone immediately and she excitedly told him her news about Cathy and how she had got it. He asked her to stop in at the station and drop a flyer in to him, although he still had no news to share about Lily. She was happy to go and see him, she felt like she needed to see a friendly face.

At the station there was the usual faces around the place, a couple of officers looked up as she walked in and smiled at her and automatically pressed the buzzer to unlock the door so she could go straight through to Matt's office. It made a nice change from the days when she used to be kept waiting for hours before anyone would even acknowledge her. Back then she was just a journalist and a pain in the neck to all of the team. Matt smiled as she walked into his spotless office, she hadn't been here for a while and noticed one new thing about the room, there was a photograph on the desk. He had never liked to have personal things in his office, she turned the frame to face her and was greeted with a picture of Mary, Patty, Lily, Summer and her, it had been taken on the day when Alex had reunited Lily and Summer two years before, that was an emotionally powerful photograph. She smiled and turned it back to face Matt. "That's lovely."

"It's a new addition, I thought it might help me focus more." He answered. "So what have you found out then?"

"Not much, yet." She handed him a flyer and whilst he looked it over she said. "Girl number six, across the bottom, her name's Cathy, she's been sleeping rough, right here in town until three weeks ago. She had breakfast with a guy in the little café 'Flint's' just off the High Street and hasn't been seen since. The guy had dark thinning hair, that's all I've got."

"So she's been here all the time, right under our noses, I'll be having a word with the beat officers, they should have seen her, we should have known about her." He reached for a file on the shelf beside him. "Her full name is Cathy Jennings, seventeen years old. We just need to find out where she is now." He smiled at Alex. "What do you have planned next?"

"I'm just going to keep talking to people until somebody tells me what I need to know, maybe the homeless community down by the bridge might remember her."

"Want me to send someone with you? I know you don't like it down there."

"No, they may talk to me but they'll smell a copper a mile away, thanks though." She smiled a tired smile at him and got up to leave.

"We'll find her Alex, I promise." He watched as Alex left the room, he hoped it was a promise he could keep.

Alex walked down to the area around the bridge where the homeless tended to hang out, last time she had been here she had been intimidated by the people hanging around but then there hadn't been so much at stake, this time she would do anything necessary to get the information she needed to find Lily. She wouldn't be put off by a mouthy woman or a sleazy bloke this time.

There were a group of the usual suspects gathered around a bench by the side of the river, she'd start there. As she approached them the looks immediately turned to mistrust, they were preparing to move away, she forced herself to smile at them to try and show them that she was not there to cause them any trouble. She handed them flyers and waited to see if anyone had anything to say. They admitted to knowing Cathy and a couple of the other faces were familiar to them but they didn't know where they were or how she could go about finding them, they weren't going to tell her anything else. They were adamant they had never seen Lily. She walked away none the wiser.

Chapter Fourteen

Cathy went into panic mode, Shaun was leaning towards her, red faced, jabbing his finger at her, shouting "You stupid bitch, how could you let this happen! Stupid! Stupid!" He just kept shouting the same thing over and over into her face, she tried to back away but he kept bearing down on her. It hadn't been her fault that June had fallen. She didn't know what to do. June had lost her balance and tumbled backwards down the stairs. Cathy had no idea why she was even trying to go upstairs on her own in the first place. In June's defence she had been feeling a lot better today, it was the first time in days that she had been confident enough to be up and about without her walking frame and she had looked healthier. Now the weather was more pleasant Cathy had been encouraging her to go out into the garden so she could smell the newly blossoming flowers and enjoy their colours. June had been happy, she even had a glow to her cheeks. When she was well June was easy to be around, it had made Cathy wonder if June had any family or friends, there were never any visitors or talk of anyone other than themselves.

When June had fallen Cathy had been in the kitchen with the radio on and had heard nothing, Shaun had come home and found June lying on the lounge floor at the bottom of the stairs, that was when the shouting had started and the accusations were thrown at her. "You stupid girl! You were meant to be taking care of her!" He was still shouting as he turned from her, he went towards

June and cradled her in his arms, trying to get her more upright to slip the oxygen mask over her face. Yet he still managed to point his finger at her menacingly. "If anything happens to her I'll…" He stopped as June began to react to the oxygen.

"You'll what?" She retorted. "I didn't know she'd try to go upstairs alone, she was in the kitchen fifteen minutes ago. Is she hurt?" Cathy was worried and defensive at the same time.

"You are here to look after her, what were you doing?"

"Preparing her dinner, looking after her Shaun!" Cathy raised her voice.

"Not very well! Stupid." He looked up at Cathy and his eyes were full of anger. She felt like running, but she needed to know that June was okay, she'd grown to like her a lot in the last three weeks, she couldn't bear to think anything bad had happened to her. She bent down to help Shaun sit her upright. "Don't touch her!" He spat the words out. "How could you let this happen, I trusted you, you're as bloody selfish as all the others, I thought you were different." As he spoke he was getting more and more wound up and then June squeezed his hand, he looked down, she was okay, she smiled at him. He looked at June with such love but looked back to Cathy with such hatred. "I'll never let this happen again." His voice had turned cold. "Get back in the kitchen, finish preparing her meal… Now!"

Cathy didn't hang around, she did as she was told. It seemed that June would be okay, maybe she would have a bruise or two but it didn't look any worse than that, so she hoped Shaun would calm down once he'd got her settled. Cathy didn't want to go back on the streets, she liked it here and she would do anything she could to make things right. She rushed around the kitchen preparing food and just waiting for Shaun to make an entrance and tell her how June was. It seemed like forever before she heard the kitchen door open but it was probably only twenty minutes. "Is she okay?" She said as she turned to face the doorway. She had no idea how he had got across the room so quickly but when she turned his face was just inches from hers. That was when the shouting and the intimidation really started. There was several minutes of shouting before he seemed to pull himself together, just as she couldn't back away from him anymore, there was nowhere left to go, he pulled away from her slightly. "You don't care, so don't pretend you do." She watched his mouth as spittle was projected in her direction.

"Of course I do, how could you think I don't care after everything you've both done for me?" She looked him defiantly in the eye, she refused to show her fear, a tactic she had learnt when she had lived at home. There seemed a change in him, his initial anger had burned out and turned into something colder, worse almost. Anger she could deal with, this new emotion was an unknown quantity to her.

"Last chance! Make sure nothing else happens to her, do you hear me?" With that he turned his back on her and left the room. Cathy felt uneasy with his flash of anger, it reminded her too much of her Mother's boyfriend but she could understand his reaction borne from panic. This time she decided to stay put and forget his temper she didn't want to run away again. She continued cooking and felt a wave of relief wash over her now she was alone in the room again.

She put the meal on a tray and took it through to June who was sitting up on the settee looking remarkably well after her ordeal, there was even some colour back in her cheeks. Shaun was sitting in the armchair opposite her with his feet up on a foot stool watching the television, engrossed in some crime drama. June looked up at Cathy and mouthed 'Sorry', she returned the smile, placing the tray down next to June on the settee. She returned with a tray for Shaun, he barely acknowledged her, he just gave a grunt, she would like to think it was his way of saying thank you.

She pulled her hair up into a ponytail and started to tidy the kitchen whilst picking at her own meal, her appetite was gone. She looked around, she liked this room it was always warm and cosy, it felt safe. A proper kitchen, that cried out to be filled with sunshine and laughter, unfortunately it seldom was. Cathy wondered why they had never had children, June seemed like she would have been fun to be around before she got ill. Her thoughts were broken by the sound of Shaun calling for her to get the trays. She collected his first then returned for June's, she was holding it at a strange angle Cathy opened her mouth to ask if she was alright but the wary look in June's eyes told her to shut up. Cathy awkwardly took the tray off her, feeling something on the bottom of the tray, a piece of paper, she looked at June and the warning to be silent was still there on her face. She kept the paper flat against the bottom of the tray until she made it back to the kitchen. She slid the paper from under the tray as she put it down on the kitchen table, the first line on the page said, '*Cathy, don't let Shaun see this.*' Cathy decided to put it away until she was sure she wouldn't be disturbed whilst reading it, she folded it up and slid it into her jeans pocket.

She finished cleaning up the dinner things and went about her evening jobs and acted just as she always did, but that piece of paper was burning a hole in her pocket. Still she made herself do the things that needed doing, trying to act normally, and then it was time to join them in the lounge and watch television for a while until they wanted their hot drinks before bed. She went into the lounge and sat down on the opposite end of the settee to June but she couldn't concentrate on the television, the note was playing on her mind. She excused herself and went to the bathroom, it was the only place she could guarantee she would not be disturbed.

The bathroom was everything the kitchen wasn't, it was cold and tired, there was a patch of mould in the corner of the room above the sink and the tiling needed re-grouting, but it was clean. Cathy perched herself on the edge of the bath as she unfolded the letter.

June's writing was clear and pretty to look at, Cathy didn't take time to study the style she needed to know what June had to say.

Cathy, don't let Shaun see this.
You're a good girl, I want to thank you for looking after me so well. I'm sorry about today, I just felt so much better I thought it would be okay.
Shaun gets angry sometimes, I hope he hasn't said anything to make you want to leave, he just worries about me and his bark is worse than his bite, I can't imagine he'd ever hurt anyone. But I know he can have a sharp tongue, many girls have left me when he's got angry and I don't want to lose you, you're the sweetest of them all. I understand your life hasn't been much fun up to date and if you feel you should go just promise me you will keep in touch. Maria was the last girl here, he shouted at her too and then she left but she promised she'd keep in touch, she never did, she was younger than you but didn't work

anywhere near as hard, she was funny though.
What I'm trying to say is I know Shaun can be hot tempered but there's no harm in him. He can get angry but it's only because he loves me.
You're a good girl Cathy.

June xxx

Cathy stood up and tucked the letter back into her pocket, she needed to get back before Shaun wondered what she was up to, she returned to the lounge, nothing had changed, Shaun was still engrossed in his program and June looked up and smiled at her. Cathy had no interest in the program now, her mind was working overtime wondering just how many helpers Shaun had picked up off the streets just like her. She wondered if she should leave, but she liked June and was feeling more confident now, hoping that all of this would blow over. Where else would she go anyway. Cathy decided to stay.

Chapter Fifteen

Tom was watching Lily as she yawned and retreated to the comfort of the blankets and curled up. He felt bad about giving her more sleeping pills but there were things he needed to do, things he needed to organise and she would slow him down. He was sure the sleeping tablets would keep her out of his way for a few hours, he waited a while until he was sure she was asleep before he got his phone out and called his wife. "I need your help."

"Hello to you too, are you okay?" Trish asked.

"I'm okay but I'm in a mess. I'm in over my head Trish and I need your help. I don't know what to do." There was a tear forming in the corner of his eye and he quickly swallowed hard to try to compose himself. He glanced over at the bundle of blankets which was now rising and falling with the movements of sleep. He told his wife everything, what had happened and how it had seemed like such a good idea at the time, he added how sorry he was that any of this had transpired.

She listened silently as he told her what had happened. "Wow you are in a mess aren't you." Was her reply.

"What do I do now Trish?"

"Stay where you are, give me the address, I'm coming over." Her voice sounded determined and Tom hoped that she had a plan. He gave her the address and turned off his phone. The bundle of blankets still seemed quite content.

Tom grabbed his jacket, phone and keys and left the flat, he needed to do some shopping, there was virtually no food in the flat, he couldn't starve the girl on top of everything else he had done to her and she would need some fresh clothes.

He drifted from shop to shop picking up the things he needed and some clothes he thought she might like, he was aware he was stalling for time, his thoughts were something along the lines of, Lily would wake up find herself alone and run away. It would answer many of his problems but somewhere in the back of his mind he knew that wasn't true, he was in this too deep now. As he wandered around he decided to get her a games console, at least it might keep her occupied and there would be no problem with her trying to connect it to the internet, as the flat didn't have any. He also picked up a bundle of pre used games to go with it, the girl behind the counter seemed enthusiastic to get rid of them, hopefully it would keep Lily amused for hours. He knew in his heart that things were not going to be that easy but he felt like he was doing something positive and that was the best he could hope for at the moment.

The shopping was getting heavy and he thought he had been away from the flat long enough, he made his way back. Stopping at a newsagents on the way to get some newspapers and a couple of magazines, he paid and tucked them into his shopping bags. Then rounded the corner into his road and saw a familiar dark blue car, as he approached it Trish got out. Relief swept over him, he put down his bags and pulled her into a deep embrace, he wasn't surprised to find himself crying as he held her.

They went up the stairs and into the flat, Trish turned her nose up at the state of the dingy little room but went straight to where Lily was still sleeping and checked that she was okay. "She's a pretty little thing, what did you give her?"

"One of my sleeping pills, in a drink." He replied, Trish covered Lily over and started to help Tom unload his shopping.

"You shouldn't give her that stuff Tom."

"I know but what else could I do? I warned you I was in a mess."

"But... Drugs... and then walking away and leaving her alone." Trish continued unpacking the shopping. Tom left the accusation hanging heavy in the air. He had no reply to it, he knew she was right. He made her a drink and sat down at the table, this was going to take a lot of explaining but he needed to tell her everything now before someone else did. Trish sat silently and listened to what her husband had done as he poured his heart out and tried to explain not only what but why it had all happened. He could see from the look on her face that she wasn't impressed with any part of his story, he could almost hear the questions crowding into her mind. They were questions he wished he'd asked himself, much sooner. She sat quietly and waited until he had told her every detail and then tried to rationalise it.

"You're a bloody fool." Were the first words out of her mouth, he hung his head but he felt her hand reach for his across the table. "We won't speak of this again but I want you to know I understand why you did it, even if it was a truly spectacular mistake. The most important thing now is that we have a young girl to take care of, she's our priority." She gave a deep sigh. "Couldn't you have just confronted this Jack bloke like anyone else would have done? It would have made things much simpler." She looked him in the eye. "So what do you want to do now?"

"I don't know Trish, I really don't know..." He got up and picked up the newspaper that was lying on the armchair. "Maybe we should look for a new place to live."

"Why… Has anyone here seen the girl?"

"I'm pretty sure no one's seen her and her name's Lily." He casually flipped the paper open and there was the story right in front of his eyes. GIRL ABDUCTED FROM WEDDING PARTY. "Shit." He put his head in his hands. "What should I do now?" He turned the paper towards Trish so she could read it too.

"Nothing at the moment, if you take her back they will arrest you, you have kids too and those kids need their Dad. If you let her run, she'll lead them back to you, same outcome." She paused, "You'll have to keep her here until things settle down, we need time to think of a way to get her home with the minimum of disruption and a way so you won't get locked up." Trish looked blankly into a space above Tom's head desperately trying to think of a way to help him. He sat watching her, feeling completely useless. The only thought that surfaced was that he hoped Jack was feeling as bloody miserable as he was.

Chapter Sixteen

Tuesday morning had come around far too quickly, Mary was reluctantly packing their cases to go home whilst Jack was getting ready to go to breakfast. "I wish we could stay here forever." She mused. "It's so peaceful."

"It's been lovely but it'll be nice to be at home with my wife too." Jack smiled at her, in fact he didn't think he'd stopped smiling since Saturday, he loved the feel on his lips of calling her his wife. They went down to breakfast together, hand in hand. The restaurant staff fussed around them making sure they had everything they could possibly want for their last morning with them. Jack got up to select a newspaper from the small table in the lobby, Mary watched him, smiling to herself, she felt so lucky to have found him again. "Time to re-join the real world." He pronounced as he walked towards her holding the paper in the air.

"Do we have to?" She sighed.

Breakfast was wonderful, they were going to miss being so pampered when they got home. Mary looked out of the window gazing at the sea beyond the cliffs, they would come back, maybe they could celebrate every anniversary here. She turned her gaze on Jack and watched him scrutinizing every news article, she thought her heart would burst with the love she felt for him. Her thoughts moved to Geoff, her first husband. When he had been alive he had always known about Jack being her first love and she thought if he was looking down on her now he would be happy for them. She still missed her late husband and had loved their life together, they had been blessed with a good family, but her heart had really always belonged to the man sitting across the table from her. She still found it hard to believe they had found each other again after so long apart. Peter had been a jealous man but it was still him she had to thank for having Jack back in her life, for that she would always be grateful to him, had the cancer not killed him he would still be in prison now but he had done at least one good thing.

"Mary, are you listening?" Jack's voice pulled her out of her memories.

"What." She looked up.

"There's a story in the paper I think you should see." He wasn't smiling as he handed her the newspaper. "I think we need to go home, now."

Mary scanned the page that Jack had handed her and there she saw a story about missing girls in the Charmsbury area, she glanced at the top of the piece, written by Alex Price was printed above it. She smiled. "She's written for the nationals, good for her."

"Just read the story!" He almost snapped.

As she read the story, her face dropped and her expression turned serious. "Oh Jack…" It took her a moment to form the words. "It's Lily, taken from our wedding party. Why hadn't Alex told us?"

"She probably didn't want to worry us on our honeymoon. I wish she had though, we need to get back and find out what's going on.

"Yes, you call a taxi and get them to pick us up as soon as they can get here. I'm going to call Alex." Mary dropped a kiss on Jack's head and went back to the room to make some calls. Jack went to the reception to get the head receptionist Kate to check on any updates on the story for him, she scanned the internet, there were none, it seemed Lily was still missing.

Forty minutes later, unable to contact Alex or Matt by phone they were climbing into the back of a taxi ready to return home and find out what had been going on in their absence.

Chapter Seventeen

Trish left Tom in the flat with Lily, she knew he would look after her well. She needed to get out, that 'bloody fool of a husband' were the words going around her head. Now he had made it her problem and left her to sort it all out. Yes, he's been angry with the tunnel community and Jack but she couldn't believe he'd been so stupid. What did he think he was going to do with a teenage girl? Oh she knew what everyone would think but he was lucky that she knew him better than that. What she couldn't understand was what the hell had been going through his mind when he actually thought that abducting a child would be a good idea. She got into the car and took some deep breaths trying to calm herself down before she drove home. The drive would take a few hours but she didn't want to wind herself up, the kids would notice and want to know what was wrong, already they would be wondering why she hadn't been at home last night. She thought the drive would calm her down she needed some distance between her and Tom at the moment.

She just couldn't get her head around what he'd done, in all the years they had been together he'd never had so much as a parking ticket and now he'd abducted a child. She thumped the steering wheel, she needed to calm down, start thinking clearly and work out a way to minimise the problem.

First of all she needed a way to keep the child quiet, they would want to move around and leave her alone at times, if she wasn't sedated the risk of her running away would be too high or she might start working out where she was and start making plans to get them caught, after all there were other people living in the same building. They needed to buy some time. The sleeping tablets had worked up until now but they were no good for her and too unpredictable for them. Her mind was rapidly sifting through all of their options, her medical knowledge made it easy to rule out many of the drugs on the market, the more she thought the more there seemed like there was only two options. By the time she was nearing home she had narrowed it down to just one.

The drive had unwound her and cleared her mind just as she'd hoped it would, now she was thinking more clearly she knew what she had to do, she had a shift at the hospital tonight and hopefully should be able to lay her hands on all of the things she needed. She just had to pray that no one would see her. She would pull a few sick days afterwards, return to Tom's flat and hopefully that would buy them enough time to come up with a plan about what they should do with Lily.

She walked into their home feeling much more prepared.

Chapter Eighteen

Alex passed on everything she had been told to Matt, who was sitting on the opposite settee listening to her, thinking how good it felt to be working together. There wasn't much to tell but over a cup of coffee she told him what she had come up with. "The homeless crew wouldn't say much, apart from acknowledging that they knew Cathy, so I walked away, a few minutes later one of them caught up with me."

"Did they ask you for money?" Matt interrupted.

"Yes but just enough for some food, anyway, he said he had seen Cathy with a guy at the café, description matched what the cashier at the café told me, average guy, dark hair, a little overweight. Not much to go on but he carried on and admitted that he'd watched them because he had been jealous that she was in the warm, eating and he wasn't." Alex paused. "I got the impression he liked her a little bit too."

"What else did he say?" Matt was getting impatient, he didn't care about the guy's feelings he just wanted the information. He sipped at his coffee.

"Well he watched them for a while and saw them leave the cafe and get into a dark blue Corsa with a 2008 plate. It turned out even though he'd been homeless for a while he still loved cars, it was one of the few interests he still had." Alex was looking pleased with her information.

"Did he manage to get any other part of the registration?"

"Unfortunately not, he couldn't remember it, just the year, but it's a start isn't it?" She looked at Matt who was writing something in his notebook.

"What was his name?" He asked.

"John was all he'd give me and I'm fairly sure it's not really his name."

"Okay I'll see what we can come up with, it's a long shot though." Matt thought that at least they had something to look into now which was an improvement on ten minutes ago, when he had nothing. The young couple from the tunnel along with Tom and Lily had all vanished into thin air but they may be able to find out something if they could turn up Cathy Jennings.

Alex's phone sprung into life, crashing into her thoughts, she looked down, it was her Nan, this time she answered it. "Hi Nan, are you having a good time?" She tried to sound upbeat and normal.

"Why didn't you tell us Alex?" She sounded really upset.

"You were on honeymoon Nan, we all just wanted you to enjoy yourselves."

"But it's Lily, you should have told us, we'd have come straight home and helped."

"Nan, there's nothing you could have done, we're all sitting around here not knowing what to do, at least whilst you didn't know you were enjoying yourselves, I hope."

"It was lovely but we're on our way back now, we're already in the taxi. We love you Alex." Mary was close to tears, Alex could hear it in her voice. "Is there no news at all?" Mary added.

"No, nothing… nothing at all on Lily but we may have a lead on one of the other missing girls, I'll tell you all about it when you get back, try not to worry we're doing everything we can." They said their goodbyes and Alex sat hugging her mug of coffee wondering when this nightmare would end.

Matt put his arms around her, kissed her and left to go back to work. She put her drink down and feeling determined she decided it was time to go to the tunnel and see if anyone could tell her anything about Tom, maybe they would remember something if they kept talking about him enough. She could only hope.

When she got there, they couldn't wait to help, anticipating Alex's visit they had already written down everything they could remember about Tom, any snippets of information that he had talked about, which unfortunately wasn't very much, they didn't even have a last name for him. He was a northerner and he'd left his family, so somewhere out there was a wife and two children that might be looking for their husband and father, it was going to be her job to try and find them. She asked them if they'd seen a blue Corsa in the area but no one had, but they all promised to keep an eye open for it.

In her head she was already planning a story, she would go into the office and write it up. If there was a blue Corsa with a 2008 registration anywhere in the area they would find it. With the tunnel community and the police out looking for it and her published story in the newspaper it wouldn't be able to move above six inches into town without being spotted, then hopefully they could find Lily.

Alex drove to the newspaper office, everyone there seemed concerned about her and pleased to see her. She headed for her desk, she didn't feel like chatting with the other journalists, today she just wanted to write, they left her alone, sensing her mood. She was quickly followed by Charlie who was looking concerned. "What are you doing here?" He demanded.

"Nice welcome Charlie, you should work on that." She replied feeling fired up for the first time since Lily had gone missing.

"Are you okay?" He may be a grumpy old copy editor who she'd given more than enough headaches to, but he had a heart of gold.

"I will be, when we find the lowlife that's taken Lily."

"Okay but you know you don't need to be here, don't you?"

"Thanks Charlie, but I have a story that needs to be written." She said. Charlie walked away shaking his head, he knew better than to try and change Alex's mind about anything. She typed furiously, getting everything down on paper, checked it once and sent it down the line to Charlie, she couldn't do anything else now, but she felt better, she felt like she had done something positive.

She left the office, got some shopping and went to her Nan's house to prepare some food for them to come home to. They would have been worried and she was sure they wouldn't have stopped for anything to eat on the way back. Her cooking was nowhere near her Nan's standards but there must be some hereditary magic she could call on and as long as she kept busy she felt okay.

Chapter Nineteen

Shaun had started watching her more carefully, she was aware of his gaze every time she moved, it felt like he no longer trusted her since June had had her fall. Cathy wanted to give him the benefit of the doubt; maybe she was feeling oversensitive since June had warned her about his temper or she thought it more likely that she was justified in feeling the way she did. He had stopped chatting with her as he normally did each morning, he just watched her with what seemed like a scowl on his face. She was beginning to feel nervous around him.

June, on the other hand was acting as if nothing had happened, but her breathing was laboured, she didn't seem to notice Shaun's mood, some days were better than others for her but she always made Cathy feel welcome, that was the very reason that Cathy had decided to stay here. Initially she had wondered if Shaun was looking for more from her than just being a carer but she found that hard to believe, seeing how loving he was with June, since she had been here he certainly hadn't tried to get anywhere near her. Now she thought as long as she kept her mouth shut and her head down and took good care of June that she would be fine, Shaun was just being moody, she hoped.

This morning he had been watching her as she prepared June's breakfast, it was as if he wanted to say something but decided against it. There were still moments she found herself torn between staying and going, June had mentioned other carers, particularly one called Maria.

Cathy thought she may try to talk to June about her when Shaun left the house. He would go out soon, he worked a lot from home but every morning he went out for a few hours. She realised that he had never said what he did for a job and she'd never heard him talk to June about it, which seemed odd as everything else he did he relayed to June in minute detail. It was something else she would ask June when he had gone out.

June shuffled into the kitchen holding on tight to her walking frame and her breath was audible, she was gasping to get some air, today was going to be a bad day for her. Cathy thought she should gauge her mood before she tried to speak to her. Shaun helped her get settled and talked to her about the things he'd heard on the news this morning before kissing her and saying he'd be back soon. She tried to say something that sounded like "Where?" Or maybe it had been when? But she was so breathless it came out as more of a wheeze than a word. He just smiled at her and left them together in the warm kitchen. Cathy placed June's breakfast in front of her and sat down on a chair opposite as she sorted out some fresh nasal prongs for her oxygen, it looked like she was going to need them today. She looked up at June who was attempting between breaths to eat some food. "June... the letter..." She asked but was interrupted by June.

"Shhh..." Was all she could manage.

"Do you think I should leave?" Cathy asked. June just shrugged. Watching June, Cathy wondered how long she could go on like this, she didn't know anything about June's disorder but it was difficult to watch her when she had days this bad. She knew in her heart she couldn't leave, June could never cope on her own, although Cathy was beginning to get the impression that if she left, she would soon be replaced by a new young home help. She was curious to know what had happened to the last girl who had been there, June had seemed concerned about her. "So you never heard from Maria again, didn't she give you any idea where she might go?" Cathy asked. June just shook her head. "Oh well I suppose we'll never know then." Cathy gave up, sometimes trying to talk to June was difficult, apart from her medical problems Cathy thought it seemed she didn't have much in the way of conversational skills. June would smile readily enough but she seemed to like her own company, if she hadn't been ill Cathy thought she would probably still have stayed in the house alone and been a recluse.

She went back to cleaning up the kitchen. The back door clicked and Shaun appeared in the room, just moments after June had moved into the lounge. "You're home early." Cathy said.

"Yes." He replied, he didn't look happy and with his one single word Cathy started to feel on edge, she'd felt like this since last night, since she had read June's letter. "How is she?"

"Nasal prongs today." She replied.

"Well that's your fault, she shouldn't have been trying to do so much… that's what you're here for." He sniped.

"I can't watch her every minute Shaun." Once the words were out she knew she should have kept her mouth shut.

"We give you a home, food, money and this is how you repay us!" He was looking for an argument.

"Money! I haven't seen a penny and as much as I like June and I really do, you can't expect me to do everything and watch her twenty four hours a day, I've not been out of this house for even an hour since I came here!" She never had known how to keep her mouth in check, but she felt better now she'd had her say.

"You've been well looked after, you ungrateful cow." On the last word his demeanour changed, the anger had passed and now it was replaced with a cold silent look. "Okay, later we will go to the bank and I'll pay you what I owe you." He turned and strode out of the room.

She didn't know what to think, Shaun's moods were erratic but at least it seemed like she would be paid after all, she couldn't help feeling uneasy about it though, she thought that maybe he'd throw some money at her and dump her back on the streets. With some money in her pocket she would survive, she'd been in worse positions.

The rest of the morning went on much as any other, there was lots of work to be done and she kept a careful eye on June who seemed to be more subdued as the morning went on. She had tried to speak to her on all manner of subjects, staying away from anything that may upset her, but today it seemed she wasn't in the mood for communicating. Cathy began to wonder if Shaun was abusive towards her but she discredited that line of thought, he always spoken about June as if she was his queen, it was hard to believe that he would allow his moods to affect her in any way.

Mid-afternoon arrived and Shaun true to his word told Cathy to get ready as soon as she had prepared June's tea and they would go off to the bank. He seemed in a better mood this afternoon. On the other hand June was incredibly quiet and wouldn't even make eye contact with Cathy, she must still be feeling awkward after her fall yesterday.

They drove into town, Shaun hardly spoke at all, so she just looked out of the window and watched the countryside roll by, she realized that they must be a long way outside Charmsbury, this was a place she'd never seen before, she didn't recognize anywhere. She had thought they were close to town, they must have been too busy chatting when he had first brought her out here for her to take much notice. They came to a town centre she didn't know, she looked for a sign but couldn't find one, Shaun just carried on driving through it. "I thought we were going to the bank?" She said.

"I have to pick something up for work first, don't worry we'll stop at the bank on the way back." He replied. That was when she remembered she had no idea what he did for a living, maybe she would find out now.

They pulled into a car park on a quiet, small industrial estate, the warehouse they were parking outside didn't look like there was much industry going on inside, they slowly crunched across the gravel and the car stopped. Weeds were encroaching on the parking area and the warehouse gave the impression of being completely empty. It had three broken windows that she could see and graffiti across a large area of the wall below the windows, apparently Mitch was very popular in the area considering the size of his tags. Shaun spoke, jolting her out of her thoughts. "Come in with me, I just have to pick something up." She looked around uncertain of what to do, but curiosity got the better of her, she wanted to find out what went on behind the walls of this dilapidated building. Her mind even played with the idea that he was a drug dealer, before she told herself to stop being stupid.

She followed Shaun as he rolled up one side of a large metal doorway, she walked into a large dirty area and heard him roll the door back into place behind her, it squealed in response to his touch. There were a few old desks but there was not much else that she could see in the gloom and there was an odd smell. She turned to Shaun to mention the strange smell just as she saw something long and heavy coming towards her, the next thing she knew was the floor coming up to meet her.

Chapter Twenty

After Alex had explained everything to her Nan and Jack they sat in shocked silence, no one knowing what else to say. Alex's phone rang and cut into their thoughts. "Matt, where are you?"

"Still at work, we got a lead on the blue Corsa, we asked around the shopkeepers and one of them said they thought they'd seen it, they checked their security cameras and we have a registration." He sounded pleased.

"That's the best news I've had all day. So what happens now?" She asked.

"We're going to find out more about the owner, you know I can't tell you any more than that." There was a hint of a smile in his voice.

"Good luck sweetheart, I'm at Nan's when you've finished up." Alex knew he wanted to see Jack and Mary as much as she had. They said their goodbyes and she relayed the news to Jack and her Nan.

The news lifted the mood enough that they started to talk about the honeymoon, how wonderful the hotel was and how spoilt they had been by the staff, they were almost glowing when they described the hotel. Alex shared her news about the job offer from London with them too, but made sure they knew it was a secret, because she hadn't mentioned it to Matt yet. She wasn't going to take the job, so he didn't need to know anything about it until all of this was out of the way. She didn't want him to feel that her life with him wasn't enough and she thought he just might see it that way, even though that was a long way from the truth.

Matt turned up at Jack and Mary's early in the evening with news that the car was being looked for, it hadn't been at the address it was registered to when some officers went to check and no one had been at home. He had stationed a couple of officers outside the house so they could check it out when and if it did turn up. It was registered to a Shaun Brown, he was unknown to the police, there had been no previous dealings with him anywhere across the country, they weren't even sure that he had done anything wrong. It wasn't yet illegal to buy a homeless person breakfast and give them a lift somewhere. He'd taken a chance putting two officers outside the house, the police budget would have to cope with it, this case was personal and if it caused any trouble for him he had already decided he would pay for it out of his own pocket, it was the only lead they had to follow at the moment.

Alex had been stunned that he had trusted her with so much information, normally he'd tell her things but not give out any of the details, she also knew that she couldn't use any of this information for a story. Matt had pointed out that this guy, Shaun Brown, may have done nothing wrong but Alex couldn't wait to find out.

They were staying at her Nan's for dinner, Alex thought it might be a nice idea to invite Mark and Summer along, she could keep them in the loop and at the moment she also thought that company would be the best thing for both of them.

An hour later everyone had gathered together. Alex was the one to pass on the news that Matt had come home with, just omitting the name. It seemed to improve their mood, Mark visibly relaxed although it was going to take a lot more to cheer Summer up, she wouldn't settle until she had her little girl back. They sat and talked everything through, there were more tears but Summer was beginning to think more rationally, which meant everyone could have a conversation around her now. It was a good sign, she even showed a little interest in Jack and Mary's honeymoon, they had all hoped that the happier conversation would offer a small distraction for her, and it did for a while. After about fifteen minutes she began to lose interest in the casual chat and turned inward again, she didn't say another word that evening but they all saw the silent tears.

It was at nine o'clock that Matt's phone rang, he looked at the display and answered it immediately, listening intently to what he was being told. After a few minutes he thanked whoever was on the other end of the line and disconnected the call and turned to face everyone else in the room. "The car returned to the house around twenty minutes ago, the officers went and spoke to Shaun Brown but it doesn't look like there's any connection." Matt looked at Summer, he felt so sorry for her.

"What did he say?" Alex asked.

"It turns out that he admitted to talking to Cathy Jennings, although he said he didn't know that was her name, he took her for breakfast and she had asked him to give her a lift to just outside Exeter, which he did and dropped her off there, he said he had just felt sorry for her. The officers thought he was being straight with them. He lives with his disabled wife and nothing seemed out of the ordinary."

"Is that it then?"

"Yes, I'm sorry it is." He could feel the previously expectant eyes turning away from him.

"Will you be keeping an eye on him?" Jack asked, up until then he had been very quiet.

"There's no reason to Jack, he's just a normal guy who's done nothing wrong from what the officers there can gather."

"Maybe he's just covering up." Alex added, trying to support Jack's point of view. "Can't you watch him for a day or two?"

"I can't do that sweetheart, there's just no grounds for it." Matt looked as downcast as everyone else.

"So what do we do now?" Alex asked after a long thoughtful silence had fallen over the room.

"We wait… there's nothing else to do. We keep asking questions and wait until we find something." Matt answered. That seemed to end the discussion. Mark and Summer made their excuses and left and the news was no further ahead than when they'd arrived. What was worse was that they'd had a small hope, now even that had diminished.

Alex and Matt went home. There was no conversation on the way, Alex was deep in thought, she had heard Matt mention that Shaun Brown lived in a small village between Charmsbury and Exeter, she knew his name and the make of car and if it was just a small village she was sure she could find out something. She didn't have the same rules tying her hands as Matt did. She felt a hand on her shoulder, Matt was leaning into her. "Are you okay?" He asked as he kissed her.

"Yes, Just thinking."

"Not thinking of trying anything daft I hope? Last time you followed your thoughts I had to track you down to Thailand." He smiled.

"Okay, but I do get results, don't I." She smiled back at him and offered a look of pure innocence.

"Let us take care of this Alex, we'll get to the bottom of it."

"Eventually." She muttered under her breath.

Chapter Twenty One

Cathy opened her eyes, it was dark, she was on a hard surface, it felt like the floor, as her mind grappled with trying to work out where she was, she put her hands down on the floor, pieces of grit dug painfully into her palms. She winced as she tried to push herself upright that was when what had happened came back to her, she recalled being hit, she must still be in the warehouse. Shaun had hit her with some kind of tube or bar and left her here, she could barely believe it as the memories resurfaced. She gingerly raised her hand to the right side of her head and found a raw, tender area just above her ear, she felt a crust under her fingers and winced at the pain that shot through her head. She must have bled from the force of the blow, she moved her fingers gingerly across her skull, feeling lumps of blood matted into her hair. She pulled her knees into her body, tightly hugging them and started to cry, loud, painful sobs.

When her crying was done, she felt exhausted but she could feel a determination building inside her, she mentally told herself to pull herself together and find a way out of here. She tried to move but her body was stiff and ached, slowly but eventually she managed to get to her feet, she felt a little light headed but apart from that and the wound on her head she was okay. Slowly she started to feel her way around the area she was in, it didn't take her long, it transpired that she was in a small room with a dirty floor and boarded over windows. She tried to get her fingers around and under the boards, she couldn't get any purchase on them, they were solidly fixed. She followed the wall around and found a door handle, a lever style but it too was solid, she couldn't make it move. She went around the room again, with more confidence this time, she was beginning to map out her surroundings, she found some pipes that were running from floor to ceiling in the corner of the room close to the door, apart from that there was nothing else in the room that she could feel. She sat back down on the floor, she'd just have to wait and hope that Shaun came back, there was absolutely nothing else she could do. Thinking of Shaun her hand shot to her back pocket and she heaved a sigh of relief when she felt the folded up piece of paper, at least he didn't know that June had tried to tell her to leave if she felt that she wanted to. Cathy didn't want him to take anything out on June, she wouldn't stand a chance against him. She slumped back against the wall and waited.

It seemed like hours and still there were no sounds around her, the absolute silence was driving her crazy, she had always hated it. She wished she'd taken more notice when they drove here, although, at that moment she couldn't think what help it would be to know where she was, when she couldn't even get out of the room. It may feel like she had been there for hours but in truth she had no idea how long it had been, there was no way of telling, no light, no clues. She wished she had a digital watch, one of those that lit up but she'd never felt the need to wear a watch, why would she, no one was ever expecting her home at a particular time. Her thoughts were becoming random and she could feel panic bubbling under the surface of her consciousness, at least talking to herself was better than the silence.

Before much longer she noticed a splinter of light coming through between the boards, dull at first but it was trying to force its way around the boards. It wasn't much, but after hours of pitch blackness it was a blessing, now she could see a gap and wondered if she might be able to prise it open a little more, now she could at least visually distinguish the shape of the room. She felt around the floor, she was looking for stones or something sharp which she could use to try and attack the wooden boards with if only to let more light in, but it seemed there were only small pieces of grit on the floor. In her frustration she cupped her hands around her mouth and shouted "Help!" She knew it was futile but it made her feel better and she had released some of her pent up emotions, she did it again. She sat down, trying desperately to think of a way to get out of this mess. Then she heard something, she was sure of it, a scraping followed by a tapping, Cathy moved towards the door, Shaun must have returned, then there was silence again, her only plan now was to hope that as he came through the door she could attack him and get away. Tap, tap and then silence again but she was sure it had sounded louder by the door. Scrape, tap, tap, tap. There it was again, her ears zoned in on the sound and she moved towards the pipes in the corner of the room and waited, the next time the tapping came she put her hand to the pipe, yes there it was, it was only a faint vibration but it was definitely there, she banged her fist against the pipe but nothing happened maybe she needed something metal. Then tap, tap, tap again, it was probably nothing but she still had hope. She reached into the small watch pocket in her jeans and slid out a coin, it was a coin she always carried with her and would never spend. Cathy knew it was kind of superstitious but she always knew she was never completely broke so long as she had that coin, probably the only useful piece of advice her Mother had ever given her. She curled her fingers around it so it jutted out between her index and middle fingers and tapped the pipe three times, it gave a hollow knock and she waited, within a few seconds three taps came back, she tapped it four times and four taps were returned, then twice and the pattern was repeated back to her. There was someone else here, she wasn't alone in the warehouse, unless it was a trick, her heart sank at the thought that it might be Shaun playing games with her or some weird way the pipes ran through the building. Cathy didn't really believe that though, she was beginning to think that this might be where she would find Maria, June's previous housemaid. Cathy shouted, there were no replies but every time she tapped at the pipe her taps were returned in the same pattern.

She sat down again with her back to the wall, the sliver of light that was trying to get into the room was getting brighter, time was passing and she realised she needed a drink and she needed the bathroom in equal measure. She hoped that Shaun or anyone would turn up really soon, Shaun must visit here regularly especially if she was right and there was someone else here too. The trouble was she didn't know that if there was someone else here would they be friendly or just as evil as Shaun. She just wished someone would turn up soon. The call of nature was becoming urgent, the corner of the room would have to do. That was when she heard the crunching of gravel, someone was outside, she shouted as loud as she could. "Help, I'm in here." She repeated the cry several times. Then there was silence, a few moments later she heard the rumbling of a metal shutter being opened. Someone was coming, she silently wished for it to be anyone except for Shaun.

"Good morning Cathy." Called a cheerful voice, as the door swung open, pouring light into the room. Her eyes slowly adjusted, at that moment she could only see a shape but as the seconds passed and her vision cleared she realised her wish had not been answered, Shaun stood in front of her holding out a paper bag. "How are you this morning?" He asked as if what he was doing was the most normal thing in the world.

"What are you doing? Where am I?" She paused trying to hold her anger down. "Why am I here?"

"You allowed June to get hurt and I didn't like that!"

"Can I go now?" She begged.

"No, but I will show you around." He was still grinning at her.

"How's June?" She asked.

"Don't worry. You just eat your breakfast Cathy, I'll show you around soon." He smiled. With that he turned around and shut the door behind him, leaving her in the dark again. Her senses were picking up the smells emanating from the paper bag, the smell was becoming overpowering and she tore into the bag, finding a bacon and egg sandwich and a small bottle of orange juice. Breakfast tasted like heaven, she sat and waited.

He returned a little while later just as he said he would, he flung the door open and said. "Come on then, I haven't got long." She did as she was told, what she really wanted to do was to kick and bite him and get away from here but for now she would go along with what he said, she thought he might seriously hurt her if she fought him, he'd already done enough damage to her. He grabbed her wrist and held on tight, pulling her along a corridor with grey walls and white ceiling tiles, it looked just like any office block she'd ever seen, she struggled to keep up. He opened a heavy door that revealed a staircase, she thought that this must be the fire escape, it was all concrete and brick and no one had bothered to make it look pretty in any way, he led her up the stairs. She counted six short flights of stairs which in her head meant they were at least on the third floor now; he pushed open a door to reveal another grey walled corridor that looked exactly the same as the one they had left behind three floors down. The only difference was there were closed doors all along this corridor and they all appeared to be locked with padlocks. Towards the end of the corridor Shaun shoved a door open and roughly pushed her inside the room, he didn't say a word he just turned and walked out, she heard the clunk of metal and could almost visualise him snapping a padlock on the other side of the door. Then all she heard were his footsteps as he walked away.

Chapter Twenty Two

Tom was sitting at the table watching Lily, she was awake and pretending to be reading a book, he was surprised that she wasn't giving him too much trouble. Only once had she struck out and bolted for the door, she had thrown her book at him and then tried to kick and hit him when she realised the door was locked and she wasn't going anywhere, she had tried standing in the window waving, shouting and trying to attract someone's attention but that had got her nowhere either, in this area people kept their noses out o
f other people's business, not wanting to get involved. The worst thing was her crying, he hated that he was doing that to her, it made him feel really bad. She was still asking if she could at least phone her mum, he kept putting her off, he didn't have the heart to say no outright. He had turned his phone to silent so she wouldn't know that he had one with him, it was a good job he had, Trish had called him and left a voicemail to say that she was on her way back and not to give Lily any more sleeping tablets. He had managed to slip out of the room and to the bathroom to retrieve the message. The problem with Lily being awake was whenever he spoke to her she just kept asking him if he would take her home or if she could use the phone. He really wished he could, he was out of his depth, he silently prayed that Trish would come up with some ideas and that she'd get here quickly.

It was early afternoon when Trish turned up and let herself into the flat, she was smiling and Tom took solace in that smile. She had a plan, he could read it all over her face. "Hi." She said.

"Who are you?" Lily asked before Tom had the chance to say anything.

"No one you need to know about." She snapped at Lily. Tom looked down at his lap, he didn't like that way she had spoken to Lily, but she was tougher than him and he hoped she knew what she was doing. Lily didn't ask her anything else, she returned her gaze to her book, glancing over the top of it trying to work out who this new addition was.

Trish made a drink for them all, in silence, Tom could see her add something to a glass of milk she was preparing for Lily. He hoped she knew what she was doing as she gestured to him to give Lily the drink. Lily drank the milk and was asleep in less than a minute. They went down to the car and brought several bags and boxes into the flat. Tom had no idea what she was up to but he trusted her implicitly, after all she couldn't make more of a mess of things than he already had.

She set up a drip stand with bags of liquid and went through her medications, she worked quickly and efficiently putting a strap around Lily's arm and wiping at a spot on her inner arm, she opened a sterilized cannula and inserted it into Lily's vein, that done she hooked up the drip. He thought to ask questions but she seemed to know exactly what she was doing. "This will keep her asleep when you need her to be, I'll show you what to do later." Trish was in charge now, Tom just nodded, he felt himself relax a little but there was a question at the back of his mind but for now it would wait, he watched Trish as she worked, then finally she slipped an oxygen mask over Lily's sleeping face. That final touch made him feel even worse about what he'd done. With her work done they sat at the table drinking tea, Tom could see that Trish was thinking over something she was going to say, he wouldn't push her, until she was ready, they sat in silence. "She will be fine Tom, don't worry the Propofol will make her sleep, you can wake her by stopping the drip at any time, but you can't keep her like this forever. You need to contact Jack and tell him what it is you want."

"What I want? I don't want anything, just all of this to be over. I just wanted to hurt him, to make him feel the way he made me feel. It was all a stupid idea, I don't want anything from him!"

"If you want this over, the only way to do it is to take something from him in return for Lily." They sat in silence again whilst Tom thought this through, he knew she was right.

"I have no idea, but I think I should at least contact someone and let them know that Lily is okay, that'll buy me some time to think."

"Okay, that'll be a start." Trish dug around in her bag and pulled out a new SIM card for his phone. "Use this, I picked it up in Leeds, so it won't be traced to this area and don't forget to set your phone to private so the number doesn't show up, we don't want to make it too easy for them." They discussed what he should say whilst they finished their tea. Tom looked around the room it was slightly unnerving now that it looked like a small hospital ward, with all of the medical supplies scattered around.

"You've thought of everything." He smiled at her.

Chapter Twenty Three

Alex heard her phone ringing, she dug around in the bottom of her bag trying to find it as she pulled into a lay-by, her fingers touched it and she managed to answer it before the voicemail kicked in. "Hi Charlie."

"Alex." He sounded breathy. "We've just had a call come into the office."

"Yes?"

"A man, he said Lily was okay."

"What! Who? Was that all he said?" Alex demanded.

"Nick took the call and came straight to me, apparently he asked for you by name, Nick told him you weren't in and he just said to tell you that Lily was okay and he'll call back."

"I'm coming in, now. Tell Nick not to go anywhere until he's spoken to me, I'll see you in a while." With that she disconnected the call and immediately phoned Matt to relay the message.

"Ask Nick if he could hear anything else, see if there were any clues to where the call could have been coming from. I'll make my way to the office, see you there later... and Alex, drive carefully." Matt sounded worried about her.

"I'll be fine, I'm not too far away. I'll ring you when I get there." Alex was agitated but she had to get to the office and find out what was going on, she turned the car around and drove slowly, trying not to panic. When she pulled up in the car park Matt was already there, waiting for her.

"Are you okay?" He asked as he put his arms around her.

"I think so... You were quick. I'm glad you're here." Alex wasn't at all sure what she was feeling, panic mixed with relief and fear was as close as she could get.

"I couldn't stay at work and wait for your call, I wanted to be here." He smiled at her, trying to comfort her.

"Should I ring Summer?"

"Not just yet Sweetheart, let's find out exactly what's happening first." They walked into the newspaper office together, heads turned as they went in and Nick walked up to meet them and they all went into Charlie's office and closed the door.

Charlie looked visibly shaken as Matt started firing questions at him and Nick, when it had all been boiled down it turned out all they really knew was what the caller had said, there were no sounds that Nick could recall to give away his whereabouts, the only thing Nick could add was that he thought the voice had belonged to a middle aged man but they were all aware that voices could be misleading, so even that was a guess, they would all just have to wait until he called back.

Matt returned to the station and arranged for an officer to be at the newspaper office for when Alex couldn't be there, then there would be no chance of a call being missed and he would organize for the team to come in to try and trace the call when it arrived. Everything was starting to move now and there was a palpable sense of relief knowing that Lily was still alive, if the caller was to be believed. They chose to believe.

Alex called Summer but it was Mark who answered the phone, she told him what she knew and left it for him to pass on the news to Summer. Now they just had to sit back and wait. A young police officer called Tina turned up within thirty minutes, it was her job to sit by the phone and catch the call when it came in but Alex wasn't ready to let someone else take over so quickly. Alex tried to chat with her and tell her some stories about Lily but Tina made it obvious she was there to do a job. Silently, Alex was pleased that she was taking the job seriously even if she was just waiting for a phone to ring. Two men turned up ten minutes after Tina with a bag full of gadgets to trace the call, but before they had even unzipped their bags the phone rang. Alex lunged at it, she wasn't going to let anyone else take this call. "Hello." She snapped.

"Relax Alex, well I assume this is Alex?" A woman's voice said.

"Yes it is, can you ring back later please, I'm waiting for a call on this line."

"I know you are, this is it." There was a pause and for a moment both women were silent.

"Why are you doing this? Where's Lily?" Then finally. "What do you want from me?"

"One question at a time Alex, Lily's fine, she's being looked after and I haven't decided what I want from you yet. As for the why…" She paused. "I think maybe you should ask Jack about that."

"What's Jack got to do with any of this?" Alex demanded. "I want to speak to Lily!"

"Sorry, she's sleeping, I'll call again Alex." Then she hung up.

Tina looked at her curiously, Alex replied to her silent question. "It was a woman this time, soft Yorkshire accent, no background sounds that I could hear but wherever she was sounded a bit empty, there was a slight echo."

"Will she ring back?"

"She said so." Alex replied. She called Matt and told him everything the woman had said, then called Mark and told him the same.

Alex left Tina in charge of the phone, she needed to get to her Nan's to find out what Jack knew about any of this. When she pulled up outside the house Matt was already there waiting for her, again, he seemed to have a knack for getting everywhere before her today, he told her that Mark and Summer were on their way too. Alex wanted to speak to Jack before anyone else arrived. Matt gave her a head start saying he'd wait outside for Mark and Summer to arrive.

She walked straight into the hall, her Nan rarely locked the door, then into the warm inviting lounge, her Nan was busy arranging flowers on the table. "Hi Alex, nice to see you."

"You won't say that in a minute Nan, where's Jack?" There was no emotion in Alex's voice, Mary looked shocked, Alex had never spoken to her like that before.

"What's wrong Alex? Do you have news?" She asked as Jack came in from the garden holding a fresh armful of flowers.

"Hello Alex." He smiled but quickly realised that both women were looking at him. "What's up?" He asked as he placed the flowers on the table.

"Sit down Jack." He did as Alex requested, the smile had left his face. She told him about the phone calls and as he listened his face grew pale.

"So this is something to do with me. How can it be? I can't think of anything I could have done in my life that would warrant this type of payback."

"Are you sure there's nothing Jack, no one you've hurt or upset?" Alex found it hard to believe that she was even asking that question, Jack was one of the kindest people she had ever met.

"Alex, you know I have no secrets, I promise there's nothing in my past that you don't know about. You wrote the book, I told you everything about my life and the community. The only bad thing I ever did in my life was to my brother and you know how that turned out."

"There must be something Jack." Alex could see Jack was struggling with this and finding it hard to believe that he was anything to do with it, but the caller had specified that this was about Jack so if they had to revisit every moment of his life they would.

"Why would they take Lily if this is about me? What could I have done that was so bad that they would want to cause this much hurt? I have always tried to be fair and kind to everyone, well with the exception of my brother, could it be someone associated with him do you think? I'm not sure there was anyone who cared that much about him to want to cause this much hurt."

"Just think Jack, please, there's something and it's important." Alex begged.

"Like I said you wrote the book Alex, there's nothing else." Jack looked so hurt it almost broke Alex's heart.

"Did you meet Tom and the new couple?" She asked.

"Yes just the once, why? I don't go down to the tunnel as much as I should anymore."

"What did you think of them?"

"Nothing much, we said hello and that was it. Why Alex?" he asked again.

"Tom and the young couple disappeared around the time that Lily went missing, the couple went in the early hours of the morning, they told Jaz that they didn't feel comfortable with all of the police around but Tom was gone long before them." Alex explained.

"Do the police think he took her?" Jack flopped into the armchair.

"The police have no idea, it's just me guessing, although I spoke to a woman on the phone. Oh I don't know Jack." Alex went to the arm of the chair, sat down and looked at Jack. "I had to ask Jack. You understand don't you?"

"Of course." He looked crestfallen. That was the moment Matt walked in, without Mark and Summer, she looked questioningly at him. "They're not here yet and I need to take a statement and get back to work." He explained.

"It's okay Matt, ask your questions." Jack knew that he would have to go through everything again for the police. Matt covered everything in less than thirty minutes but they were no closer to an answer when he had finished, that was when Mark and Summer turned up. Jack repeated everything for them too without getting in the least bit irritated, Alex appreciated that this had taken a lot out of him, yet he was still being kind and patient with everybody. That was just how Jack was, so why would anyone blame this on him? Alex thought.

After everything had been said Summer looked up with tearful eyes. "Do you think if we find this Cathy girl that we'll find Lily too?" The question had been directed at Matt.

"Honestly Summer we don't know but I hope so." That was the only answer he had for her. Alex moved to sit next to Summer and gave her a hug, she couldn't begin to imagine what Summer was going through. There was a knock on the door and Angie and Mel joined the gathering, they sat down and everyone discussed everything they knew again. Angie was every bit as distraught as Summer, Alex moved away so that Lily's two mum's could console each other. As she watched them her mind drifted back to the shared happiness of them finding each other two years previously when Angie had agreed that Lily could meet her biological mum after eleven years of separation and they had all lived like one big family ever since, Lily being the glue that held them together. Mel nudged her and brought her out of her memories and back to the room, she nodded towards the kitchen, Alex got up and followed her. "How are you doing?" Mel asked.

"Better than they are." Alex nodded towards the lounge where Angie and Summer were barely holding it together.

"Do you know anything yet?"

"Only what I've told them. Why?" Alex frowned.

"I just thought there may be things you were keeping from them because they are so fragile at the moment."

"Mel! This is Lily we're looking for, not some stranger."

"Sorry… I just thought..." Mel sulked.

"It's okay, we're all a bit touchy at the moment. What's going on in your life? It feels like forever since we've been out and had a chat." Alex tried to lighten the moment.

"I've met someone and he's gorgeous." She smiled. "You're the only person I can tell at the moment with all of this going on."

"I'm pleased for you Mel, just don't rush into anything." Alex said, not really interested in discussing Mel's love life.

"You're never going to let me forget the Lee incident are you? Carl's different, you'll like him."

"Just be happy Mel, that's all I'm saying." Alex turned away, she hoped that this one would work out for Mel, she didn't have much luck when it came to men, but now wasn't the time to celebrate her new relationship.

Returning to the lounge the mood seemed to have lifted a little bit as Angie and Summer were asking Mary about the honeymoon, it was good to hear them talking about something more positive. Matt had already left and gone back to work, Jack was still sitting in the armchair, he looked smaller, somehow older and tired, Alex was worried that this might break him, she hoped her Nan would be able to hold him together, however this turned out. Alex said her goodbyes and left them all to talk things through, she needed to get back to the office and wait for another call that hopefully would throw more light on things.

Chapter Twenty Four

Cathy looked around at her new prison, it was almost as if it had been designed as a cell. At least in this room there was a window, it was glazed with frosted glass so she couldn't see anything outside but just having some daylight filtering in was a vast improvement on the previous room. From the shadows she could see through the window it looked like there were bars outside the glass. She noticed how quiet it was up here, there was no sounds at all. There was also a room off to the side without a door, Cathy walked towards it surprised to see a small bathroom with a toilet and a sink, there were no mirrors or decorations, just plain grey plaster, there wasn't even a bulb in the light fitting, the running water was a blessing and she set about cleaning the wounds on her head. Back in the main room the walls were the same grey plaster and there was an old stained mattress on the floor with a green sleeping bag that had been haphazardly thrown on top of it. She checked the door, unfortunately it was definitely locked, she sighed, thinking 'how on earth did I get into this mess!' She noticed a mug had been thrown on the sleeping bag. She had to smile, it's the small touches that make it home, she thought wryly.

After a while the tapping started again, it made her jump, when it started it was much louder up here than it had been downstairs, this time it didn't stop, there was a sequence of taps and then the same pattern was repeated, she thought it sounded like a conversation was going on. She randomly hit a pipe with her coin and the tapping abruptly stopped. She tapped again a few times and it was repeated back to her. There's more than one other person locked up in this warehouse, she thought. Horrified at the thought, she recalled the other doors with padlocks on she had seen as Shaun had brought her here. "Hello... Can you hear me?" She shouted as loud as she could. The tapping started again and she was sure she had heard a voice, it was faint but definitely someone replying to her. "I can't hear you, shout!" She yelled at the top of her voice.

"Yes... Hello." A faint voice came back to her and she felt a rush of relief, she was no longer alone.

"What's your name?" It hurt her throat to shout so loudly but it that was overshadowed by the relief of knowing that there was someone else there.

"Maria." Came the distant reply. "You?"

"Cathy. Are you okay?"

"Yes." They shouted to each other for just a few minutes, she was also aware of another voice joining in the shouting, they must have been further away because Cathy couldn't make out the words but Maria seemed to be passing the conversation on to them. Cathy had to stop shouting, it was hurting her throat too much but she felt better knowing she was not alone. She went to the bathroom and ran the water, filled the mug and drank deeply, her throat thanked her. Then she went and lay down on the mattress and surprisingly the thought that with other people here they may be able to find a way out relaxed her enough to sleep. She smiled before she closed her eyes thinking that June would be pleased, she had found Maria.

Chapter Twenty Five

Alex had waited around long enough at the office and so far there had been no follow up call, she decided it was time to go and do some of the groundwork that Matt couldn't. She left Tina holding the fort at the newspaper office with a promise to contact her immediately if a call came through, it didn't need two of them. They'd had a little more time to get to know each other whilst they had been hovering over the phone willing it to ring, Tina had turned out to be much more amiable than Alex had first thought. She had admitted to Alex that she had been nervous of doing this job because Alex was her boss's girlfriend and she didn't want to get anything wrong. Alex had put her at her ease, it couldn't have been easy for her and she just wanted to do a good job.

Alex had spent some time looking through local maps and trying to remember exactly what it was that Matt had told her. She had hoped that Tina might let more details slip but it turned out she didn't know very much about the case, she'd just been put on the phone duty. Alex knew the type of car Shaun Brown drove and that the address was in a small village between Charmsbury and Exeter, she tried putting his name into a search engine but that showed up nothing and she tried the local phone directory, there she found plenty of Browns but none that specifically shouted out the name Shaun to her. She would carry the directory with her to refer to as she travelled around trying to find the right man. Matt hadn't been away long when he had gone to check out the address so she thought it may be closer to Charmsbury than Exeter but with the amount of small villages in this part of the country it didn't narrow it down much for her. She still had a pile of flyers in the car, there were enough there to get her started today, she could always go and see Rob and get some more if she came home empty. She was determined to keep going until she discovered something, she looked back at the map and decided to start from Charmsbury and work her way outwards.

She jumped in her car before she could tell herself how much of a lottery this was and the chances of finding Shaun Brown were incredibly slim, but she felt that she had to try. She drove into the first village she came across, stopped at a local shop, they shook their heads at the flyer, knew no one who drove a blue Corsa or anyone called Shaun Brown but they had tried to be helpful and had taken a flyer for their window. This routine replayed itself throughout the afternoon with some people showing more interest than others, it seemed everyone was willing to help, but couldn't, simply because they didn't know anything.

At six o'clock her phone rang, it was Matt, he had got home and was wondering where she was. She crossed her fingers to dispel the white lie and told him she had been out shopping and was on her way home.

An hour later she arrived at home, when she went into the house Matt looked at her "Successful shopping trip?" he asked. "Where did you go?"

"Oh, just window shopping, I didn't see anything I liked." She lied.

"Alex you're a terrible liar, what have you been doing? You've been so worried about Lily there's no way you'd go shopping, so where have you really been?"

She flopped down onto the settee, she'd been caught out and there was no point in continuing the lie. "I've been trying to track down Shaun Brown but I couldn't find him."

"Why would you want to do that? I've already told you he's not involved with Lily."

"Because I think you might be wrong." She said quietly.

"I know you're worried but please leave this to us, we do know what we're doing, he's just a man with a disabled wife, who bought a homeless person a meal and gave her a lift, there's nothing else to know about him."

"How can you be so sure, did you look around his house or check any other buildings?"

"No Alex, this guy has no record, he's never done anything wrong, there's nothing to suspect."

"But what if he does have Lily, shouldn't you look?"

"I'd need a judge to sign this off and no judge would sign a search warrant with no reason to, we just don't have any evidence." He understood what Alex was going through but he really couldn't do anything else. "Do you want me to go and talk to him myself, would that make you drop this vendetta against him?"

"Yes that's exactly what I want and I want to come with you to look him in the eye and see if I believe him."

"No. You've got to let this go. I'll go and see him again if it will ease your mind but not with you and you really must let this go." He was serious and Alex could see it in his eyes.

They rarely argued but when they did Alex always knew it was time to stop whatever she was doing, Matt was normally really laid back but this case was pushing everyone's buttons. She also knew she wouldn't be able to follow him to Shaun Browns house, he would spot her in an instant but she had an idea and went out to the car before sitting down to a meal that Matt had cooked for them. They didn't say much to each other that evening, each of them lost in their own thoughts and worrying about upsetting each other if they talked about the case anymore. Matt dropped a kiss on her head and went to bed early, it was easier that way.

When Alex woke up the next morning, Matt had already got up and left for work, he had let her sleep or he was trying to avoid discussing things with her any further, she thought the latter.

Chapter Twenty Six

Matt was concerned about Alex, she seemed to be taking the whole case on her own shoulders and she wouldn't listen to him or anyone else. He needed her to realise that the police were doing everything they could but it just didn't seem to be enough for her. There had been no news from Tina who was still stationed at the office, so this morning there was nothing to move the investigation forward. Maybe just to quiet Alex's worried mind he would take a trip out to see Shaun Brown, just to ask him a few more questions and take a look around. If nothing else at least it would make him feel like he was doing something.

He drove through the town of Stooke, hardly a town at all, just a smattering of houses, a pub that looked like its heyday had been around the 1940's, a church and a newsagent. As sleepy villages went it was the sort you read of in books about forgotten places, it was surrounded by fields and a river but there was nothing else for miles. He turned right and drove up a track that led to the Brown's house, the car wasn't there but he hoped Shaun's wife would be in, she could answer his questions. He knocked on the door and waited, he knew she was disabled and maybe it would be awkward for her to get to the door, he could wait. He knocked again. There were no sounds coming from inside the house, he looked around, there was a barn by the side of the house, not the old wooden type but a newish metal construction. He wandered over to it and banged his fist against the door, silence, it didn't sound like he could disturb anything here. He walked around it and peered in through the dusty windows, all he could see were garden tools, some wood and what looked like a motorbike, nothing of much interest in there. He turned and went back to his car, he waited for a while with the stereo on, filling the time with Coldplay, meanwhile his mind turned to Lily and trying to work out where she could be. He was disturbed by the sound of a vehicle coming along the track. He watched as the blue Corsa pulled up in front of the house and Shaun Brown got out. He was dressed in overalls and what hair he had was messy, he looked like he had been doing some manual labour, as far as Matt knew this man didn't have a job. He opened his car door and went to meet Shaun. "Hello." He extended his hand.

"Hi, can I help you?" Shaun took Matt's hand in a firm friendly handshake.

"Yes I'd just like to go over some details about the missing girl, Cathy." As he spoke he looked towards the house and saw a face peering out at them from the window.

"Oh I didn't realise your wife was at home, no one answered the door."

"She doesn't like visitors, it tires her." Shaun answered, his tone flat. "What can I tell you?"

"Could we go inside." Matt wanted to take a look around, he waited as Shaun thought this over.

"Is there some kind of problem?"

"No, just that the girl is still missing and my officers may have missed something that you could enlighten me on." Matt smiled warmly, trying to confer friendliness.

"Okay, come in." Shaun walked towards the door. Matt turned and took a quick look inside the car, it was clean, incredibly clean for someone who had been out working manually, but there was nothing out of the ordinary. Then he followed him into the house. "I'm sorry I can't give you long but there's so much I need to do for my wife, so what's this about?" Shaun said as they walked through into a lounge area, everything was clean and tidy but it was cold, there was an open fire but it hadn't been cleaned out since the last time it had been used. "Don't you have any home help?" Matt asked.

"No, just me." He answered abruptly.

"Well I won't keep you, this is just a follow up, can you tell me about the girl you picked up in Charmsbury about a month ago."

Shaun started to tell Matt, at first reluctantly because he had already spoken to some officers but soon he settled into his story and tried to be helpful. Whilst they were chatting, a lady who Matt assumed was Shaun's wife came into the room using a walking frame, she nodded at him but didn't say a word. Shaun introduced Matt but still she didn't speak, she just politely smiled, Matt noticed her breathing sounded laboured as she sat down on the settee and listened to his questioning of her husband. Whilst Shaun was telling of how he had dropped the girl off just outside Exeter, he wasn't sure exactly where because he didn't know Exeter that well, Matt glanced over at June. She seemed unaware of him looking at her, her eyes were settled on her husband and they seemed to be questioning what he was saying, it made Matt think that just maybe Alex was right to be suspicious of this man.

Twenty minutes later, Matt was returning to his car after thanking Shaun for his help. He was uneasy, something didn't feel right, but there was nothing that he could do, Shaun's story was watertight and exactly the same as he had told the previous officers that had questioned him. It was just that look in his wife's eyes that alerted Matt to something being not quite right, even if she had nodded in all the right places. He shook himself, he was there to deal with facts, not feelings and the story had checked out. Matt turned up his Coldplay CD and drove back to Charmsbury.

Chapter Twenty Seven

Alex had checked in at the office but there was no news there, she sat with Tina for a while before she decided to go and see Summer and Angie, she just wanted to know they were okay and then she would drop in on her Nan.

She got to Angie's house and found her and Summer together, talking about Lily and all the things she had got up to, they were helping each other through their pain and Alex felt like an outsider, almost like she was spying into a private world, they were pleased to have her there but she couldn't add much to their memories and shared love for Lily but at least they seemed better together than apart. After seeing that they were coping she was happy to leave them and go to check up on Jack, she couldn't imagine how awful he must be feeling.

The house looked just the same as always from the outside, no one would guess the trauma that was going on behind the front door. Alex took a deep breath and went inside, there was no smell of baking today. Alex went through the hallway into the lounge and the first thing she saw was Jack sitting in the armchair, looking aged and sad. "Alex, hello." He said as she walked in.

"Hi Jack, how are you?"

"I've had better days. Your Nan's in the kitchen keeping busy." He tried for a smile.

"I've just come to see if you're okay, and if you remember anything."

"Nothing, I wish I could, then we could sort this mess out but I really can't think of how this came about or who it might be." He looked bemused. "Not a clue." He added under his breath.

Alex squeezed his shoulder. "We'll find her Jack."

Then she went through to the kitchen to see her Nan, she was standing over the kitchen table chopping vegetables, she looked up at Alex and smiled. "I'm making soup, Jack's getting fat from all of my cakes." The smile didn't quite reach her eyes it was overshadowed by sadness and worry. They didn't say anything else but Alex gave her Nan a hug and returned to Jack. She felt so bad for them, this should have been the happiest days of their marriage not the most worrying.

"Your Mum and Dad came by last night." He said.

"Really, I haven't been to see them since the wedding, I suppose I should." Alex felt a little guilty, she wasn't very good at keeping in touch with everyone.

"They understand that you're busy, don't worry, they came to see if everyone was okay and hear our news about the honeymoon." He looked up at her. "Has Matt got any news yet? Any more phone calls?"

"Nothing yet, it's only a matter of time. Everyone's doing everything they can. Try not to worry too much Jack."

With that said there wasn't much else for them to talk about, Mary made coffee for them all and they sat and looked at each other until Alex couldn't bear it any longer. She made her excuses and left, she wanted to go and see Matt.

Back in her car she rang him, he answered straight away. "Hi sweetheart."

"Hi Matt, any news yet?"

"I've been to see Shaun Brown, had a look around and there's nothing there, sorry sweetheart, I know you thought he was the one."

"Are you back now?"

"Yes, I'm in the office."

"Okay, I'm going over to the newspaper office to see if there's anything happening there then I'll try and come over."

"Oh, okay. Any reason?"

"Do I need one?" Alex replied.

"I guess not, see you later." She could hear a smile in his voice as they said their goodbyes. Alex was relieved to know he was back and wanted to get to see him as quickly as she could before he went anywhere else. She decided to go to see Matt before going into the office, after all they would contact her if a call came in and she wouldn't be too far away.

Alex drove into the police station car park and pulled up next to Matt's car, if anyone from the station saw her they wouldn't think twice, they'd just assume she was visiting Matt, which she would, if they spotted her. She got her notepad out of her bag and went round to the driver's side of Matt's car, she saw one of the blinds twitch, she'd been spotted. She carried on with what she was doing it wouldn't take a second. She cupped her hands around her eyes and squinted through the window of the car then jotted down the numbers she read from the milometer. She threw the notebook in her bag and went into the station to say hello, she had thirty seconds to come up with an excuse for being here to see him. She was buzzed through and went up to his office. "Hi." She smiled at him.

"Alex, are you okay?"

"Sure, why?" She answered innocently.

"You seem a bit off today."

"I guess I am a bit, we rowed last night and I just wanted to make sure we were okay."

"Of course we are." He smiled and visibly relaxed.

"Good. What have you been up to today, any news?"

"Nothing so far, I've been out to... Okay you're not going to get me to give you Shaun Browns address that easily but nice try." Now there was a broad smile on his face.

"Can't blame a girl for trying." Any awkwardness was instantly diffused as they both laughed, Alex had pretty much the information she had wanted anyway, she hoped. "I'm just going into the office and then I'm going home, see you later." She leaned over the desk, gave him a kiss then turned and waved as she walked out of the room.

She drove her car into the newspaper office's car park and got her phone and her notepad out. She had taken a reading of his mileage the previous evening, if she took off five miles as his drive into work and any possible detours. She should be able to work out the village he had driven to or at least narrow it down. She smiled to herself; if he had wanted someone who wouldn't interfere he shouldn't have got involved with a journalist.

She looked at the numbers and discovered that Shaun must live a bit less than forty miles away and she knew the direction so he shouldn't take much finding now. Feeling pleased with herself she went into the office to see if there was any news from Tina. There still hadn't been another phone call but everyone knew it was only a matter of time, they would have to ring back and tell them what it was they wanted. Alex still couldn't believe it would be anyone from the tunnel community that was doing this but had to admit that Tom looked guilty, but she couldn't work out who had a link to Jack, the more she looked into this the more confusing it got. Her money was still on Shaun but she couldn't work out a link, Jack said he didn't know anyone by the name of Shaun, but plenty of people had lived in the tunnel who hadn't used their real names. She felt that her focus on Shaun was correct, there was something not right about him even if Matt thought different.

She returned to her car and set off in the direction of Exeter, setting her odometer to zero.

Alex drove through the Somerset countryside for forty miles until she came across a small village, she stopped and took a flyer with her into the local pub. She asked after Shaun Brown but no one knew the name and she showed them the flyer, she got the usual response, a shake of the head and a moment's concern flitting across their faces. She was sure she would have got it right this time, she headed back to her car, there must be other villages around here. Although the landscape looked like it was fields as far as the eye could see. There was no point in her going any further afield but maybe she had just come a little too far. She grabbed her map from the back seat and looked over the area and in a small arc from where she was, it looked like there were twelve possible villages, everything else looked like it was too far out of the way. She could do that in the time she had before she needed to get home, her mood picked up again. She was determined to find him before the day was out, Matt wouldn't be happy but she needed to do this, if Shaun had Cathy and Lily she was going to find out where and bring them home.

The next village she tried only had a small shop but they didn't know anything so she moved on. This continued through the next four villages, Alex was beginning to lose heart again, then it was as if fate had offered a helping hand, she spotted a blue Corsa in her rear view mirror, she took a look at the driver, short dark hair, she crossed her fingers. Glancing at the registration she noted it was a 2008 plate, it must be him, surely this must be Shaun Brown she thought. She pulled into the next lay-by and allowed him to pass, then pulled back onto the road, dropping well back from him, it wouldn't be a problem there was virtually no other traffic on the road so she could stay well back and still follow him. It did fleetingly cross her mind to message Matt and tell him where she was, just in case anything went wrong but he'd never forgive her for getting involved, she couldn't tell him where she was. After a couple of minutes they entered the village of Stooke and he turned onto a track, she couldn't follow him down there, he'd see her straight away and demand to know who she was and what she wanted. She parked up further along the road where she could still see the entrance to the track, she got out of her car and walked back along the road until she got to where he had turned in, she needed to see where it led.

Alex walked along the track, it was rough with stones, potholes and tree roots, with hedges on one side and trees on the other. She thought that the state of this track there couldn't be much traffic that used it so it was probably the way to get to his house, she remembered Matt saying he lived out in the sticks. She walked around a bend and saw the house just a little bit further along the track. It looked like it stopped at the house; if she waited on the road she wouldn't miss him, it looked like it was the only way out. She stood against the hedge so she would be hidden from view of the house and looked around, there was the house, in need of some work but a standard farm house and a metal barn, nothing else around the house no other outbuildings, just flat land. She'd like to have a look around that barn but Matt had been here and if there was anything suspicious he would have checked it out. No, she thought, he must be keeping Cathy and Lily somewhere else, away from the house. She would wait for him to leave home and see where he went. Turning around she walked back down the track returning to her car to wait for Shaun to make a move.

Alex started to think about all of the things that could go wrong but she still couldn't bring herself to ring Matt, he would just tell her to go home and now she'd come this far she wouldn't let it go. Her phone rang, it was the office. She answered it with trepidation, "Hello."

"Alex, we've had a call." Tina's voice came through clear.

"Okay, what did they say?"

"It was the man again, we asked him his name but he wouldn't give it, he said Lily was well and that he wanted Jack's phone number."

"Did you give it to him?"

"No, not until we've spoken to Jack and can get ourselves over there. He said he would phone back again later. It looks like we're moving forward, albeit slowly. Do you want to speak to Jack or shall we?" Tina asked.

"You talk to him, tell him I'll be round later to sit with them."

"Okay, are you okay? You sound anxious." Tina enquired.

"I'm fine, I'll catch up with you soon… And Tina."

"Yes."

"Any idea where the call came from?" Alex looked towards the track as she asked, he could be in there now having just hung up the phone.

"No, it was a mobile, no idea where he is and again no background clues."

Alex was sure she was on the right line now, Shaun had just got back to the house and they had had a phone call. She wasn't going to leave the village until he came out of that house again.

From where she was parked she could see a small shop around one hundred yards ahead, she thought she'd go and see if they recognised any of the girls that were on the flyer. She walked into the old fashioned corner shop and was instantly transported back to her childhood, sweets in jars on the shelves and cans of cheap pop next to boxes full of packets of crisps. The lady standing behind the counter looked like she'd been there for fifty years, no smile or warm welcome but Alex wasn't about to be put off, she approached the woman and asked for a bag of pear drops, trying to keep one eye on the doorway in case a car went past, pear drops had been her mum's favourites and Alex had always got into trouble for stealing all of her mum's sweets. "Can you help me please?"

"If I can." She replied with a faint look of, do I have to.

"Do you recognise any of these faces, I'm trying to find these missing girls." Alex handed her the flyer and watched her face.

"No I'm sorry I don't, I thought she looked familiar but I'm not sure." Alex looked towards where she was pointing, it was at a girl called Jane.

"You've seen her around here?" Alex questioned.

"No... Yes... I'm really not sure." She replied. Alex believed her, the look on her face matched the words coming out of her mouth.

"Thanks for looking." Alex motioned that she should keep the flyer and paid for the sweets, she didn't want to stay in the shop too long in case Shaun decided to leave home.

She returned to the lay-by and continued to watch for his car to appear.

Chapter Twenty Eight

Jack was distraught, a policewoman had just spoken to him and they wanted to give the man who had Lily his phone number. He had no problem with them passing his number on but he still couldn't work out how any of this could be his fault and now he was frightened, he hadn't told Mary but he had started having some chest pains, he hoped it was just stress but at his age nothing could be ruled out. What really hurt him was the moment he got the one thing he had wished for into his life, his one great happiness, it was as if someone wanted to balance the scales by giving him some real pain, something terrible to worry about.

Now he would do anything to get Lily back and chest pains or not, he would get to speak to the one person who wanted to hurt him this badly and ask him why. He still couldn't think of a single reason why this could be happening.

Mary was milling around making tea and trying to keep him calm when there was a knock at the door, he answered it and let the police officers in. After a short discussion they handed him a mobile phone to use, rather than give out his home phone number. They hadn't been able to trace the call when it had come in as the caller had blocked his phone number, maybe they'd have better luck with him calling a mobile phone, they should be able to glean more information that way. All of this technology made Jack nervous and he didn't really understand what they were talking about. They were throwing acronyms around and everyone else seemed to know what was going on, they were all nodding in agreement, he was in the dark, he was just going to have to trust them. They said they had left Tina at the newspaper office to pass on the phone number when he rang back and she would let them know when that was done. So now it was a waiting game.

Jack helped Mary organise cups and plates for everyone, they chatted whilst they organised tea, cake and biscuits and set them down in front of the officers. They were both surprised that Alex wasn't here to oversee what was going on. She would understand what everyone was talking about and she would want to know what was happening.

One of the officer's phones rang he listened for a moment and he nodded to his partner. "Jack, the number's been given, we just have to wait for a call now." He said. Jack went over to his chair, sat down and waited, this call would be where he might find out where all of this stemmed from. Around him were men in uniforms drinking tea and eating Mary's infamous chocolate brownies. Still they hadn't heard from Alex, Jack wondered why, he wanted her here. The new mobile phone sat on the table and Jack was watching it as if it would explode any second, his heart was thumping in his chest. He jumped when a hand touched his shoulder. "It's okay, we're here, don't worry we'll find him Jack. We'll have Lily back where she belongs really soon now." It was a reassuring voice but deep down it didn't make Jack feel any better. He sighed and sat back down in the armchair, they were right of course, these were people who were really good at their job and this was all in a day's work for them. They chatted amongst themselves whilst Jack couldn't lift his gaze from the phone, they told jokes and laughed, trying to include Jack but he was only interested in one thing.

The phone leapt to life, lighting up and buzzing, one of the officers, Jack thought his name was Dan, picked the phone up and nodded at Jack, Jack nodded back, he was ready for this. Dan handed him the phone. "Hello." Jack said.

"Ah... Jack... you won't remember me but I'm going to be your worst nightmare." The voice wasn't familiar to Jack, the accent seemed to be one he should know, but not the voice.

"Who are you and why have you taken Lily? Is she okay because if you hurt her, I'll find you and I promise you'll never hurt anyone else as long as you live." Jack had no idea where that had come from but it was truly how he felt and he felt infinitely better for having voiced it.

"Calm down Jack, Lily's fine, just a little sleepy."

"Let me speak to her." Jack demanded.

"Business first Jack, business first." The words he used were confident but the tone of the voice sounded a little stilted almost as if he was reading his lines.

"What do you want?" Jack asked.

"Money and to be left alone once Lily is home."

"I can't promise that." Jack hesitated. Dan was waving his arms about to get Jack's attention, Jack watched Dan as he mouthed 'give him anything he wants'. "But I can try." Jack added. The officer breathed a sigh of relief.

"I want fifty thousand pounds and to be left alone. Then you get Lily back totally unharmed."

"Okay, what about the other girls?" This was unscripted but Jack was getting confident now, they could raise the money, even though most of it would have to come from Mary, he would pay her back, every penny. The officers gave him the thumbs up.

"What other girls Jack? You're only interested in Lily, there's no other girls, just get the money I'll ring you back tomorrow morning to arrange everything."

The phone went dead, Jack looked up and was greeted by smiling faces, they were happy and they thought they had enough to find out who the provider of his mobile phone was, they seemed confident that with one more call they may be able to trace him, the technical guys were sitting together going over everything they could find and talking on their phones to other people. All of a sudden it seemed that there was hope and there was a buzz around the room.

"Did you recognise his voice at all?" Dan asked.

"No, it doesn't sound like anyone I know. I really want to find out who it is because I don't have a clue."

"We'll find them, I'll stay here if that's okay with you both, just in case another call comes in, the others have work to do back at the station. I think I must have got lucky, Matt's always talking about Mary's baking." Dan smiled, trying to lighten the mood.

"Of course you can stay. Get Lily back safely and I'll bake for you whenever you want." Mary added.

"I'll hold you to that." He smiled.

Jack sat back in his chair and closed his eyes, he hoped Dan was right that they'd find her, he spoke confidently and Jack wanted to believe him.

Chapter Twenty Nine

Alex sucked on a pear drop savouring the sharp sweetness as she watched the track. She'd been sitting there for over an hour now and nothing had happened, she hoped there wasn't a back way out, it certainly hadn't looked like it but she didn't know this area.

Jack was playing on her mind she couldn't wait any longer to speak to him, she wanted to know if anything had happened, she had planned to go and see them tonight and maybe she still could, but she felt a need to know what had been happening and Jack would be wondering where she was, expecting her to be there to oversee the phone calls. She picked her phone up and pressed the photograph of her Nan and Jack exchanging their vows. It gave two rings and then she heard Jacks voice. "Hello."

"Jack, have you heard anything yet?"

"Yes, he rang, he says that Lily is fine but sleeping. Where are you Alex?"

""Just looking into something, I'll see you later. He must have drugged her, they said Lily was sleeping when I spoke to them. That's assuming that she's okay and still with them, and he's not lying." She mused. "What else did he say?"

"He wants money and a get out of jail free card, the police think they can trace the call."

"That's great news Jack." She said slightly distracted as she watched Shaun's car appear and pull out onto the road. The phone call timings fitted with Shaun being at home, now she felt sure this was who they were looking for.

"Where are you Alex?" Jack asked again.

"Just out, I've got to go, I'll ring you later." She paused. "Jack, don't worry, okay?"

"I'll try. See you later." They both hung up on the call and Alex clipped her seatbelt in and drove after the blue Corsa.

Shaun drove out of the village at a steady pace and on through a small town where there were an abundance of traffic lights, Alex was worried she would lose him here, but she managed to keep sight of him as he went straight through the town and continued out into the countryside. They entered another village, a couple of minutes later and he pulled into a car park in front of a row of seven small shops and got out of his car. Alex pulled in by the side of the road, just far enough away that he shouldn't notice her. She knocked her hazard lights on and watched as he went into a shop specialising in walking aides for the disabled, he didn't even glance her way, she remembered Matt mentioning that his wife was disabled, so that seemed like a normal thing to do, he came out with a small box, there were no clues as to what was in the package. He continued on a few shops down to a bakery, after a couple of minutes he came out with two full bags. He threw everything onto the back seat of his car and pulled out of the car park but not in the direction of home. Alex entered the traffic again, getting a beep from someone's horn as she cut in front of them, she'd been thinking about Shaun and not enough about the road. She looked around at the driver about to mouth the word sorry only to see a young woman waving her hands around gesticulating and then sticking her fingers up to her. She didn't bother with the apology she just looked ahead for Shaun and kept him in sight. She sighed, there

117

was no way she was apologising to someone who reacted like that behind the wheel even if it had been her fault.

He drove on for a few miles then turned right on a roundabout and drove into an industrial estate, well it would have been an industrial estate at least a decade ago, the railings along the side of the road were rusty and there was greenery climbing around them, they drove past a unit where there was still someone working but it looked like a small garage business, there were three cars parked outside. After that there was a small furniture makers in the next unit which appeared to be closed, there didn't seem much going on here. Shaun kept driving, but slower now, Alex kept following him but she slowed right down to put more distance between them, he would spot her immediately if she was to get any closer, they were the only cars on the road. He slowed to a crawl and turned into a car park in front of a dilapidated building, there was graffiti and broken windows, some of the windows had been boarded up from what she could see. She pulled her car up to the curb just past the car park entrance and parked on the road, scanning the area to see if there were any CCTV cameras on lamp posts or the side of buildings but there weren't any visible. Getting out of the car she walked up to the railings where the overgrowth of weeds hid her from view, she could see Shaun getting out of his car. He was older than she had initially thought and was carrying a bit of weight, he looked like any average fifty year old man, there was nothing about him that would make him standout to anyone, she understood why the descriptions from people had been so vague, he was mister average.

He opened the back door of the car and retrieved the two bags he had picked up from the bakery but not the package from the disability shop, slammed the car door and locked it. He turned and walked to the side of the warehouse. Alex slipped inside the car park, he wouldn't see her, he was walking in the opposite direction. She ran up to the side of the building, past his car and watched him from the corner, he bent down and pulled at something, then she heard the rumble of metal shutters being opened. It didn't go on long so he must have just pulled them up far enough to get in, she watched as he disappeared inside. Now she thought, was the moment she should call Matt and tell him what was going on, she didn't, she wanted to get a closer look first. She listened as the roller door unfurled itself and she assumed, closed. She stepped out, away from the building and looked around. The warehouse was three floors high and looked just like any other warehouse, there was nothing unusual about it except the graffiti, which in her opinion improved the building. She took her phone out and snapped a few pictures of the car, where it was parked and the warehouse itself. Now she was ready to follow Shaun inside, she went to phone Matt but again hesitated, she was torn, knowing that he would just tell her to leave it alone, he would be less than pleased with her involvement. She wanted to present the finished job to him, then he would forgive her for interfering.

She walked to the shutters, they were almost closed but there was a gap at the bottom, she was sure she could roll underneath it, it would make too much noise if she tried to open it up. Bending down on the ground she peered in, he wasn't there so she lay on the floor and easily slid underneath.

The area she was in was dirty and dim, there were a few desks and not much else, a filing cabinet in the corner and a smell, she couldn't place it but it wasn't pleasant. There was no sign of Shaun, she walked across to the filing cabinet and opened it, there were just a few scraps of paper in one draw and nothing in any of the others. She picked the papers up and looked at them, it had been a phone company that had used this warehouse, the thought of phones made her realise she hadn't turned hers off, if it rang now she could be in all sorts of trouble. Taking her phone out of her back pocket she flicked it to silent, at least that should keep her out of trouble and pushed it back into her pocket. She heard a door close further along the building and footsteps, she pulled herself tight up against the filing cabinet and made herself as small as possible. Shaun walked through the open plan room and pulled up the roller doors and went out closing the door after him, Whatever was in the bags had been left here and she wanted to know what it was. Alex heard the lock engage.

She had no idea what she was going to do now, but she wasn't going to waste this opportunity, worrying about locked doors would keep until later. She came out of hiding from behind the filing cabinet and went in the direction the footsteps had come from, there were office doors along a corridor, she poked her head around a couple of them but there was nothing to be seen, just more grubby rooms, most of them had their windows boarded over and the smell was getting increasingly sour, it smelt like someone had been keeping animals in there. She opened another office door and the room was filled with light, the windows were intact here, opposite her she could see Shaun pulling his car away from the building, she froze, hoping he hadn't seen her, no he couldn't have, he was reversing his car. She dropped to the ground and stayed there until she heard his car crunch across the gravel, the sound diminished until there was silence. Her heart beat wildly in her chest as she listened, nothing, she sighed with relief, he hadn't seen her. She hoped he wouldn't notice her car on the road either, there weren't any other vehicles in the area. Alex stayed where she was for a few minutes just in case she had to get out quickly but it seemed that nothing had happened, he hadn't come back, she was free to explore and see what it was he was doing in this warehouse. When she felt certain he wasn't coming back she continued looking through the offices, there was nothing here just empty rooms, she flicked a light switch on in an office, nothing happened, no electricity, she shouldn't have been surprised.

She walked back into the hallway and looked around, on the other side of the hallway there was a heavy door, possibly a fire exit or the stairs to get to the other floors. She pulled the door, she had been expecting it to be locked but it yielded immediately, she walked into a brick and cement stairwell, it was cold in here but the smell was better. She ran up two flights of stairs to the first floor, taking the stairs two at a time. Again she was confronted with rows of office doors, it didn't look like anyone had been here for a while, some of the doors stood open, she looked around but there were just some old desks and old style desk phones and lots of wires lying around on the floor.

Suddenly she felt her phone vibrate in her pocket, she hoped it wouldn't be Matt she wasn't ready for him to come and rescue her just yet. It wasn't, it was Mark, she answered it. "Hi Mark." She kept her voice quiet, for no reason she could think of.

"Alex, where are you, we're with Jack, he's been telling us about the phone call." He sounded a little less wound up than he had last time she'd spoken to him.

"It's good news isn't it, at least he's asking for something now. That means she's okay." Alex hoped.

"Yes but where are you now?"

"I'm just following a lead, I'm on a disused industrial estate on the road to Exeter, don't worry I'll be home soon." She felt much more confident now she'd told Mark what she was doing.

"Need any help?" He asked.

"No, just don't tell Matt, he'll flip."

"Okay, we'll all be at your Nan's when you get back."

"See you later, Mark." She smiled as she ended the call. She slipped the phone back into her pocket. She hesitated, there was a noise, had she missed Shaun coming back? It would serve her right for feeling so proud of herself. She listened hard, it was a tapping, she couldn't work out where it was coming from, it seemed to come from all directions at the same time. She stopped and listened, it sounded like central heating pipes banging, but there was no power here so how could there be heating and even if there was how could it have been turned on. She listened closer, moving towards some pipes in the room, she put her hand on them, they were cold but she could feel a vibration that matched the sound.

She went cold, there was someone here, it was the only explanation. No, no it's probably just rats, she thought as she let a breath out that she hadn't realised she was holding. The tapping happened again, there seemed to be a regular rhythm to it then it would stop and be repeated, that was no rat, there were definitely people here. She shouted "Anyone there?" then repeated it louder but there was no reply.

Alex went back to the stairwell and climbed up the next two flights to the next floor, she pushed open the door and was confronted with the same layout as the previous floor, she moved through it swiftly, checking rooms but they were just empty, caked with dust and grime, there was nothing here either. There was only one more floor to check, it would probably be a waste of time but she'd come this far, and somewhere deep inside her she knew there was something here to find. She wouldn't leave until she had discovered what it was. She returned to the stairs and ran up the last two flights. She reached out to open the door from the stairs and suddenly a hand clamped down over her mouth, she tried to bite it but whoever it was, was too quick for her. Before she knew what was happening, her arm was pulled out to her side and a foot tapped the back of her knee with some force, sending her down to the floor, she rolled a little and looked up into the face of Shaun Brown. "Well! Who the hell are you?" He barked at her.

"Alex." She whimpered, her arm hurt, he could easily break it from this angle.

"And... what are you doing here Alex?" He said sarcastically. She didn't answer, she was too stunned, she hadn't heard him come back.

"Owwwww!" She cried as he pulled on her arm.

"What the fuck are you doing here?" He demanded.

"Just looking."

"For what?"

"Somewhere to sleep." She thought quickly, it was the best she could come up with.

"Why, when you have such a nice car outside to sleep in!" It wasn't a question, he was just shouting at her. "Get up."

"What are you going to do?" She asked.

"Find you somewhere to sleep... where no one will find you again." He added this statement coldly. He half dragged her through the doorway into the corridor.

Chapter Thirty

Matt looked at his watch, Jack had told him that Alex would come straight to them when she got back from wherever she had been. He had gone straight round to see Jack and Mary after work to meet her and pass on the news that the phone provider had definitely been traced and the phone number was registered as being in a batch that had been on sale in Leeds, it was a pay as you go SIM and it had been topped up with cash at the same shop it had been purchased at, which meant the number was not registered to anyone named. They couldn't be sure at the moment where the call had come from but now they had the phone details they would capture the whereabouts of it from the next call, there had seemed to be some problem with finding its location on this call. It was mostly good news and all they had to wait for was that mobile phone to ring again. Dan had still been there when Matt arrived and they chatted for a while, but Alex still hadn't turned up. He had also just missed Mark and Summer they had been with Jack and Mary all afternoon but they had gone home, Summer had been feeling the stress of the day and Mark wanted to get her settled for the night, they would be back in the morning.

Matt sat next to the fire, opposite Jack and they talked, about anything they could think of but there was a nagging feeling at the back of his mind that something was wrong. Alex had never let Jack or her Nan down before and even Mary had no idea where she was. Alex always told her Nan where she was, especially when she didn't want him to know. This time he could tell from their worried looks that they weren't covering for her, they really didn't know.

As the night drew on they all started to get concerned about Alex's whereabouts, she seemed to have disappeared without a trace and she wasn't answering her phone, which was unusual, she normally had it glued to her hand. Matt phoned the station but no one had heard about any incidents involving Alex, he waited. He continued to ring her mobile which was still going to voicemail, he left message after message, he waited longer, then rang home, nothing. He could feel panic setting in.

Where had she gone and what was she up to? Last time she disappeared he had ended up going out to Thailand to save her skin, although, she had seemed to be doing quite well on her own. This time he had no idea where she may have gone. Then the penny dropped, she'd gone to find Shaun Brown, it was the only logical thing he could think of. "I've got an idea." He said to Mary. "Don't worry, I think I may know where she is."

"Where?" Mary asked to Matt's back, he was already grabbing his coat and heading for the door.

"Stooke.' He shouted back.

Jack and Mary looked at each other. "What on earth is Stooke?" Mary asked. Jack shrugged in reply. He was reeling because this was all going from bad to worse. He wondered what else could go wrong, and what he'd ever done to deserve all of this.

Matt jumped in his car and drove out to Stooke, he knew his way but it all looked very different in the dark, he took a wrong turn along the twisting turning country lanes but realised his mistake and put his GPS on to correct his route. He eventually found the track and bounced along it until he reached the house. As he stopped the car what greeted him was a fully lit up house that looked perfectly innocent and cosy, it almost shouted that nothing bad has ever happened here.

He got out of the car and went towards the front door, when he got there the door was opened to him before he even had chance to knock. Shaun was standing in the doorway. "Hello again, can I help you?"

"Hello Mr Brown, yes I hope you can, could you tell me if you've seen this woman today?" Matt reached into his pocket and pulled out his favourite photograph of Alex. He looked into Shaun's face and noticed a scratch just under his eye.

"No, should I have?" He asked, he looked at Matt questioningly.

"We know she was out this way earlier today, I just wondered if you'd seen her, nothing more. Oh that's a nasty scratch." Matt said pointing to his face.

"I'm beginning to feel like you're targeting me. I thought we'd cleared everything up, am I now going to be the first person you come to every time someone goes missing?"

"Not at all, you're the only person I know in this area so I thought you might be able to help, that's all." Matt tried to sound innocent and hoped he'd succeeded he could do without a complaint about him going to the station.

"Would you like to come in and check?" Shaun was starting to get riled.

"That would be very nice Mr Brown but I haven't got time to socialise, I need to find this woman. Thank you for your help." Matt watched Shaun's face, he didn't seem to know what to say next, Matt had diffused the situation perfectly and left Shaun feeling unnerved. If he was involved in this he would feel compelled to make a move now and Matt would be waiting for him.

Matt turned away and got back into his car and drove away from the house. When he got to the bottom of the lane he pulled into a lay-by where he could watch to see if Shaun left home, he waited.

After an hour he thought he might have got it wrong, Shaun hadn't left the house as Matt thought he might. Matt waited for another long hour and he became even more certain that he must have it wrong. Shaun hadn't moved out of the house.

Matt drove home, despondent.

Chapter Thirty One

Shaun had dragged Alex along the corridor, sworn under his breath a couple of times and finally let go of her arm. She instinctively shot forward and went for his face with her nails, he was quick but not quick enough, she caught him just under the eye, she had been a centimetre off target. He swung his leg and kicked her mid-thigh, she went down again, holding onto her leg. "You little bitch." He shouted as he dabbed at his eye. "Why are you here?"

Alex raised her head and spat at him, he grabbed her roughly and made her stand up, holding her two hands together behind her back with his one hand and went through her jacket pockets with his other. He didn't find anything except for a piece of paper with a phone company logo on it, he threw it on the floor. Then he checked her jeans pockets, he found what he had been looking for, he pulled the phone out, threw it on the floor. "Now break it, go on, you stamp on the phone." He pushed her forward until she was standing directly in front of the phone, still holding her wrists tightly.

"No, I won't! Let me go." She struggled to get away but it was no good he was too strong. She could smell his sweat, he may be strong but he wasn't used to exerting himself, she continued to squirm and struggle, but to no avail.

He pushed her along the corridor in front of him and as she passed her phone on the floor he came into line with it and raised his foot, slamming it down, shattering the phone, then he kicked it along the corridor. She was in front of him and saw the phone go flying up the corridor ahead of her, she couldn't see what he was doing but when they stopped she heard metal against metal then the door opened and she was thrown inside. "There's somewhere for you to sleep Alex. It was what you were looking for… wasn't it?" He laughed as he slammed the door, there was a clunk and then she listened as he walked away.

"Come back you coward." She shouted after him but the footsteps travelled away until there was no trace of them left.

She turned and ran at the door, it was locked, he'd locked her inside, she couldn't believe it. She rubbed her leg, that was going to leave a huge bruise, then looked up at her surroundings.

In the corner of the room crouched in the corner, with her knees pulled up to her chest was a young girl with large frightened eyes. Alex immediately forgot about her sore wrists and leg. "Hello." She said approaching the girl. The girl tried to pull herself even further into the corner. "Don't be frightened, I'm not going to hurt you." Alex said quietly. "What's your name?" She got no reply but the girl now looked up at her as if she was debating whether she should trust this new addition to her surroundings.

Alex looked away from the girl and scanned the room, it was small but it had a window although it had thick frosted glass and what looked like bars outside. There was a tiny washroom off to the side and a sleeping bag in the far corner. There was a paper bag on the floor, she bent to pick it up. Suddenly the girl launched herself forward and snatched the bag off her "Mine." Was all she said.

"Okay, okay, I just wanted to look, I'm sorry." At least now she knew the girl could talk, it was a step forward. "How long have you been here?" She asked.

"Long time." The girl growled in response.

"Why?" Alex asked, the girl just shrugged and opened the bag. It was food, Shaun had been to the bakery to buy bags of food, he had been carrying two full carrier bags when he got here. "Are there others here?" The girl nodded in response. "How many?" The girl just shrugged again. Alex thought this could drive her mad if she couldn't get the girl talking. "I'm Alex. Will you tell me your name, maybe we can help each other?"

"Beth." It was almost a whisper, but Alex caught it.

"Hello Beth, want to tell me what's been going on, so we can try and get out of here." Alex tried for a confident tone, the poor girl looked terrified. She couldn't have been above seventeen years old, Alex remembered an Elizabeth from when she did the flyers but this girl looked nothing like her.

"Beth how long do you think you've been here?"

"Months, no, longer, I don't know." She replied tearfully, the sadness in her voice almost broke Alex's heart, all traces of her bravado of moments ago were gone.

"It's okay Beth, don't cry." Alex moved forward to instinctively put her arms around her but Beth tucked herself back against the wall. Alex backed off immediately, wondering what this poor girl must have been through. She went to the door and shouted as loud as she could. "Hello, anyone there?"

"Yes, who's that?" A quiet voice came back.

"Alex. Who are you?"

"Cathy."

"Maria" Another voice added.

"Are you okay?" Alex shouted.

"Okay." Came two replies in unison.

"Are you together?"

"No." One of the voices said.

So she had found three of the missing girls, Alex wondered if the others were here as well, maybe they had had their spirit broken by being here like Beth. "I'm here with Beth." She yelled. There was no reply, they were probably trying to process the information that there was a new person here. "Did Shaun bring you here?"

"Yes." Came a reply, she would have to get used to their voices.

"Cathy, he said he dropped you off in Exeter, what happened?"

"He offered me a job." From the sound of her voice, she was physically the closest to them, they had to shout but Alex could easily hear her.

"I've been looking for you Cathy, do you know who else is here?"

"Maria, and another, I don't know her name, can't hear."

Alex now knew there were at least four women, trapped in this building, all she had to work out now was how to get them out. She knew the layout of the building but couldn't get out of the room. There must be a way, she just had to find it. She turned to look around the room and noticed that Beth had moved closer, she seemed to be edging towards her. Alex was stunned, this was the behaviour of a frightened animal not a young woman, what the hell had that man done to her. She could hear the women still shouting to each other in the other rooms but now her attention was on Beth, "Do you want to talk Beth?" She asked gently. Beth nodded and Alex watched a tear tumble down her cheek. "Can I sit with you?" Again Beth nodded, Alex slowly squatted down beside her, close enough that they were almost touching. Beth suddenly grabbed Alex's arm and hung on to her tightly. "You're real." She whispered.

Alex wanted to cry for her, instead she pulled her arm free and wrapped it around Beth's shoulders. "We'll be okay Beth, we can get out of here."

"Promise." Beth's wet eyes shone with hope.

"I promise." Alex answered, hugging Beth whilst also mentally crossing her fingers, she really hoped she could get them out of there, she wished she had called Matt and told him where she was too. This was such a mess.

Chapter Thirty Two

Matt woke up on the settee as dawn was just beginning, he had been exhausted when he returned home, then it came back to him, Alex, where was she? He needed to go and check if she had come in and gone to bed. He hadn't heard her but he'd been so tired when he got in he hadn't been able to stay awake. If she'd come in and seen him asleep she would have left him there rather than waking him. He crept quietly up the stairs missing the step that creaked, he didn't want to wake her. He opened the bedroom door but his worst fears were realised, she wasn't there, the bed hadn't been slept in and the room was in almost darkness, unchanged from the way it had been left in the early hours of this morning, now he really had no idea where she might be.

It was just past five o'clock in the morning and still the dark side of dawn outside, he couldn't ring Jack and Mary yet to see if she had turned up there and he didn't want to worry them if she hadn't. He thought he had got it right last night that she would be at Shaun's but to his surprise she hadn't been and he didn't know where else to look. He made a coffee and thought things through, he would ring the station and see if they had heard anything, any incidents or accidents, he would ring the hospitals too. He picked up the phone, no one at the station had any news, it had been a quiet night but they said they would ring around for him. He sat at the table with his hands wrapped around the steaming mug of coffee and then an idea came to him, Mark. Yes, she would have spoken to

Mark if she was up to anything, she always confided in him and got him to help her. He picked up his phone and dialled the number, it was answered after seven rings a groggy voice said. "Hello."

"Morning Mark, do you know where Alex is?"

"Matt, no, isn't she at home?" Mark sounded like he was waking up quickly.

"I haven't seen her since yesterday morning, have you spoken to her?"

"Well…" Mark played for time whilst he thought about what he should say, Alex had asked for his discretion but she might be in trouble, he couldn't keep the conversation to himself.

"Mark, if you know anything, tell me! She hasn't been seen since yesterday morning. Now, where is she?" Matt's temper was coming through loud and clear.

"She spoke to me yesterday afternoon, she was looking around an old, disused industrial estate on the road to Exeter, that's all she told me, she was fine when I spoke to her, it did sound like she was inside somewhere, her voice sort of echoed. She said she'd go round to her Nan's when she got back." Mark told Matt everything he knew.

"Is that all she said. It was definitely the road to Exeter?"

"Yes. I don't know anything else, shall I try and ring her?" Mark asked.

"You can, but it just goes straight to voicemail every time I call. I've got to go and look for Industrial Estates, thanks Mark."

"Let me know if there's anything I can do." Mark said, fully awake now.

"Just ring me if you hear from her." Matt put the phone down, Mark wound him up for no real reason, he hated how Alex always went to Mark first. He understood it, but he didn't like it.

His phone rang, the station had rung around for him but there was no news on Alex. He asked them to look out for her car and treat her as missing. They promised to keep an eye out for her, there was little they could do until she had been missing for twenty four hours and Matt knew the routine only too well. He also knew the guys at the station would do their best for him.

The morning was drawing on now and by the time he got ready to leave the house it would be a more reasonable time to wake Jack and Mary, he knew they wouldn't mind once they knew why. He showered, dressed and drove across town, by seven o'clock he was sitting in his car outside their house, he looked around but couldn't see her car here. He got out of the car and knocked on the door, he waited for five minutes before Mary sleepily answered. "Matt, it's early, are you okay?"

"Not really, is Alex here?"

"No. We haven't seen her. Should she be here?" Mary started to sound worried.

"I was just hoping she was, she didn't come home last night, I'm worried Mary, I know something's wrong."

"Come in and speak to Jack. Don't forget she went missing last year and she was fine."

"This just feels different." He added.

They went into the lounge, waking Dan who had been fast asleep on the settee with his legs dangling over the arm rests, settees weren't made for people of Dan's stature to sleep on, Matt would have smiled had he not been so worried. Mary went and told Jack to hurry along. Once they were gathered together they sat and pooled their ideas about where Alex may be, there were plenty of dilapidated industrial estates in Somerset, but Matt was still convinced this had something to do with Shaun, he

135

knew Alex had been sure Shaun had got Lily or maybe she was lying somewhere hurt, Mark had thought she was inside somewhere, could she be in the same place as Lily. He wanted to go and look for her himself but they were due to take a phone call this morning from whoever it was that had Lily and that was just as important.

Matt was torn he didn't know which way to turn, Mary brought in fresh coffee and they continued chatting. "Dan can stay and take the call with Jack, you go Matt, go and find Alex." Mary suggested. Dan nodded in agreement with her.

"You know I can handle things here." Dan added.

"I know." He sighed "But I feel responsible Dan." Matt looked around, they were all watching him.

"Go Matt." It seemed the decision had been made for him.

"Ring me when you get the call, I need to be kept up to date." Matt added.

He picked up his jacket and went to find his map in the car, he needed to get a list of old Industrial Estates between Charmsbury and Exeter. Thirty minutes later he was on the road with a list of estates to check out.

Chapter Thirty Three

Alex was cold, she opened her eyes, it hadn't just been a bad dream as she had hoped. She had fallen asleep from sheer exhaustion with her head on her knees, her back propped up against a wall. She gently stretched her leg out. "Ouch." She cried, holding her hand to the tender place where she had been kicked, she unfurled herself slowly, it seemed everywhere on her body ached. The whole of the previous day came flooding back to her as she looked across the room. Beth was curled up in the sleeping bag, gently snoring.

The previous night, Beth had fallen asleep crying, it had taken Alex a couple of hours of cajoling to get her to open up and when she finally did tell her story, she sat and cried but it had seemed to start a new fire in her and as she began to act stronger, Alex could begin to see the girl on the flyer reappearing just a little. It would be less challenging to speak to her today, a friendship was forming between them through the circumstances they found themselves in. Alex hoped that together they could come up with a way to get out of here, although she thought Beth had probably already entertained most ways of trying to escape. Looking around at the room Alex was amazed that anyone could spend months in here, alone. It was clean but barren, Beth had told her she tried to keep it that way because at least it gave her something to do, a routine to keep her mind clear for at least a few minutes every day. Then there were the few moments every day that she spoke to Shaun, as much as she hated him just a hello meant there was some human contact, then there were the other girls, but she had given up the shouting, it hurt her throat too much. She was the girl that tapped the pipes to communicate, she had told Alex that she did it when she needed to know there was someone else there, just to know that she wasn't totally alone.

Beth stirred, she was just turning over in her sleep, as she moved she pulled the sleeping bag with her, it revealed a book on the floor which had been previously hidden, Alex inched forward to take a look. It was a paperback copy of an old Agatha Christie book 'The Murder of Roger Ackroyd', with a torn and dog-eared cover, Alex smiled, Agatha would have loved a story like this to get her teeth into. She slid it back to where she had found it. Now she needed to start looking for ways out of here. The windows were barred and the door was solidly locked, she was going to need to be a bit more creative and look further than the obvious. Slowly the room brightened with the onset of the new day and Alex was determined to find a way out.

When Beth woke up Alex asked her about the book. "Shaun bought it for me, he knows I hate being alone, he thought a book might give me some company, it did for a while."

"If he knew you hated being alone why did he put you here in the first place?"

"I told you, June didn't think I was working hard enough so I had to go."

"So why didn't he just let you go home or drop you in a town somewhere?"

"I don't know." She threatened to cry again but managed to hold it in. Alex didn't want to upset her but she couldn't understand why he was bringing the girls here.

"What was June like?" Alex asked hoping to get back onto more solid ground.

"Bossy, lazy, she wanted a slave not a helper." Beth said.

Alex still didn't understand why he hadn't just let her go, why lock her up here and turn her into little more than a caged animal. What did he have to gain from the girls being here, they could have gone back to their lives and never mentioned Shaun or June again. As she thought about the whys and wherefores she went around the room, tapping walls and doors, desperate to find a weak spot. The door was a heavy solid construction, not like an average office door at all, she wondered if Shaun had replaced the doors to make sure they couldn't be broken down. The walls seemed solid too, no vents or grills, just walls, there were the pipes, she wondered if she could try and open up the holes the pipes came through. Her first problem was she had nothing to try and make holes with, all that was available was a mug, book, sleeping bag and empty food cartons. Which made her realise she was hungry. She sat down feeling defeated before she'd even started. It crossed her mind that maybe one of the other girls may have something in their cells, she went to the door and started shouting. After checking with the other girls that could hear her, it sounded like their rooms were the same, they had nothing that might help either, which left only one alternative, they would have to work together to try and distract Shaun when he turned up. Beth said he turned up every day with food, he'd never missed a day but the time could change. They would have to try and overpower him. It wasn't going to be easy and Alex already had a bad leg from her last tangle with him but they had to try and now there were two of them to take him on. They sat and waited.

Chapter Thirty Four

Matt had been driving around looking at industrial estates for a couple of hours and he was beginning to despair, he had no idea what he was looking for. He had followed the road to Exeter, some of the roads on the estates were packed with cars and people and some were completely barren and empty of both. He had no idea if he should be looking for a desolate estate of just a disused building. He needed a clue, something to push him in the right direction. He knew Mark had told him it was a disused estate but what if he had it wrong, Matt needed to try everywhere. He tried to ring Alex's phone again but it went straight to voicemail, he couldn't leave another message, she obviously wasn't getting the previous one's he had left. He rang Mark but he hadn't had any luck either. Alex never went anywhere without her phone, that made him absolutely certain that there was something wrong.

He phoned the station wondering why he hadn't thought of it earlier. "Dave, can you contact the phone company that Alex uses and ask them to trace her last calls?"

"She's still not turned up then?"

"No and I'm worried, speak to Stacey and ask her for a favour for me, she'll sort it out, I need to know where her phone was last used."

"I'll ring her and get back to you." Dave put the phone down and Matt felt a wave of relief. He knew this could pinpoint her.

He drove on to the next estate, it was buzzing with people on their tea break, he got out of the car and showed a couple of people her photo, it was a long shot but he had to try, but no one had recognised her. He returned to his car and drove into Stooke, he hadn't meant to come here, but it was on the road to Exeter. He still had an inkling that was making him think that this was something to do with Shaun.

He pulled into a car park opposite a small village shop as his phone started to ring. It was Jack. "Any news?"

"Nothing." Matt answered feeling defeated.

"We've had a call from the man who has Lily, he wants me to meet him the day after tomorrow with the money, he will bring Lily. He said no police."

"I bet he did. Any idea who he is yet?" He asked.

"No, not a clue, but your tech guys are confident they can trace Lily before the deadline. Dan's gone back to the station to do the paperwork, he's going to see Summer on the way." Jack told him.

"That's great news."

"Matt, she'll be okay you know, Alex is tough."

"Sure she is… But what if someone else it tougher Jack, what if she's in serious trouble? I need her back." Matt was on the verge of tears, the strain of the day was beginning to tell on him.

He got out of the car, he needed to stretch his legs and pull himself together, he wasn't used to feeling this overwhelming emotion, last year she had disappeared but it felt different, this felt wrong and frightening. He walked towards the small shop, he felt like he needed a cigarette, although he had given up eight years previously, but today the craving was worse than ever. He went up to the counter and bought himself a pack of his favourite old brand, as an afterthought he picked up a packet of mints, it was his old routine and he was slipping back into it seamlessly. "Are you okay?" A voice came through to him as he was musing over his choice of mints.

"Sorry?"

"You look miles away, are you okay?" The lady asked.

"I've misplaced my girlfriend." He answered, trying to make it sound less important than it was.

"And you're looking for her around here, second person in two days looking for missing people, this village will be getting a reputation." She smiled as she said it.

"Oh?" Matt was interested now.

"A woman came in with a flyer, looking for a girl. Now you looking for a woman. Coincidence?"

"Maybe not, was this the woman?" He pulled out the photograph of Alex.

"That's her, she was looking for some missing girls, she bought some pear drops. She left this flyer." The woman looked pleased with herself for remembering as she handed the familiar flyer over to Matt.

"Do you have any idea where she was going, did she mention anywhere?"

"No, sorry my love, she wasn't here above a few minutes, I couldn't really help her."

"Did she seem okay, not worried?"

"No love she seemed fine, just interested that I may have seen one of the girls on the flyer."

"So you knew one of the missing girls too?"

"No, the face just seemed familiar, I could have been getting it confused with a customer or someone on telly, you know how it is." Matt didn't but he nodded in reply.

"Thank you, you've been a big help." Matt said, now feeling like he was actually on the right track and it confirmed that she had been here to check out Shaun. There could be no other reason to come to this sleepy little back water, he had no idea how she had found her way here but she had. "Before I go, are there any old industrial estates around here?"

"Not this side of town, there are a few before you get into Exeter though, all sprung up with the boom in electronics a fair few years ago and disappeared just as quickly."

"Thanks for your help." Matt turned and left the shop, putting the newly acquired cigarettes into his pocket, he no longer felt the need for one, he was inspired to get back on the road. He got back in his car and continued through the village casting a sideward glance down the track to Shaun Brown's house, he would go and see him, but after he had already mentioned he felt like he was being targeted, Matt thought he should stay clear today. "But I will target you if anything's happened to her." He said to the empty car, "And that's a promise." He added, meaning every word.

He drove through a town, no longer taking much notice of where he was. Everything he was focused on was beyond these shops and these people, busying themselves with their everyday lives. Somewhere beyond this picture of normality was Alex and he was going to find her.

Chapter Thirty Five

Jack stood with his arms around Mary as she gazed out over the garden, she was looking but not seeing, her head was full of disquieting thoughts. All of this had taken its toll on her and she was tired and scared. Since their wedding, two of the most important people in her life had disappeared. Janet and Paul were coming over this morning, she'd had to ring them and explain what was happening, they hadn't taken the news well, their daughter was missing now, as well as Lily. They were aware of the affect that it was having on everyone, not just them. The police were still looking for the missing girls and now potentially had another missing person to find; the boss's girlfriend. Mary pulled Jack in closer to her, feeling a safety radiate from him that she needed at that moment, she knew Jack was beginning to think that all of this was his fault and she tried to be strong for him but she honestly believed that none of this was of his doing. Now Alex had gone she needed him to be strong for her, they were going to need each other more than ever. She had to wonder if this was the price that they had to pay for their happiness, that another aspect of their lives had to be devastated. She shook her head to get rid of such stupid thoughts. "Are you okay?" Jack asked, his voice full of concern.

"Yes." She whispered. "Just thinking." Jack turned her round to look at him whilst his arms still encircled her.

"Alex'll be fine, Matt will find her, she's probably still trying to track down Lily."

"Then why isn't she answering her phone Jack." Mary hadn't meant to be sharp with him. She realised when she saw the hurt look on his face that he was already blaming himself enough without her adding to his feelings of guilt. "Sorry... I guess we're all strung out." She looked up into his handsome face and kissed him. They stayed in their embrace until a few moments later when there was a knock at the door.

Mary answered it to Janet and Paul who bowled into the lounge demanding answers. Mary sat them down and explained everything she knew. Paul was angry at everyone and Janet was tearful. "You know Matt will find her, he's not going to let anything bad happen to her, she's everything to him. Trust me if anyone can find her it's going to be him."

"I'm going to go and look for her myself." Paul stood up and headed for the door with a face like thunder.

"Paul, please, sit down. Where would you even begin? Matt's out there doing everything he can. He'll ring if he needs help, You'll be the first to know." Mary begged him. He reluctantly returned and sat down next to his wife, he knew Mary was right he just didn't want to sit around doing nothing, he didn't like this feeling of helplessness.

"Why couldn't she have stayed at business school, why did she have to go into journalism?" Janet chipped into the conversation whilst aggravating a loose piece of cotton on her jacket.

"Because she's doing what she loves, sweetheart. You can't deny her that."

"I know but I didn't think she'd get herself into so much trouble. She seems to have a knack for getting into tight spots."

"That she does, but she sorts everything out too." Mary smiled remembering the praise Alex had got for her writing over the last couple of years. "Why don't you both stay here, it'll be easier if we're all together." Mary was relieved when they agreed, she needed her family close by. She thought that they needed her too whilst they waited for news.

The phone rang whilst they were sitting talking about what Alex used to get up to when she was small, it was helping them to avoid thinking of some of the things that could have happened to her now. It was Charlie, "Mary, hello, I'm trying to find Alex, she's not answering her phone."

"Sorry Charlie, we don't know where she is either." Mary said.

"Is this another of her solo stories." Charlie joked.

"Charlie she's looking for the missing girls, but she's gone missing herself now, I'm sure she'll get in touch when she can."

"Oh I'm sorry Mary, I thought it was odd she hadn't put out a story, she'd been so busy writing the past few days, so that everyone knew about Lily I couldn't understand why she had just suddenly stopped."

"Matt's out looking for her and she will officially be missing this afternoon so more police can get involved then, but they're doing everything they can now." She winced as she realised that Janet was listening to her side of the conversation. Charlie made more apologies and sounding more than a little embarrassed, he offered any help they may need and got off the phone.

All they could do now was wait for news. Mary took Janet into the kitchen and they started baking, at least it would keep them busy, Jack and Paul sat looking at the television but neither of them was watching it.

About an hour later the phone rang again, it was Matt. "Jack, I've got a lead, not a great one but she was seen in Stooke yesterday, the shopkeeper told me there were old industrial estates closer to Exeter, so I'm on my way to take a look around now."

"At least we know where she was yesterday, that's a start, good luck Matt, keep in touch."

"I will, but now I think she might have been right, Shaun Brown's involved in this somehow. Try and think if you ever met anyone of that name Jack, I need all the information I can get." Matt paused. "And Jack, can you tell Dan where I'm heading just in case I need him."

"He's not got back yet Matt but I'll tell him as soon as I can."

"Ring the station, he'll be there." They said their goodbyes and Jack put the phone down, then he phoned Dan immediately.

He returned to his chair, churning the name Shaun Brown over in his head, it meant nothing to him but Matt and Alex were certain this was the man they were after. Beyond the problems with his late brother, Jonathan, and his death, he couldn't think of anything else, sure there'd been spats between people at the tunnel over the years but nothing that stuck in his mind, they all used to rub along quite well and any altercations were sorted out amicably.

Everyone was relieved to hear that Matt had a clearer picture of where Alex had been, but the words that had been left unsaid were that he still didn't know where she was now, although they were all thinking it.

Chapter Thirty Six

Tom and Trish looked at each other across the table. "There, don't you feel better now you can see an end to all of this?" Trish asked.

"I suppose so, I just hope there's no police waiting for me when I get there. Why couldn't he just leave the money somewhere for us to pick up?"

"This isn't a movie Tom, just give the girl back and get the money and we'll get the hell out of here. We need to get home. If he leaves the money somewhere the police will definitely be waiting when one of us goes to collect it, it's better this way."

"Her name's Lily!" He hated it that she couldn't use Lily's name. "I suppose you're right about the money though."

He looked across the room, Lily was still lying there with the drip in her arm, asleep. He thought she was looking thinner and pale, he hoped she was okay, if she got ill it would be something else he could beat himself up over. Trish had assured him that she was fine, to be fair Trish was looking after Lily well and monitoring her regularly, waking her and making sure she ate and drank enough, he thought the reason she couldn't use Lily's name was that it would suddenly make it personal for her. He had noticed her smiling at Lily when she thought he wasn't looking. He wondered, once this was all over if their marriage could survive his stupidity, would Trish forgive him once Lily went home?

He was surprised that Jack hadn't put the police straight onto him, when he had called the number he'd been given he had half expected to be speaking to someone who just wanted to keep him talking whilst they traced the call. Did they even still do that? He wondered. There was always news about how technology was helping criminals, the police couldn't keep up with them. Could they even track a mobile phone if they didn't have a number. He had no idea and it was too late to worry about it now, if they could, surely they would have turned up with their flashing blue lights by now and taken Lily home and him to prison. Tom looked over at Trish whilst she was fussing over Lily, he thought that Trish was every bit as frightened as him, it was just that she refused to let it show, she had always had the harder shell out of the two of them.

It was almost time to wake Lily, she needed to shower and eat and have some time to read or play her computer games, although she would probably spend her time awake just continually asking to speak to her mum as she always did, she had fought against the drip yesterday, she understood what they were doing, but Trish was stronger than Lily and used to dealing with unruly patients. He was trying to make the best of a bad situation for her, but he couldn't just let her start talking to people. She would be home and safe in just two days and hopefully they could try and put this behind them, just the thought of all of this being over was a relief to him. He still bitterly regretted what he'd done and wasn't looking forward to facing up to Jack but they had come this far and it looked like they might come out of this with a fair bit of cash too, if everything went to plan.

Maybe that would be payment of a kind.

Chapter Thirty Seven

The phone rang, Matt pulled the car over to the side of the road and took the call, it was Dan. "Hi Matt, I've spoken to the phone company, they've just got back to me with the information you wanted, I was stunned they were so quick."

"And they said what?" He questioned impatiently.

"Okay, well the last call from that phone was yesterday, early afternoon, they have tried the phone and they can't get a signal now, the phone is either turned off or out of battery."

"Come on Dan, I know this stuff, where is she?"

"Okay, I'm coming to that, at the time of the last call they got a triangulation reading from the call and she was at an address on Small Woods Industrial Estate, they are running another program to be certain of the address, I'll get back to you when I have the information."

"Thanks Dan, you know where I'll be."

"Matt, the Results are due in from the other call within the next few hours, it's been more difficult for them to trace on that call, some of the masts in the area have been down whilst they've been carrying out work on them for the last few days, but they will be able to give us an idea of where to look, they're hinting at it being fairly local."

"Good, let me know when the results come in and have some of the officers ready to take with you, I'll get there just as soon as this is taken care of." Matt knew that wasn't strictly true, first of all he had to make sure Alex was home and safe, he wanted her where he knew she couldn't get into any more scrapes.

"Okay, I'll keep in touch." Dan said.

Matt checked his road map and pulled back onto the road, he wasn't too far from Small Woods, he just hoped she was still in the area. He swore to himself that when he found her he would marry the infuriating woman and keep her close to keep her out of trouble, they would be blissfully happy, it was a promise he was determined to keep.

He came to a roundabout and turned right into Small Woods industrial estate, there were a couple of units that had businesses in them but on the whole the area looked quiet. He pulled up in front of a garage where two men were looking under the bonnet of a ford fiesta. "Hi, have either of you seen this woman?" He pulled the photo of Alex out and showed them. They both shook their heads and went back to looking at the engine of the car. "It looks pretty quiet around here, I thought it would be busy with people on their afternoon breaks." He smiled as they looked up again with expressions that said can't you leave us alone.

"Sorry mate but this area hasn't been used for five, maybe six years. No one except driving schools and a few kids come down here, it's quiet for new drivers see."

"Yes I understand, so none of the buildings here are occupied?"

"Just us and next door, rent's cheap because the places are falling down. Anything else I can do for you?"

"No I guess not, thanks." Matt walked back to his car and got in. He looked back to see the guys were back with their heads underneath the bonnet again, he wished them luck, mechanics was something he had never really understood. He turned his engine on, now he'd come this far he thought he should have a drive around and see what the rest of this estate looked like.

It was desolate, there was nothing but overgrown weeds and rusty railings and it didn't look like anyone had been around here for years, but Dan had specifically said that the phone call had come from this estate. Matt parked up by the side of the road, trying to work out what could have been going on that would bring Alex here.

He phoned the station. "Is Dan there?"

"Matt? No he's gone out to see Jack, can I help?" Jules asked.

"Yes can you get him to ring me, urgently. I haven't got his number on me."

"Yes, but do you want......" Matt hung up on her, he didn't feel like talking he just wanted to know where he had to go next. He would sit here and wait for Dan to call him.

Twenty minutes passed before his phone rang, he snatched his phone from the dashboard. "Dan, where is she?"

"Matt, it's unit twenty three, the last listing I can find for it was a telecommunications company called JoJoTel, they moved out just over five years ago."

"Okay I'm going to find it, I'll ring you back later, thank you Dan."

"No problem, just call if you want me to come out there."

"No, I need you to wait and see if the other call came from the same area. Ring me as soon as you know anything."

Matt disconnected the call and drove along the road looking for numbers, he looked around but there were few clues, some of the buildings still had business names but he couldn't see any numbers, he pulled out his phone and opened up the internet. The GPS map showed number twenty three was just a short distance back the way he had come in, on his left. His pulse increased a little, finally he felt like he was doing something. He saw an old broken sign on the gates as he approached 'JoJoTel', at last he thought. He parked his car at side of the road and walked into a large car park, he didn't want to risk a puncture, there appeared to be a lot of broken glass and debris scattered around. The warehouse that loomed in front of him was old and as the guys at the garage had said the places were in dire need of repair. There was graffiti all over the lower half of the building, which was being encroached on by the overgrown weeds that were trying to take hold and climb up the side of the building. Most of the windows at ground level were broken and patched with bits of wood. He wondered who would have covered the windows if no one came here, he looked up, the windows on the top floor were caged with bars. It didn't look very inviting, he walked around the side of the building and tried pushing and pulling a couple of the doors but the place seemed to be locked up tight. He stopped and listened, nothing, it was in complete silence, just the breeze rustling the leaves on the trees at the far side of the warehouse.

He heard a car on the road but it carried on past, just another learner driver, he supposed, getting ready to practice their emergency stops. He pulled out his phone and rang the station. Tina answered. He told her what he needed. "I'm at unit twenty three, Small Woods Industrial Estate. Can you get someone to contact the owners of this warehouse? I need to get inside, as quickly as possible."

"Yes I'll get back to you." Tina said. Matt liked Tina she was going to grow into a great officer, efficient, mild mannered and eager to get the job done. He hung up, now all he could do was wait. He continued to look around the immediate area but there wasn't much to see, a lot of weeds, trashed buildings and graffiti.

There was the sound of another car on the road, the sound changed and Matt heard tyres crunching across gravel, the car must be heading into the car park, either someone was turning up with the keys or maybe for a private rendezvous, he hadn't expected someone to turn up here with the keys so quickly, so this probably wasn't a visitor for him.

He walked to the side of the warehouse and peered around the corner, he watched as the car pulled up to the front of the building, then reversed so it was facing towards the gates. He stayed where he was and just watched, silently, as the car door opened and Shaun Brown got out.

Chapter Thirty Eight

Matt watched as Shaun opened the boot of his car and pulled out several bags, they didn't look heavy. He confidently slammed the boot of the car, glanced around and started to walk towards the warehouse, he'd been here before.

Matt stayed out of sight whilst he watched him walk around to the side of the building, after a moment he heard the rumble of metal shutters and made his way around the building to get a better look, when he reached the corner and looked around it Shaun had already disappeared inside the building, but his first mistake was leaving the shutters open. Matt moved closer, the shutters were up just a foot or so but it was just enough that Matt could get into the warehouse. If there was something going on in there he wanted to know about it. He squatted down and looked under the shutters, there was no sign of Shaun, it looked like a normal empty warehouse, he looked again just to be certain, there was absolutely no sign of Shaun. He lay on the ground and rolled under the shutters into the empty room. He moved directly to the side of the room as fast as he could, hidden by a filing cabinet he watched and listened, he calmed himself and waited, he knew Shaun was in there and sooner or later he would make a sound and give himself away, then Matt would know which direction to start looking in. He looked around the area he was in, there was little to take any notice of, there was a smell he couldn't quite work out but the place probably had its fair share of rats or mice scurrying around.

He heard a door close to his left, he waited a moment to be certain Shaun wasn't heading his way and when he didn't appear Matt moved towards were the sound came from, he walked along a corridor with all but one of the doors standing open, he looked into some of the rooms, they were just empty offices, a number of them with boarded up windows. The door that was now to his right was the closed door and he had no idea what was on the other side, with it being a heavier door he hoped it was a fire exit or at least a way upstairs. He gingerly pushed it hoping Shaun wasn't stood on the other side of it, he had been right and everything was quiet, he slipped through the door and into the cold, dull stairway. He hoped Shaun wouldn't appear now, there was nowhere to conceal himself, he took the stairs two at a time to the first floor. He put his ear against the door, there was no sound coming from the other side, all he could hear was his own heartbeat thundering through his body. He pushed the door and it opened without a sound, he entered the corridor. It was empty but at least on this floor it was lighter and easier to look around, the offices had windows instead of boards, some cracked but nothing worse and there was nothing to see here. He went up to the next floor, still with no idea where Shaun had gone, it was all quiet there too and again there was nothing but empty offices, some with desks, most without. As he walked back towards the door to enter the stairwell he heard some noises coming from above him, he couldn't make out what was going on but there were definitely voices. It went quiet again, he waited. If he went upstairs now he didn't know what he would find, he truly hoped it would be Alex and Lily but what if he was wrong. No, he would wait here until he could find out what was going on. He pulled the door open slightly ajar, hopefully not enough to be noticed if anyone were to come past. He needed to get more information before he went any further. He waited, he heard the voices on and off, but still no detail. He jumped as a shudder ran up his spine and he felt something run down the back of his neck, he put his hand up and felt sweat, he was nervous, he had to get this right he couldn't let anything happen to either of them upstairs, the more he thought the more sure he was that they were both there. A door closed hard above him and footsteps came tripping down the stairs, through the crack in the door he could see Shaun pass by him, he was rubbing his back as he continued downwards. He waited for a minute, Shaun didn't come back up the stairs, so Matt opened the door and ascended the final flight. At the top he paused at the door, mentally preparing himself for whatever lay beyond, then he went into the corridor. He heard the distant rumbling of the shutters closing from downstairs.

He looked around, it was the same layout as the other floors but this one had padlocks attached to all of the doors, he frowned. "Alex." He bellowed.

"Here." Her voice came back to him, it had never sounded sweeter. He rushed to the first door but the padlock had been snapped shut. He looked around but there was no key anywhere obvious, he pushed at the door, then put his shoulder to it but it wouldn't give. He needed something heavy. He looked around the floor, there was nothing to use that he could see, his eyes fell on the broken phone, it was Alex's with the silly sparkling cover, which he had always joked about having been made for a ten year old princess.

"Are you okay?"

"Matt, is that you?"

"Yes, have you got Lily with you?"

"No, but Beth's here and Cathy in another room, Maria too." Alex yelled.

"Okay look I'm going to find something to open the locks with, I'll be back I promise." He shouted down the corridor, unsure of exactly where her voice was coming from.

"Okay." She replied. "Matt."

"Yes sweetheart."

"I love you."

Matt felt a lump in his throat, this was no time to get emotional, he turned and ran down the stairs as fast as he could, searching for something that would open the doors. In the corner of the stairwell he saw a brick, not ideal but it would have to do, he picked it up and ran back up the stairs. He hit the lock several times, the brick crumbled a little but held up to the task, finally the lock gave up and fell away from the door. He pushed the door open and there was Alex waiting for him, he ran towards her and held her, then he noticed another woman in the corner of the room huddled inside a sleeping bag. "Who's this?" He paused "Where's Lily?"

"Beth, she's been here for a while, It's Elizabeth, one of the girls you've been looking for. There's more people here in the other rooms, we've got to get them out." She looked up at Matt pleading for him to get moving. "I haven't seen Lily yet."

"Okay." He paused whilst he thought. "Beth will you be okay here on your own?" Matt asked gently. Beth nodded.

"It's okay Beth, Matt won't hurt you, he's going to get us all out of here." Alex smiled at Beth to try to give her some reassurance.

Alex and Matt went into the corridor and started working on the next lock, "Who's here?"

"Cathy."

"Cathy, stand away from the door." Matt shouted, as the lock gave way and he kicked the door open and moved on to the next locked door.

Alex stayed to check on Cathy, they hugged and when she was sure Cathy was okay she caught up with Matt at the next door. When she got there he had already opened it, she went inside and found Maria, she was a pretty dark haired girl, young and painfully thin but the smile Maria gave her as she went into the room was worth every moment of being here. "Jane's in the next room." She said. Cathy was standing behind Alex and immediately said. "Maria I've heard all about you." She moved forward to comfort the girl.

Alex moved on with Matt and left them to calm each other, she looked back to the room that she had been in and saw Beth cautiously looking out from the doorway, she looked almost scared to leave the room, within a few seconds Cathy and Maria were moving towards Beth to make sure she was okay.

Matt had the lock off the next door. "Alex, come and help." He shouted as he moved on again. She pushed the door open, there was a young woman who looked to be in a similar mental state as Beth, cowering in the corner. Alex lowered her voice. "Hello, you're safe now, do you want to come out?" The girl just sat in the corner with her hands over her face. "I'm Alex, who are you?" She waited patiently for a reply. Eventually it came.

"Karen. Can we really leave?" It was a small voice but she sounded in control, her hands stayed firmly over her face.

Karen, yes we're going to get out of here, once we have everyone together, are you okay."

"Yes."

Alex followed Matt again, he was already in the next room with a girl who looked healthier than all of the others and immediately came out of the room to meet up with the other girls. Matt looked at Alex. "That's Jane, how many more are there?"

"There's more rooms, keep going Matt, I didn't know there was this many of us up here." She looked down at his hands and noticed they were bleeding from using the brick with the force of his hands against the locks, the brick was breaking up and now half the size it had started out at. "Are you okay? Here let me try."

"I'm fine, just make sure the girls are alright and ready to get moving. We'll go as soon as I get these doors open." Alex could tell he was in pain, but he was determined to get everyone out in one go. She went and checked on the other women, they all seemed okay and were talking and hugging each other, trying to come to terms with what was happening.

"No one in here." Matt shouted down to her. He banged on the next door, there was no reply but he couldn't leave anything to chance, he winced as the brick bit into his hands as it hit the metal plate behind the lock, there was blood everywhere now freely pouring from his hands, he took his jacket off to wrap around the brick but it was no good he couldn't use it wrapped up that way. Alex took the brick from his hands and started bashing the lock, he let her. He hadn't got the force anymore to get this last lock off. It eventually gave up and Alex squealed. "Gotcha." Even through the pain Matt had to smile to himself. She threw the door open but there was just another empty room.

"Where's Lily?" Matt asked.

"Not here, I haven't seen or heard her."

"There must be somewhere else he's keeping her, we've got to keep looking."

She returned to the group and started to usher them down the stairs, Matt followed behind them, making sure they all got out safely. He looked back at the corridor and couldn't believe that they'd been kept here like this, at that moment the jewelled cover on Alex's phone caught his eye, he went back to pick it up and tucked it into his inside pocket before catching up with the women. They were almost at the bottom of the stairs when he reached them, he was relieved to see that on the whole they looked okay, Beth and Karen were still visibly shaken and Karen still wouldn't take her hand from her face, at least she was still moving and that was good.

He looked at Alex and then down at his bleeding hands, it had all been worth it.

Chapter Thirty Nine

Alex was running on adrenalin, she was still shocked that Matt had turned up and rescued all of them, all of them being more than she could have believed, she'd only been aware of four people. They had made it to the bottom of the stairs and she looked back to see Matt standing behind them all, he was looking down at her, she smiled, everything was going to be alright now. Her eyes ran over the other young women here, on the whole they looked okay and they weren't questioning anything, they were all eager to be getting out of here and they were moving as fast as possible. Beth was holding Alex's hand with a vice like grip, it would take her a while and a lot of love to get over what that man had done to her. Alex looked around, Karen was also very subdued and was still covering her face. Alex watched her for a moment and wondered what it was that Shaun had put that poor woman through, then she wondered where Shaun could be keeping Lily.

They all went through the door and into the downstairs corridor, it was darker down here and the group started to feel more nervous about being out of the relative safety of their rooms, Alex did her best to reassure them, but the fading light due to the dusk outside and the boarded windows on this floor weren't helping, it felt like she might lose their trust at any moment. She started to lead them to the open area and towards the metal shutters, where hopefully they would be able to make a quick exit.

Matt was the last person to come out of the stairwell, he walked towards her, then suddenly stopped. "Alex."

"Yes, come on, we have to keep moving."

"Do you smell anything?"

"Yes it smells bad, let's get out." She just wanted to get free of this place.

"I've just remembered what that smell is." His voice fell to a whisper. "It's death." He took off in the opposite direction, throwing doors wide open to reveal nothing more than empty offices. Alex ran behind him leaving the women in a huddle by the shutters. There was a door at the far end of the corridor, it was the last room on this floor. Matt pushed it open with one hard shove, They both instinctively put their hands over their mouths, the smell was coming from in there and it was foul, they had to control themselves to stop from gagging at the smell. In front of them were concrete steps going down but they couldn't see anything beyond the third step, the room was in darkness. They looked at each other not daring to speak what was going through their minds. Matt grabbed his phone and flicked an icon, wincing as he did so from the cuts on his hand, it lit the torch which in turn flooded a small area of the room in intense blue light and they looked down into a small room, this was where the rat smell was coming from, Alex turned to look at Matt, looking away from what the torch was highlighting. "There was another woman here! I can't look... tell me it's not Lily." There was no reply, her words hung in the air. "Matt!"

"No...I just don't know... there's not much left to identify, look, the rats." He said quietly.

Alex glanced back at the body lying on the hard stone floor, she didn't want to look for a second longer but she had to and she could see the rats scurrying away from the beam of light that Matt was moving around the room, she could hear the squealing as they tried to get away. Matt turned the torch off and closed the door. "There's nothing I can do to help her." He said. "I'll call the station." They both stood silently for a moment processing what they had seen in the beam of the torch, Alex leant against the door frame feeling like she was about to pass out from the horror of what she had seen.

"Let's get everyone outside, I need some fresh air and I think they would all like their freedom." She said as she got her breath back, Matt had nodded in agreement. Alex was shaking, frightened that it might be Lily but not wanting to think it was possible, now she had to be brave for the other women here.

They tried to get the metal shutters open but they wouldn't budge, they pulled and pushed frantically they hit buttons that were to the side of the shutters but it was all to no avail. Matt suggested they try and prise some boards from the windows, it would be the only way out of here now the door was locked solidly. Between Matt, Cathy and Alex they managed to uncover a broken window, Matt knocked the remaining glass out with his elbow and started to help the women out of the window. Fifteen minutes later they were all out and standing in the car park breathing fresh air and hugging each other, as much with relief as trying to keep warm. Alex went over to Karen and placed her hand around her shoulders, she was still covering her eye. "What did he do to you?" She asked gently. Karen moved her hand away from her face revealing an ugly infected wound from her eyebrow to her cheek, she was lucky to still have her eye. "Does it hurt?" Alex asked, as soon as she had, she knew it was a terrible question, of course it hurt. Karen nodded. "We'll get you to a hospital, it'll be taken care of." Alex leant in and hugged her, Karen allowed the human contact and Alex could feel her sobbing onto her shoulder.

Matt was watching her as she went around the women making sure they were alright, she looked up and caught him looking at her. She walked over towards him and he put his arms around her, kissing the top of her head. "Are you okay?" He asked.

"I will be when we find Lily." She thought for a second. "That's not her in there Matt, whoever that was must have been down there for a long time."

"I agree." He said. "First we need to get these ladies somewhere safe and warm." He pulled her closer to him. "Then I'm going to find Lily." He added. He looked down at her and knew he would never let her go again.

"I'm okay, go and phone the station, at least two of them need to get to hospital as soon as possible." She smiled up at him.

"I'll be two minutes, okay."

"Okay." She replied, watching him as he walked across the car park towards his car. Something seemed wrong. My car, where's my car she thought, I parked it right there. Matt had parked his almost exactly where hers had been but there was no sign of her car now. She sighed, that'll be another job for the police. She walked back towards the huddle of women as she heard a car engine, revving, loud and close, she looked over towards Matt, he was still walking across the car park, she tried to gauge where the was sound coming from. Before she had time to even register what was happening headlights swept across the car park as a car drove in from the road, too fast, it was going far too fast. "Matt!" She screamed at the top of her lungs.

The women scattered, diving for cover. Alex ran towards Matt, she couldn't see him, the glare of the headlights hurt her eyes. The car kept coming, she leapt out of the way, throwing herself to the ground, face first into the gravel. The car screeched to a halt, slammed into reverse, turned around sharply and exited the way it had come in and at the same speed. After the incredible noise it was as if the world had stopped for a second or two, she didn't know what had happened. She looked up trying to seek out Matt in the rapidly darkening evening, it was almost fully dark now. She got up and walked towards the road. Matt was lying face down in the gravel. "Matt… Matt." Nothing, no reply. "Matt…" She screamed. She pressed her fingers to his neck, yes she was sure there was something there, a pulse, slight but it was there. She needed to get her phone, then it came back to her she no longer had one, Matt's phone would do, where was it? He had been about to use it, she needed to hurry, she needed to get an ambulance here. She quickly searched his hands and his pockets, all the time talking to him, she pulled a phone out of his pocket, along with a packet of cigarettes, for a moment the thought of Matt smoking stopped her train of thought, she looked down at the phone but it wasn't his, it was hers that Shaun had smashed, she fumbled with it trying to get it to light up but it was dead. The tears started and she couldn't stop them, the other women were still hiding wherever they had fled to because she was sat alone over the crumpled body of the man she loved. It couldn't end like this she wouldn't let it, she looked down and it registered with her how much blood there was spreading across Matt's shirt, she screamed "No!". She didn't want to leave Matt but she needed to find his phone. "Where are you all." She screamed through the tears. "Don't leave us here. We need you now." A hand from behind softly touched her shoulder, it was Cathy, in her hand was what was left of Matt's phone, shattered by the impact from the car. Alex cried even harder, how would they get help now. "I've got to get an ambulance here."

"I'll go." Cathy said.

"There's a garage on the corner, see if there's anyone there." Alex said.

"Which way?" Cathy asked.

"Oh never mind. Talk to him, don't stop talking, I'll go." Alex instructed. She tenderly kissed Matt's forehead, stood up and ran, she had never moved at that speed or run that distance before in her life but she approached the garage in what felt like seconds, the shutters were all down. She stopped, with her hands on her knees she gasped for breath then she started crying again, hot angry tears. This couldn't be happening. She stood up and beat her fists against the shutters and started screaming out of sheer frustration. The shutter rumbled and opened up, startling her. A man stood in front of her. "What's up with you?" He said.

"Phone the police, now. Please, Charmsbury 634792. Ambulance, police, now." She gasped for breath.

To his credit he didn't ask any questions he made the call then he said. "Now calm down, where's the problem? I'll drive you back, come on."

"Did you see a car come past here maybe ten minutes ago?" Alex asked.

"No, no one's gone along this road since this afternoon as far as I know, just a guy asking if we'd seen his girlfriend." He looked over at Alex, it's you isn't it? He was looking for you.

"Yes. Now he's in trouble." Alex was pleased this was a man that knew how to talk and drive at the same time. "Someone drove into the car park and ran him over. We need to help him." As she said this they pulled into the car park and Alex ran from the car to Matt who was still in exactly the same position she had left him in, with Cathy holding his bloodied hand and talking to him. Alex sat down and shooed Cathy away, no one else should be with him now just her, she needed to be there for him.

She cried silent tears as she talked to him, rubbed his hand gently and dropped kisses on his face and hands. The man from the garage, she hadn't thought to ask his name, came over to them with a blanket from his car. He looked at Matt and took his pulse, frowning he said. "We can't move him, he may have internal injuries, I'll go and wait on the road for the ambulance, shout if you need me. Keep talking to him." He was looking around at the women standing around the car park, wondering where they had all come from. Alex continued to talk to Matt whilst trying to gently tuck the blanket around him, she wanted to take him in her arms but the man had been right, they just couldn't risk moving him yet. Everything around them was silent, she didn't think she'd ever heard such deafening, unwelcome silence before in her life. "Please Matt, please, talk to me." She whispered into his ear. "I need you, just talk to me, say anything, tell me it'll all be okay." She wept. "I love you." As she looked down onto his broken body and handsome face. "Matt, please, just say something." In response she felt him squeeze her hand, it was gentle but it was there, he was going to be okay.

Then in the distance she caught the faint sound of sirens, please let them be for us she silently prayed. Slowly the sound came closer and the silence was broken, then suddenly everything seemed to happen all at once. There were arms around her pulling her away from Matt, she fought them and turned to argue and saw the familiar face of Dan, she crumpled into his chest, "Save him Dan, don't let anything happen to him." Dan wrapped his jacket around her and turned to Tina.

"Get the women together, get their names and get more cars out here, we need to get them back to the station." Tina touched Alex's arm and swiftly went off to organise the other women who were standing in a huddle now dazed by everything that was happening. "Alex what happened can you tell me?" His voice was kind and patient.

"There's another woman, dead, in there. The cellar." She pointed to the warehouse. As she turned she saw two paramedics standing over Matt, putting an oxygen mask over his face. Dan looked over.

"We're taking him in, now, he's in a bad way." The paramedic said to Dan.

"We're going with him." Dan said immediately guiding Alex towards the ambulance. "Tina, wait for backup then take the car back to the station, I'll ring you later. When they arrive get them to check the warehouse, Alex said there's a body in the cellar." With that he tossed the car keys to her and joined Alex in the ambulance.

Suddenly Alex's head was filled with sirens and machines beeping, all she could do was hold Matt's hand, cry and pray that he would be alright. Nothing mattered now except for Matt, the people around her had taken over and were in charge over his life or death.

Chapter Forty

Shaun drove as if the hounds of hell were after him, he saw an ambulance and police car, sirens blaring and lights flashing, driving in the opposite direction, they weren't about to stop him for speeding but he wasn't taking any chances, he pulled over to let them safely drive up the centre of the road at high speed. He wasn't sure what to do next, he wanted to go home, get June and get the hell out of Somerset but he knew she would ask too many questions and slow him down, she'd still be packing her damn bag whilst the police turned up and arrested him, he couldn't take that risk, prison would kill him. He had just driven directly at a police officer certainly harming him and for all he knew he could have done far worse damage, why did Inspector Jones have to get involved? All he knew was someone was sneaking around the warehouse, he thought they must have found where he had dumped that last bitch's car and gone snooping, he had sat in his car watching to see if anything was happening, eventually he had seen all of his girls in the car park, someone had got them out. He hadn't realised who it was until he had him in the beam of his headlights and by then it was too late to turn back. The police would come looking for him very soon, he had decisions to make and quickly. They would be especially hard on him now he had harmed a police officer. He was thinking too quickly, he needed to calm himself and work out what to do next.

He slowed his speed, took deep breaths and regained some control, he couldn't stop his hands from shaking, he just held on tight to the steering wheel, his knuckles showing white. He decided that he couldn't go home, at least if June didn't know anything she couldn't be implicated, he knew they would go to the house first to look for him, so that was the one place he couldn't be seen.

He turned the radio on as he sped through the dark country lanes of Somerset, he needed to hear the news, he was praying that Inspector Jones was still alive. It seemed like he had to wait forever but finally the news came on. It was headline news and the woman's voice sounded like it was accusing him directly as she read out a list of facts and they spilled into his car.

'A police officer has been seriously injured at the site of a disused warehouse on Small Woods Industrial estate in Exeter tonight, a car drove into him, seemingly with intent to harm the officer.

We are led to believe he had discovered where a number of missing young women had been kept as prisoners, he was in the process of getting the women to safety when the incident happened.

A police spokesperson has reported that the police officer and three of the women are in hospital being treated for their injuries. The police are looking for a local man to help with their enquiries.'

He turned off his radio and the woman's accusing voice, at least Inspector Jones was still alive.

He kept driving into the night.

Chapter Forty One

Alex sat in the stark, unforgiving lights of the hospital waiting room, she felt so helpless, there was nothing she could do, yet she felt like she needed to be doing something, anything that could help. The doctors and nurses had taken over now, she could only wait. The police had started their investigation, it shouldn't take them long, they knew who was responsible for the carnage that she now found herself in the middle of. They would have Shaun in custody before the night was out, he wouldn't get away with this, the police would make sure of it. She sat silently not wanting to let anyone into her thoughts except for Matt, he had to come through this. She knew she would have to talk to the police soon, they needed to know what they were dealing with. She got up and made her way to the nurse's station. It seemed to her they wouldn't look her in the eye but maybe it was just her imagination, it was easy to think the worst, but they were just too busy taking care of a hospital full of sick people. All she wanted was some paper and a pen, finally the nurse smiled at her and gave her what she asked for. She returned to her plastic chair and recalled the events of the last couple of days in the way she knew best; she committed every word of it to paper.

At some time through the evening Dan joined her on the uncomfortable plastic chairs, he put his arm around her and handed her a cup of sweet instant tea but he didn't say a word, she sipped it, winced at the taste, placed the cup on the floor and continued to write whilst

Dan watched, she logged every last detail that she could remember and it had filled the waiting time. It was the worst hours of her life, waiting for news. Her and Dan's eyes looked enquiringly at every nurse that passed, hoping that they would find out what was happening but so far all of them had just walked past not even glancing in their direction.

"You should go home and rest Alex." Dan said in a gently tone.

"I can't, not until I know he will come through this."

"I'm going to find the doctor." She let him go, he could get far more information than her, when he approached people they listened and answered, it was the uniform, it worked every time. Alex watched him as he stood at the desk talking to a nurse, she was nodding and explaining something to him but Alex couldn't hear what was being said.

The waiting room was suddenly filled with people, they were milling around her, she looked up and her Nan was heading towards her with her arms open. Alex gladly let them comfort her to a chorus of questions. Jack was by her side and when Alex looked up again she saw her Mum and Dad there with Mel, Mark and Nick and Charlie from the paper too, it was too much for her, she couldn't hold it together any longer, she held onto her mum and cried.

Dan returned to the group nodding and smiling at the sudden company. He looked at Alex. "They don't know anything yet he's still in theatre, they've promised to tell you the second he comes out. I've got to get to the station, it seems Shaun Brown's not at home." He turned to leave.

"Wait." Alex called after him. "Take this it's everything I remember."

"Thanks." He took the papers from her. "We will find him."

"Find Lily, please, someone must know where she is." Alex's eyes pleaded with him, something good needed to come out of all of this, she was due some good news. Dan nodded and walked away.

Alex fielded questions from everyone, whilst still watching every nurse that passed just in case they needed to talk to her, eventually they were all talked out and they sat together as a group, silent, just waiting for news. They were all absorbing the details of what had happened at the warehouse. Then Jack broke through everyone's thoughts with an update on Lily and the phone calls. "So you mean by now they should know where the call came from?" Alex was surprised no one had told her but maybe they had thought she had enough on her plate, she couldn't blame them.

"Yes, now they have the phone number they can triangulate the data and pinpoint where the call came from." He added.

"I need to speak to Dan, does anyone have a phone?" She looked around. Suddenly five mobile phones were thrust towards her, she smiled, it felt good, it was the first time she had had anything to smile about in what seemed like an age. She plucked Mark's phone out of his hand, for no reason other than it was the closest and she dialled the police station. "I need to speak with PC Dawes."

"I'm sorry he's not available, how can I help?" The voice came back.

"Get him to ring me as soon as he can, do you have a record of this number?"

"Yes but who wants him?"

"Alex Price."

174

"Yes, of course, I'm sorry I didn't recognise your phone number, is there any news yet?" Alex didn't want to make small talk.

"No, I just need Dan." Then she cut the call off and handed it back to Mark. "He'll call soon." She said to him. She turned to Jack and got him to give her every bit of information that he had.

Fully updated and armed with all of Jacks information she started to wonder if she had been wrong all along, Lily hadn't been at the warehouse, she had no idea where else Shaun might be keeping her, if it was Shaun at all, she shuddered when she remembered the body at the warehouse. She was sure the police would soon find out, Shaun couldn't run forever and if what Cathy and Beth had said was true he wouldn't leave his wife for too long. She thought Lily would be home very soon and possibly without Jack having to give any money away. Would he even risk the swap after what he'd done to Matt? Mark's mobile rang and he handed it to her. "Dan, any update on Lily's whereabouts?" She asked.

"Yes, the phone people can't get an exact pin point, they've been working on some masts, updating them, but it's local somewhere around Blunsford by the looks of it, they're still trying for an exact location, it'll take them a while."

"Blunsford? That's the other side of Charmsbury, nowhere near Stooke or Exeter." Alex was stunned she must have got it all wrong. "Have you got anybody out there?"

"Alex don't worry, of course we're taking care of things, any news yet?" Dan asked.

"No nothing, I'm trying to believe that no news is good news."

"I'll be back with you as soon as I've finished here."

Alex relayed the news to Jack who looked confused too, they had all wanted to believe that Shaun was involved in this, alarm bells should have rung when Jack said he didn't know anyone of that name or description. They would just have to wait.

They sat around for a while longer, it was Mark that broke rank first, he said he had to get back to Summer, he had left her with Angie and Steve and wanted to get back, he took Mel with him, Charlie and Nick went minutes later. Now it was just family left to sit and wait. She wondered if Dan had contacted Matt's Mum, Matt didn't have much to do with her since she had moved to Spain with her new husband but she ought to know, Alex would ring her as soon as she got home. Silence fell over the group again as they sat and waited.

They didn't have to wait much longer, a young, clean shaven doctor approached the group and asked Alex politely to step into a side room so they could talk, Mary and Janet got up to accompany her but she shook her head, she needed to do this alone. She followed him as he held the door open for her, she couldn't tell anything from his face, he was giving nothing away, until she sat down.

"I'm sorry, there was nothing more we could do." He said quietly and thoughtfully.

"No." She screamed.

Chapter Forty Two

Mary and Janet heard the scream and rushed into the side room, Alex was standing up, screaming and crying with her arms wrapped protectively around herself, the doctor was trying to console her and explain what happened, unsuccessfully. They moved towards her and took over from the doctor and wrapped themselves around her like a protective barrier.

"I'm sorry, he just didn't have the strength left for the operation, there was too much internal bleeding and we couldn't stem it."

"Thank you doctor." Janet said. All they wanted at that moment was to be left alone.

"Is there anything you would like to ask me Alex?" He said, he could see that it was taking all of their strength just to accept what had happened. "I'll be available whenever you want to talk, you will have questions, please stay here as long as you need to." Mary shook her head and he slipped out of the room, leaving them to grieve.

The women stayed together for some time before Janet left the room to pass the news on to Jack and Paul but the doctor had already given them the bare bones of what happened. Everyone was shocked that now this was a murder enquiry.

Alex asked to see the doctor again, he entered the room almost immediately. "Can I see him?"

"I'm sorry but we can't do that now, you can come back tomorrow and we will have him ready for you then."

"I need to see him." She sobbed.

"I'm sorry. I wish there was something I could do." He added as a nurse gestured to him to follow her. Alex watched him walk away.

Twenty minutes later Dan turned up with Tina, both of them were trying to be professional but their puffy red eyes told the truth, they took their turns in consoling Alex. No one could believe what had happened and they were determined to find Shaun Brown, they had over half of the officers working that night out looking for him. A voice broke through the sadness. "Alex, come here and let me hold you, you poor girl." The voice belonged to a tall, large lady with the kindest eyes Dan had ever seen, she pushed her way forward. "Come with me sweet girl, talk to me." Alex allowed her to lead the group towards a quiet room. Janet and Mary were pleased to let Patty the midwife take over, a familiar face amongst the nurses was what Alex needed, someone who could really help. Patty had worked at the hospital for twenty five years and had delivered Alex, she was a family friend. Mary let them go forward and kept everyone else back, mouthing to them the words, 'let them go'. The women of the family knew Patty would have many words of wisdom for Alex, she was an incredible woman and had had her own fair share of pain in her life. Alex poured everything out to Patty who sat patiently and listened whilst holding her hand. "Now you have to go on Alex, for Matt, make him proud. He loved you so much, you know that don't you?"

"Yes but he died saving me, how could I let that happen?"

"It wasn't your fault, he loved you, he was protecting you sweetheart and those other girls." She said gently.

"And now they won't let me see him, I want to hold his hand one last time Patty and they won't let me." The tears ran down her face.

"Honey, that's for the best, see him tomorrow when he's ready to be seen."

"I just want to tell him I love him. It's all that matters now."

Patty pulled Alex into her ample bosom and hugged her, she didn't want Alex to see she was crying too. She made her mind up. "Come with me." She took Alex by the hand and they left the room. She left Alex with Janet and went to speak to a nurse, in less than three minutes she was back. "Are you ready?" She said to Alex.

"Alex looked up her wide eyed." Something passed between them and Alex nodded. They walked through the hospital together and took the lift down to the morgue. Alex took a deep breath as they entered the cold, bare room, there on a trolley to the side of the room was Matt, his body covered with a sheet but his face looking peaceful as if he was no more than asleep. Alex ran to him with no hesitation, smoothed his hair back from his handsome face and took his wounded hand in hers and told him how much she loved him, she spoke to him like it was the most natural thing in the world. Patty stood by the doors to ensure they wouldn't be disturbed, now it was Patty that was weeping, just watching the strength in Alex.

After ten minutes Patty went to Alex's side and took her hand, "It's time to go now sweetheart." She gently urged, Alex leant down and kissed Matts forehead and walked a few steps backwards, not wanting to turn her back to him. They left the morgue, Alex stopped and looked up at Patty. "Thank you." It was all she said but

Patty saw that Alex's eyes were dry now and that was thanks enough.

Less than half an hour later Alex and the family left the hospital, Jack had insisted that she stayed with them for the night, they wanted to be able to take care of her, she didn't argue, she thought it would be the best place for her too.

Chapter Forty Three

Alex opened her eyes and the light flooded in, for just a moment it was a normal day. She realized that this was her Nan's house and questioned why she would be there instead of at home. That was the moment the reality came crashing in on her. She lay in bed and recalled the events of yesterday, so much had happened but Patty had allowed her to say her goodbyes to Matt and for that she was truly grateful. She knew that she needed to get up and face the day, it was going to do no one any good for her to just lie around in bed, she would only feel worse for it, the answer was to keep busy. If she was doing something constructive she would be too busy to feel sorry for herself. She got up and headed for the shower, she needed an update on Lily too, whatever had happened Lily was still out there somewhere and Alex was determined to find her and bring her home.

It was still early, her Nan and Jack were still asleep, Alex opened up her Nan's computer and started to search social media for news on Lily, she got side tracked by the news coverage about Matt, this wasn't going to be as straight forward as she had hoped, every time she saw a story or a comment about Matt she could feel the lump in her throat and tears welling in her eyes, she needed to pull herself together. This would be nationwide news now a police officer had been killed and the whole country would be on the lookout for Shaun Brown, it would be there every time she turned on the television or a radio. She turned off the computer and went to the house phone, she needed to get in touch with Matt's mum, it wasn't a conversation she was looking forward to but she wanted to get it done before Jack and her Nan got up and before his mum turned on the news and learnt of her son's death through the media. Alex felt a pang of guilt for not ringing her sooner.

The call was every bit as difficult as Alex had expected but his mum had been patient and kind with her, she said that she would be travelling over as soon as she could get a flight, they would finally meet, Alex had hoped for better circumstances but at least she would be here to say goodbye to Matt.

She heard movement from upstairs and put the coffee on for them when they came down; they were surprised to see her up and getting breakfast ready. Her Nan gently suggested that she should be resting but Alex said no, she had things to do. Alex caught the look that passed between her Nan and Jack. "I'm okay, I promise. I need to be doing something, we still have to find Lily and Matt would want us get her home safely." She caught a lump in her throat when she mentioned his name but again she fought the tears.

"Then let us help you." Her Nan had said. Alex nodded in response. She knew she would need all the help she could get.

After they had eaten Alex made a few more phone calls to friends and to the newspaper, then she sat down to talk to Jack about having to get the money for Lily. "Fifty thousand, that's a lot of money Jack."

"It's okay we can get it. Don't worry."

"Did he say where you were to meet him?"

"No, I assume he will ring again it's all a big power trip for him." Jack said. As they were talking Dan walked into the room, to see how Alex was.

"Dan your timing is perfect, we were discussing Lily." Alex said.

"Well I have news too, but first how are you?"

"Okay I think, I rang Matt's mum this morning and explained everything to her, she's coming over as soon as she can get a flight."

"That's good." He paused. "Alex it might be a bit soon but when you're ready will you stop by the station and sort out Matt's personal stuff, we want to be sure you have everything and nothing gets thrown away by mistake." He looked at Alex gauging her response.

"Sure." She replied, not knowing what else to say, her heart felt like it was breaking.

"I'm sorry Alex, I don't know how I should be handling this." He hesitated. "We have all available officers out looking for Shaun and that's all we can do at the moment, everyone at the station is in shock, although they are determined that he won't get away with this." He added, trying to give Alex reassurance that everything possible was being done.

"None of us know how to handle things Dan, it's fine, we'll find our way through it all together." She smiled at him. "Is there any news on Lily?"

"Yes, that's the news I have for you. We think we've got the area, we will have to wait for another call to pinpoint them but we have officers in Blunsford looking now."

"Will you keep me in the loop? I know it's a lot to ask but I need something to focus on right now Dan."

"I'll do what I can Alex." He smiled at her. It was the same answer that Matt always gave. Alex knew Dan would try to help, he was one of the good guys.

"I need to go home, I've got to get changed, then I'm heading over to Blunsford so I'm on the spot if there's any news."

She glanced over at Dan as she remembered what she wanted to ask him. "Did anyone find my car?"

"Yes, it's at the station now, it had been moved down into a side road, out of sight, away from the front of the warehouse."

"Thank you, I really didn't want to go back to the warehouse. I'm not sure I could have faced that. Are the other women all okay?" She asked, Dan nodded in response but before he could elaborate her Nan interrupted.

"If you're ready to go home Alex" Mary asked obviously concerned. "I can come with you"

"No it's fine Nan, I have to go back sometime on my own and I want to go. I can't stay here forever."

"You can, as long as you want to… but I do understand, as long as you know we're here for you."

"Of course I do." Alex smiled. "And your brownies." Which got everyone smiling.

Dan offered to take her over to the station to collect her car, she jumped at the offer, now was her chance to find out what was happening with Shaun Brown.

Alex sat in the car whilst Dan drove, there was an awkward silence for the first mile, it was difficult to know what to say to each other without stepping on each other's memories, it was Alex that broke the silence. "Is Matt's car at the station too?"

"Yes, they brought it back at the same time as yours. Do you want to take it home? I can get someone to drive it over for you whenever you want it, there's no evidence to collect from it."

"Thank you that would be great."

"Alex are you really okay to go home?"

"Yes, really, I want to be there, it's the closest I can be to him now." She said. There followed another lull in the conversation. She broke the silence again. "Is there any news on Shaun? Have they any idea where he might be?"

"Nothing yet but all ways out of the country have been blocked to him and every police force is on the lookout for him, it's only a matter of time. He won't get away with it Alex, I promise." His voice was full of bitterness.

"So he didn't turn up at his home then?" She was surprised.

"No we have officers posted there around the clock, no one's seen anything unusual. His wife doesn't seem to know anything about what's been going on. She's nervous, won't or can't really say anything much and she seems genuinely worried about her husband."

"She should be worried! Does she know what he's done?" Alex asked.

"If she does, she isn't saying. She seems quite shocked that he hasn't been home." He said blankly.

They pulled up at the car park, her car was parked next to Matt's. "I'll take Matt's car if that's okay Dan."

"Okay I'll get the keys, hang on." He disappeared into the station. Two minutes later he returned with the keys. "One of the guys will drop your car round to you later."

"Thank you." Alex said as Dan looked at her carefully.

"You will be okay won't you?"

"Of course I will, don't worry." She managed to smile at him.

Alex turned away from Dan and slid into Matt's car. For a moment she just ran her hands over the steering wheel, and breathing deeply she took in the faint lingering smell of Matt's aftershave. She put the key in and the engine jumped into life, the CD player instantly kicked in, playing his favourite Coldplay album just as he would have left it. She cried a little but sang along with the music, just as Matt would have done. She felt close to him here, she slowly drove home, absorbing all the sensations of what he would have felt when he had been on his way to make sure she was safe.

She arrived home, everything was exactly as she had left it except for a bunch of flowers on the doorstep. She picked them up, the card said they were from Mel, she carried them inside and put them on the coffee table in the lounge, she looked up at the painting on the wall taking in the view, Buddha Mountain in Thailand, they had been happy there, she smiled.

Chapter Forty Four

The phone rang, it sat on the table but no one heard it. Mary was in the kitchen, baking, Jack was in the garden, they were both doing things to try to stop themselves from thinking about everything that had happened. The phone continued to ring and flash up the name Lily, just as Dan had programmed it to.

Tom sat looking at his mobile phone in disbelief. "They're not answering." He said to Trish.

"What!" She was surprised too. "Have they given up on her?"

"I guess they'll see that someone has rung, we will have to ring back later." They were both shocked that the world seemed to have stopped revolving around them. "Maybe they're onto us?"

"How could they be Tom, they'd have been here by now if they knew anything. How could they anyway, we haven't left anything to chance, we've been careful, really careful." Her voice trailing off thoughtfully.

"You're right." He capitulated, still slightly worried. Lily was again sleeping, it was getting more difficult to keep her under control when she was awake now. She was getting braver and a few times had bolted for the door trying to get out, she had even tried to attack him earlier today, he would be glad to get her home, he was beginning not to care about hurting Jack anymore. Trish was threatening to leave him to it, she needed to get back to work before someone realised she wasn't at home in bed with the flu. She'd been mentioning more often how stupid he'd been keeping up his vendetta against Jack, she'd even mentioned that his father would have been ashamed of what he was doing had he been alive to see it. He thought he would have a lot more to deal with once Lily had gone home, Trish was never going to forgive him for this. He let ten minutes pass before he picked the phone up again and pressed the redial button.

"Jack, Jack... the phone." Mary shouted. Jack was out in the garden. Mary approached the phone, looking at it suspiciously, Jack hadn't come in and she needed to know what was going on, she made a decision and answered it. "Hello."

"Put Jack on." The voice said.

"You'll have to speak to me, who are you?"

"That's not important, tell Jack tomorrow twelve o'clock, in the park."

"Which park?" She asked trying to keep her cool just as Jack appeared in the doorway and took the phone from her.

"What do you want?" He asked gruffly.

"You, tomorrow, the park, twelve o'clock by the bridge. No police." The phone went dead. Jack immediately phoned Dan and relayed the information.

"Okay Jack are you ready for this?"

"Of course I am if it means we get Lily back."

"I'll contact the bank and arrange for the money and be with you first thing in the morning. It's all going to be okay so try not to worry."

"Easier said than done Dan."

Mary stood looking at him whilst all of this was going on, he was looking older since all of this had started and she was worried about him, she had noticed his hand straying towards his chest on occasions, she prayed that he was as well as he kept insisting he was. She hoped that tomorrow this would all be over and she could concentrate on getting Alex through the next few weeks and Jack could settle down into married life as he had hoped they would.

Dan was at the station trying to get hold of the mobile phone supplier, he needed them to have pinpointed Lily's whereabouts, then he wanted to check on Alex, it would be tough for her to be in the house alone so soon after Matt's death and Matt would have wanted him to keep an eye on her. The phone company said it would take them a little while to check the coordinates but they promised to get back to him as soon as they could and yes they were aware how important this was. Now he'd heard from Jack he was fairly sure that he wasn't looking for the same person that killed Matt, he was almost certain that they were trying to find two separate people. He had put out alerts for Shaun Brown and there were dedicated officers out looking for him. It was only a matter of time before they would find him, he couldn't keep running forever and when they did catch up with him he would pay for his actions for a long time to come. For now, for him it was a waiting game and he decided to go and wait it out with Alex, she needed people around her at the moment and until he heard from the phone company there was nothing he could do, the women that had been kept at the warehouse were being interviewed and giving their statements, they were being well looked after by the female officers and accommodation had been arranged for them in town, keeping them all together seemed like a good idea at the moment.

He got in his car and drove across town only to find that Matt's car wasn't there and neither was Alex. He turned around and went back to the station, he could start sorting Matt's things out, it was a job that Alex shouldn't have to do.

Chapter Forty Five

Alex was keeping herself busy, she had decided that she needed to drive out to see June, maybe the woman in Shaun's life would know more about where he might have gone, more than she was prepared to tell the police. Alex just had to get her to admit it.

The first thing she needed to do was to buy herself a new phone, she wanted to be able to stay in contact with everyone. She entered a phone shop, there were people milling about everywhere, all going about their day like nothing had changed, she wished she could feel like them instead of the numbness that was casting a veil over her, she felt as if she was going through the motions, trying to push herself through a dense fog. She spent a few minutes looking through the huge array of phones on offer and quickly got bored with trying to work out the merits of each of them, there was a time nothing would have given her more pleasure, but not today. She decided to go for a new state of the art phone, she couldn't be bothered to pick and choose, she paid and left, relieved to be getting away from other shoppers. She opened the box and slipped her own SIM card into the phone, it worked, finally it felt like she was back on the grid now. She spent the next thirty minutes in the car setting the phone up and making sure all of the information she needed was still there. Most importantly she managed to pull her precious photos of Matt and the wedding down from the cloud storage and back onto her phone, she looked at each photo in turn, smiling and crying, he really was gorgeous, what was she going to do with her life now. She finally dried her eyes, composed herself and set out determined to find some answers.

This time when she drove into Stooke she didn't hesitate to drive down the track, she was surprised by a police car being parked in front of the house. She remembered Dan mentioning that they had posted someone here waiting for Shaun to attempt to return home so they could pick him up. To her relief the police officer was someone Alex had never seen before, maybe he was from another area brought in to help with the case, when a police officer is murdered they pull out all of the stops. She went to speak to him, she was in luck, he didn't know her either so there were no awkward questions. She approached him as a reporter, he wouldn't tell her anything but she didn't get the impression that he was going to do anything to stop her from approaching June, his only interest was in waiting for Shaun to appear. As she turned away from him she noticed the firearm at his side and shuddered. She walked towards the front door and saw it was already ajar, she knocked but there was no reply. She glanced back towards the officer who now only seemed to be focused on the driveway she pushed the door and walked inside, "Hello." She shouted, "June, are you here?" There was no reply. She hoped June would be here somewhere and hadn't been spirited away by some well meaning relative, if she had been surely the house would be locked up, no, she must be here, she thought. Beth had mentioned that June never left the house and that she had never met any relatives of theirs, never even heard any spoken about. Alex looked to her left, into a comfortable looking kitchen but it was empty. Then pushed a door in front of her, it opened to reveal a large lounge, June was sitting on the settee, she turned to look at Alex with an expression of surprise but said nothing. Alex took in the scene, a middle aged woman, overweight with pale skin was slumped on the settee in front of her, the woman was wheezing, it seemed she couldn't get her breath. "Are you okay?" Alex asked sounding more concerned than she felt.

"No." It sounded like more of a breath than a word. June pointed to a bag on the other side of the room. Alex went to get it for her. It was heavy, she unzipped it, inside was all manner of medical equipment, Alex took it to June, she would know what she needed. Junes fingers moved quickly over the tubes and bottles and within a few minutes she had sorted out, nasal prongs and attached them to a small oxygen bottle. "Thank you." She wheezed. "Who are you?"

"June, where is Shaun." Alex didn't feel like making small talk or waiting around until June felt well enough to fob her off with any lies.

June shrugged, "Who are you?" She asked again.

"Alex, reporter." She hesitated. "Shaun killed a police officer, you know that? Well that police officer was my boyfriend." She swallowed back the welling emotion.

"Sorry. I don't know, he's not here. You shouldn't be either." She wheezed.

"Do you know where we might find him?"

"No."

"You know about the women he had locked away?"

"No." A fleeting look of surprise showed on her face.

"June you must know something. Do you know what happened to the women who he brought here to help you?"

"No."

"You don't know or won't tell me?" Alex was losing patience. The woman in front of her may have health issues but she also didn't seem to care much about what her husband had been up to. Alex wasn't in the mood for this, she knew she shouldn't have come here. "Sorry to have bothered you." She said with a certain amount of sarcasm as she got up, making it obvious she wasn't sorry at all. She was aware the woman was ready to say something but at that moment she couldn't care less. She had a moment of lucid thought and knew she shouldn't be here, she needed to do the work that no one else seemed to be doing, finding Lily. She looked back to June, "Did you know a young girl called Lily?" June shook her head. Alex walked out of the room, past the police officer and got back in Matt's car, he watched her as she left. She wasn't going to let anyone get away with anything today and she was determined to find Lily, she was aware the anger was kicking in and she welcomed it, it was more constructive than the heavy cloud of sadness.

She drove back to the police station, she wanted to know what the women had been through, she hoped that there would be someone at the station that would be willing to talk to her but she wouldn't hold her breath.

She walked through the glass double doors and the faces in front of her changed, she could read pity in them. She looked them in the eye. "Is Dan here?" She directed the question at Tina.

"No, he's out following a lead."

"Shaun or Lily?" She asked outright.

"We can't tell you that, sorry." Tina really did look sorry too. Alex knew the score however much she didn't like it.

"Okay, well are the women still here that were in the warehouse with me?"

"Yes they're being interviewed now."

"Can I see them?"

"Sorry, no."

"Okay so do you want to interview me?" She asked trying to think of every way she could of getting access to Cathy and the others.

"No, you wrote everything down for us and the other women are corroborating what you told us. We don't want to make you re-live events unless we really have to."

"Tina, I need a way to get some information, I have to find Lily." She looked Tina in the eye, hoping that honesty might get her a result.

"I understand Alex but I can't tell you what's going on, you know that. In fact I could lose my job for telling you that Shaun had nothing to do with Lily, the girls had never heard her name mentioned." Tina offered a sly smile.

"So do you know who the dead victim was?" Alex was pushing her luck now Tina had offered one piece of information.

"Yes, it's not Lily."

"Where did you say Dan had gone?"

"I didn't but he's in Blunsford." Tina was still smiling and this time Alex returned the smile, she mouthed the words 'thank you' and turned to leave the station. "Alex."

"Yes."

"I'm sorry… if you need a friend…" she let the end of the sentence hang in the air. Alex continued out of the station, Tina's kindness had threatened to bring the tears again. She got into the car drove out to Blunsford with Coldplay's 'Fix You', blasting from the stereo.

Chapter Forty Six

Dan had just arrived in Blunsford and he was waiting for a phone call, he pulled in to a supermarket car park and saw the other two cars he had sent out here, he just hoped he was doing the right thing otherwise the guy at the top would be wondering why he was using up police resources to sit around a car park. He was sure that this was right though, the calls had come from this area, Lily was here somewhere and all he needed now was the exact location, now they were ready to go as soon as the information came in. His mind drifted to the carnage of the previous day, a police officer going about his business, had Matt let emotion get in the way? He had no idea, but it certainly seemed like he had done everything by the book. Then there was Alex, how would she cope with it all, the world seemed to be throwing everything at her at the moment. He had envied Matt, he had never managed to get into a really meaningful relationship, he knew it was tough on the partner of a police officer, there was always some sort of problem even if you got lucky and it was just the hours you had to work. There was a tap on his window, he turned to see Dave, one of the officers he had put out here, he opened his window and caught the smell of fried chicken. "Been eating again Dave?"

"Just a snack." He replied smiling. "Any news yet?"

"I'm expecting a call any minute."

"Want us to have another drive around?"

"Yes, why not, it's better than you eating yourself to death in a car park. I'll call you as soon as I hear anything."

"Okay. Is there any news on the scum that killed Matt?" He wasn't smiling anymore.

"Nothing, but he won't get away with this." Dan replied.

"Not if I get my hands on him he won't!" With that Dave returned to his car and his partner and drove out of the car park, the other police car stayed in sight, parked up. They could do nothing else but wait.

Dan watched everything that was going on around him, people parking up and going shopping, there was a group of young men meeting up, maybe the beginning of a stag party going for lunch before a long day of drinking. He missed those carefree days, most days now if he was lucky he might get a pint at the end of his shift before falling into bed exhausted. He was musing over what he would do if he had the time when he looked up and saw a familiar car driving along the road in front of where he had parked. It was Matt's car and Alex was at the wheel, what was she doing here? He knew from talking to Matt that she had a great nose for a story and would always interfere at the exact moment you didn't want her to, he thought he may have mentioned the calls being traced to this area, he was sure he had but what else did she know, he racked his brains for exactly what he had told her and he knew whatever it had been it was too much, he also knew she was determined to find Lily, he should have kept the update to himself. He put on his seatbelt and pulled out of the car park and followed her, was she taking a chance being here or did she know something, Dan had no idea but he felt like it was his job to keep an eye on her, he felt a responsibility towards her for Matt's sake. He followed her up and down roads, trying to hang well back, he didn't think she'd appreciate being followed. It didn't seem like she was heading anywhere in particular, it felt like she was just randomly driving around the town he let her disappear into the distance.

He headed back to meet up with the other waiting officers, it wasn't too long before his phone rang. "Hello PC Dawes?" A woman's voice asked.

"Yes."

"This is Veronica, we have been tracing a call for you, we now have the coordinates."

"Okay fire away." He felt his pulse increase, could they get Lily back before Jack had to part with fifty thousand pounds?

"The call came from twenty four Warren Way. Do you need anything else?"

"Thank you, can you trace any other calls that have been made from that number?"

"Yes, there were three calls made to a Charmsbury number three days ago and a few calls to the number you provided us with from yesterday and the day before."

"Anything else?"

"Yes just one more that was made to a hospital in Yorkshire, the Northern General, that was three days ago too."

"Thank you."

"If there's anything else you need just let me know."

"Thank you Veronica." Dan ended the call. The three calls to Charmsbury were the ones that Alex took at the newspaper office and the others to Jack but a hospital in Yorkshire didn't fit the bill at all, although that was close to where the SIM card was bought. He tapped the address twenty four Warren Way into his GPS, it was on another industrial estate, he put a message out to the other cars, turned his lights on and cut through the traffic en route to get Lily.

The GPS took him directly to the address he had entered into it but it hadn't been what he was expecting, he pulled up in front of the bowling alley and got out of the car. He went inside and asked for the manager. A young man with blue hair and several lip piercings came out to see him. "Can I help?" His name tag showed he was called Spud. Dan couldn't help but smile.

"I hope so, have you seen a man here who looks like this?" Dan handed the manager a photograph of Shaun Brown. "He may have had a teenage girl with him." He watched as Spud scrutinised the photograph whilst singling out one of the lip piercings to chew on.

"Nope, I've never seen this guy. We get lots of Dad's bringing their daughters here though, but I've never seen him." He added thoughtfully.

"What about this girl?" He asked as he handed Spud a photo of Lily.

"No, sorry. I've not seen her here. Wait. Isn't that the girl that was in the paper, the one that's gone missing?"

"Yes and she's been missing for a week now. Have you seen any new faces, older men with young girls?"

"This isn't that kind of place." He leapt to the businesses defence. Dan liked that about him, loyalty was always hard to come by. "Gone a whole week… that's not good is it?" Spud added.

"We'll find her." Dan replied. "What I meant was have there been any new faces around, anyone you've never seen before or have come in for some other reason except for bowling?"

"All the time, people on their holidays, you see them once then never again. Lots of people walk in just to check admission prices or have a drink."

"You have cameras here, do you keep the footage?"

"Yes for two weeks, do you want it?"

"Please."

"It's a digital file, I'll download it for you. Hang on, it won't take a minute." Spud rushed off to organise the footage that would keep a couple of police officers busy for a few days. True to his word he returned minutes later and handed a couple of memory cards to Dan.

"Thanks for your help." He hesitated, struggling to bring himself to say it. "Spud."

"You're welcome, come back with your family one day. Hey I really hope you find the kid." Spud smiled and wandered off to check on his customers. Dan liked him, unfortunately he hadn't been much help and now he didn't know where to go from here. Whoever had Lily must have just come out here to make the calls, he'd shown Spud Shaun's photograph on the off chance he might have seen him too. This was turning into a real mess, now it seemed like they were back at square one and on top of that he'd lost Alex.

Chapter Forty Seven

Alex had driven out to Blunsdon oblivious to almost everything except for the music and the smell of the car; the smell of Matt. There were tears rolling down her cheeks but she still managed to sing along with every track on Matt's favourite CD, she didn't think she'd ever change it. Her mood was swinging between sadness and anger, she couldn't pin her emotions down to one thing or the other, she thought she should take some time off for herself but first she wanted to find Lily, then she could have the luxury of fixing herself. The thought of Lily being out here somewhere close was driving Alex to distraction, it was all that was keeping her focus, without it she thought she might fall apart. She was very aware that she was taking on a one woman mission to get Lily home safely and then to find Shaun, but she was determined to end this whole nightmare and make Matt proud of her. That was when the tears started again, she pulled over, she had no idea where she was beyond being in Blunsdon, she didn't know this town well enough. The road she had pulled into was a quiet one, well away from the bustle of the main roads, she sat in the car quietly and tried to pull herself together. She had hoped to find Dan out here somewhere but it was just a wild goose chase she had no idea which part of the town he was heading to and she was far from sure he would want to see her.

After about fifteen minutes Alex was aware of a couple of net curtains twitching, it looked like the local neighbourhood watch were on to her, if she didn't move on soon they would be out with their brooms to shoo her away. She didn't want to have to explain herself to a busybody who would in turn feel sorry for her when they saw the state she was in, it was too much to contemplate. She pulled her seatbelt around her, rubbed the heel of her hands into her eyes to dismiss the tears and moved away from the curb. She would drive around for a while and keep her eye open for Dan or any other familiar faces.

She drove in what seemed like circles, blindly, just keeping moving, at one stage she had seen a police car a few cars behind her and thought it was following her but it turned out it wasn't, it hadn't followed her when she turned off into the side road. Eventually she thought she could fill a little time by going and getting something for her dinner tonight, she needed to eat after all. That had been a disaster, she had shopped like she normally did, only realising at the checkout that from now on she would be cooking for one, the tears came freely again, she really needed to pull herself together. As she left the supermarket she had seen the tail end of Dan's car pulling out of the car park. She jumped into the car and tried to follow him, he was easy to spot he had his blue lights flashing, her heart lurched, praying that he had found Lily. She followed him through the traffic as he pulled into the car park of a bowling alley, she parked up alongside his car and waited.

Twenty minutes later he reappeared and got into his car, she went to join him. She opened the door and slid into the passenger seat, surprising him, thankfully, he smiled. "Alex, what are you doing here?"

"I saw the blue lights and followed you here, any info yet?" She tried to sound bright, the last thing she wanted was for Dan to have her to worry about on top of everything else. "It's the journalist in me." She added.

"Nothing of any use so far. Where have you been?"

"Just driving around, hoping to magically summon up Lily I suppose. I don't even understand why all of this is happening Dan."

"We never do until it's all over, and it will be over soon Alex, we'll find her."

"So where to next?"

"I've got some calls to make, you should go home."

"I can't, I'll just tag along with you."

"No Alex, you can't and you know it, I have a job to do." He said. She could instantly see that she had pushed him too hard, his face set in a grim frown.

"Sorry, I just…"

"I know." He softened his voice. "We will do everything we can, go home, try to relax a little, you need to look after yourself." His face relaxed as he spoke, he knew he had been too harsh with her. She climbed out of his car and back into her own. Dan drove away, he had thought it was the kindest thing to do, he just wanted her to go home. Matt had always said she was stubborn and now he was beginning to see it for himself. He would try to be kind but he needed to let her know that interfering was not acceptable.

Alex sat in her car watching Dan drive away, she followed him as he drove through the town. She hoped he hadn't noticed her behind him but she also didn't think he was stupid, he pulled into a supermarket car park alongside another police car and got out, she parked up in an opposite car park out of sight and got out of the car to watch him from the road. Whilst she waited she phoned Jack. "Hi have you had another call yet?"

"Alex are you okay?"

"Yes, just trying to track down Lily, has he called again?"

"Yes a while ago, I have to meet him tomorrow in the park, so don't worry she'll be home soon."

"If you can believe what he says Jack, how do we know he won't just take the money and run?"

"The police will be there, even if he tries, there'll be nowhere to run."

"I hope I'll find her before it comes to that."

"Be careful Alex, you should be at home, leave this to the police."

"Okay Jack, maybe I will." She said it just to stop him worrying but she was beginning to get a bit tired of everyone telling her what she should do. She looked across the road into the car park, Dan was still just sitting in his car, he wasn't doing anything.

She walked along the main road and found a row of shops, she headed straight for the newsagent, they always knew the locals better than anyone else in town. She no longer had any flyers but she had photos on her phone she stopped and scrolled through her downloaded information and found the file which had been transferred to the new phone and there it was, a photo of the girls and ones of Lily from the wedding. She went into the shop and asked if they had seen her and showed them the photographs, again all she got was a shake of the head. She would work her way around all of the local shops, if Lily was in this town she was going to find her.

After visiting every shop in the street she was already disheartened, no one seemed to have ever seen Lily, not even a maybe. Could the police have it wrong? She walked back to the car, she wondered why Dan had been at the Bowling alley, he had had his lights on too. Was that where she needed to start looking? She could have kicked herself, she needed to start thinking clearly again, she was being too emotional and missing the clues. He had said there was nothing of any use there when she had asked him but had he tried hard enough? She would go and see for herself.

Chapter Forty Eight

She got to the car park but there were no spaces by the bowling alley, she cursed and drove around looking for a space to park, eventually she turned into a road a few minutes walk away, she was determined to go and ask her own questions.

The bowling alley was dull and quiet and smelt of cheap disinfectant, maybe people didn't use it too much in the day, she had always thought of it as an evening thing herself, the whole place seemed a bit grubby but she walked up to the bar area, ordered a drink and asked the barman about Lily. "The police have already been in asking the manager questions, so who are you?" The middle aged man behind the bar asked.

"Just a friend, I'm just trying to help."

"You should leave it to the police love."

"Well, you have to help where you can." She said through gritted teeth, she really was sick of people telling her what to do today. She forced a smile at him.

"We don't know anything here and that's the same as the boss told the police."

"Will you just have a look at a photograph and humour me?"

"Sure." He sighed as he ran his fingers through his curly black hair, she thought he'd do it just to get rid of her. She showed him the photo on her phone of Lily at the wedding, he glanced at it. "Nope never seen her before."

"Please take a closer look, then I'll go... promise."

He took the phone from her and looked carefully at the photo, "Nope as I said never seen her." He started to hand the phone back to Alex then suddenly pulled it back towards himself. "But that guy in the background looks familiar."

"What guy?" Alex hadn't even realised there was anyone else in the picture.

"Him." The barman had zoomed into the picture and pointed at the screen.

"Tom." She said in amazement.

"You know him?"

"Kind of, just a friend of a friend." She didn't know how else to explain it. "Has he been here?"

"A couple of times for a drink, he hasn't stopped here for long, he just comes in gets a drink, makes a call and goes. He was here earlier today."

"Do you know where he lives?"

"Not a clue, but if it helps give me your number and when he comes in next I'll ring you." This time he smiled at her and it was a real smile. Without hesitation she scribbled her number down on a piece of paper for him.

"Thank you." She meant it, finally there was something happening. She left the bowling alley a lot happier than when she went in, now she knew why Dan had been here, this is where the call had been traced to. She had no way of knowing whether Tom drove there or walked but she thought that he was trying to use somewhere anonymous and the chances were that he lived locally, she hoped very locally. Alex rang Jack back. "Jack it's Tom, that's who's got her, I'm certain now. Please think if you've ever met him before, anything, even just an inkling."

"Oh Alex I've thought this in and out so many times, I have no idea, I'm sure, apart for him being at the tunnel I've never met him."

"Okay, well if you do think of anything, ring me." She ended the call. She could feel the adrenaline pumping around her body and it felt good, she knew she was onto something now and hoped it wouldn't be too long before she would hear something from someone. He was close, she could almost feel him, she had a lot of anger brewing and she wanted to find him whilst she still felt like this.

She returned to her car, common sense told her she should tell Dan what she knew even though she didn't want to. She drove back to the car park to find him but there wasn't a police car in sight, right now she needed Matt, he would have been able to help her. She didn't know what to do next so she returned to the bowling alley, it was the only place she knew Tom had been seen, so she would go there and wait. The barman looked up at her and smiled but didn't bother her and apart from ordering a drink they barely spoke. She did get the feeling he was keeping an eye on her but she batted the thought away, after all she probably looked quite a state, she hadn't given her hair or make up a thought for days. She couldn't blame him for thinking she may potentially be troublesome to him. She sat in the same place for three hours before the barman finally approached her. "Look love, go home. I promise I'll ring you if he shows up. You look like you could do with a good night's sleep."

"You're probably right." She conceded, knowing full well she wouldn't get any sleep, but being there wasn't helping her mood, she'd got too much time to think. "By the way, I didn't ask, what's your name."

"Steve. Are you okay to get home?" He sounded genuinely concerned. Alex softened towards him.

"Sure, I'm fine. You promise…"

"Yes I promise I'll ring you." He finished the sentence for her.

With that she knew he was right, she was no use here and if he called she could be back fairly quickly.

She got into the car and slid in the CD, then immediately slid it out, she'd cried enough for one day, she couldn't listen to that music again, she put the radio on and pointed the car towards home. The news came on the radio before she made it back to Charmsbury, as she listened to news about the upcoming election and some juvenile political point scoring her phone rang. She pulled the car to the side of the road. "Alex, where are you?" It was Dan.

"Almost home, why?"

"We've found him." He sounded like he was smiling.

"What... who?"

"Shaun Brown, he'd made it up to Liverpool, he was trying to board a ferry to Northern Ireland. Apparently the police got in a bit of a scuffle with him. They had no intention of letting him get away."

"Where is he now?" She asked for no reason other than she couldn't think of anything else to say. It felt so unreal.

"They're bringing him back to Charmsbury, where we'll interview him, there will be some big names coming from London to do it. I just wanted you to know."

"Thanks Dan." She couldn't say what she really felt about Shaun over the phone, she hated him for taking Matt from her but ranting at Dan wouldn't make her feel any better and she didn't feel like celebrating the fact that they'd caught him. So she disconnected the call. She felt numb. The phone immediately rang again, she glanced down at it, it was Dan again. She ignored it and pulled back onto the road and drove home.

Chapter Forty Nine

Jack was beginning to get nervous, he'd arranged the money and would collect it from the bank in the morning, he was amazed at how quickly the banks could move and how accommodating they could be when the police got involved, even accepting him on a Sunday. He felt ashamed that it was Mary that had to put up most of the money but it was hardly his fault, well at least he didn't think it was and he had promised that he would pay her every penny back. It seemed whoever was doing this thought it was totally down to him and he still couldn't work it out. Tomorrow he hoped this would all be over, just as long as everything went to plan and finally he would discover what all of this was about.

Mary did her best to make the evening pleasant, she cooked his favourite meal and opened a bottle of wine but he wasn't in the mood for conversation, feeling relaxed seemed wrong under the circumstances, he went to bed early, he knew he wouldn't sleep but he didn't feel like chatting the evening away and he knew Mary was fretting over him. He couldn't sleep which was hardly surprising so he turned the radio on in the hope that it may lull him off to sleep, it was what he used to do sometimes when he had lived in the tunnel and it had always worked for him. He lay in bed as the music finished and the news came on. That was when he heard that Shaun had been picked up by police in Liverpool, he was surprised they hadn't heard from Alex, he thought she may have wanted to stop with them tonight given the situation but she hadn't shown up. He got up and went to the phone, once he'd spoken to her he thought that he might be able to settle down for the night he just wanted to know she was okay. The phone rang out a few times and he thought that maybe she had managed to sleep but then she picked up. "Hi Sweetheart, how are you feeling?"

"Hi Jack, lonely but okay, the hospital and the funeral directors have rung." She paused. "Have you heard the news?"

"I've just heard on the radio, why don't you come over here and let us look after you? I don't like the idea of you on your own tonight."

"I'm fine Jack, I want to be on my own and I want to be here. I feel closer to him here, you do understand don't you?" She sounded so young and vulnerable it almost broke his heart but Jack couldn't force her to come to them.

"Of course I do sweetheart, just come over if you change your mind."

"Thank you. After we've got Lily home I've got to go and sort everything out for the funeral, they were so kind and said there was no rush. They said that I should just relax for a while. How can I do that Jack?" She said, her voice thick with emotion.

"Do you want us to come with you? We can all get through it together." He offered.

"Yes please, I don't know what to do Jack, I'm not sure how to handle any of this."

"Oh sweetheart, we're all here for you, we can all help."

"I know and I will need you but for now there's Lily to think of, how are you feeling about tomorrow?" Alex asked trying to change the subject before she dissolved into tears again.

"Nervous, frightened of stuffing it up. I still have no idea who this guy is Alex, not a clue."

"You'll be fine Jack, we'll be there for you too, Tom, or whoever he is will pay for this. You should get some sleep or at least try to."

"You too Alex, I feel better now I've spoken to you. Goodnight Sweetheart." He really did feel better now he knew she was safely at home, she needed time to heal. He returned to bed and surprisingly slept solidly through until six o'clock the next morning.

Mary was already up and bustling around the kitchen, keeping herself busy, there was nothing else she could do today, it was down to everyone else but she could make sure there was food and drinks for anyone who came to the house today and she had a feeling there might be a lot of people to comfort. Alex turned up on the doorstep at eight o'clock and was immediately made to have some breakfast. "You need to eat." Her Nan had said thrusting a plate of waffles in front of her. Admittedly her stomach growled at the smell of them, she realised she had hardly eaten yesterday, she hadn't bothered to cook when she got home last night, she had spent the evening hovering over her phone waiting for a call from Steve, but it hadn't come. The waffles were delicious and she immediately felt better for eating, now all she needed was a gallon of coffee and she might feel somewhere near normal. "Nan, is Dan coming over this morning?"

"Yes I think he'll be here soon, he said he would come to the bank with us. Angie and Steve will meet us there, they have insisted on putting up half of the money."

"Let's hope you all get your money back before the days over." Alex said as she dived into a big mug of hot sweet coffee. She knew that this money was her Nan's life savings and she was going to do everything in her power to make sure it came back to where it belonged. "You don't mind if I hang around to see Dan do you?"

"Of course not, you can stay here all day if you want to."

"I've got to write a story for Charlie or he'll think I've forgotten about him."

"Charlie knows what's been going on, he knows there's more important things going on for you at the moment, don't you worry about him."

"No, I must put a story together, everyone needs to be on the lookout for Tom and Lily and whoever the woman is that's involved in this too."

"The only thing you must do is relax Alex. Lily will be home again soon." Her Nan said pointedly. Alex pulled her laptop out of her bag and started writing. Mary just looked at her and sighed, it was no good trying to tell Alex anything.

An hour later Dan turned up, Alex grabbed him as he came through the door. "Dan I need to show you something."

"Morning Alex, why did you ignore my call last night?"

"Because I was tired of everyone telling me what I should be doing and knowing you'd found Shaun, well I just didn't know what to feel. Sorry."

"It's okay, I was just worried about you. What do you have to show me?" He looked at her quizzically.

"This photo, I didn't notice it until yesterday but when I showed it to Steve he saw it immediately." She pushed her phone into Dan's hand. "Look."

"It's a photo of Lily."

"Yes that's why I showed him but he noticed the guy in the background, it's him, Tom."

"And this means what... and who's Steve?" Dan looked confused.

"Tom's the one who has Lily. Steve's a barman."

"You can't know that Alex, this is a guess at best."

"No, Steve recognised him." She said.

"Okay, go back a bit Alex, Steve's a barman and how does he know Tom?"

"Tom went into the bowling alley a few times, had a drink and used his phone, then would leave. You traced the calls to the bowling alley didn't you?" She asked but she already knew the answer.

"You know all of this stuff … how?" Dan looked at Alex, Matt had been right when he said she had a good nose for a story and she was always interfering.

"I followed you, it didn't take a detective to work it out."

"Okay so I will need that photograph so we can see if we can clean the picture up and get a better look at him."

"I've sent it in an email already." She smiled at him.

"Can you leave it to us now?"

"Sure." She said and returned to her coffee.

Mary overheard the conversation and smiled. She was so proud of Alex, today should get a little easier if they knew who they were looking for and Alex was always happier when she had a story. Dan started making calls to the station to get the photograph blown up, then sent to all officers and checked that the back up team was ready to meet them at the park at eleven o'clock, he wanted everyone in place early. They left Alex at the house whilst they went to sort out the money, the bank had been incredibly helpful to allow them to withdraw the money on a Sunday. Alex finished her article and sent it to Charlie. Even just a little bit of routine made her feel much more normal.

Chapter Fifty

Alex pulled Dan to one side, out of earshot of Jack and Mary. "Dan, have you finished taking statements from Cathy and the other women?"

"I don't think so, it'll take a while. Karen's still in hospital and they haven't had a chance to speak to her at all yet. Beth is traumatised and is still with a counsellor at the hospital too, it's too much to expect for her to tell her story just yet."

"Can I speak to them, I just want to know how they're doing?"

"I'll ask them but I don't see why not, you were all in there together. Just as long as you're not doing it for a story."

"Dan! How can you think that after all those poor women had been through, we all got out of there together, I want to know that at least something good has come out of this." Alex was truly shaken that he would even think that of her.

"I'm sorry but those women are so delicate at the moment." He stopped when he realised that it was Alex that was probably more shaken than all of those women. "I am sorry Alex." He could see from the look on her face that he had hurt her. "I'll talk to them today, okay?"

"Sure." She didn't want to speak freely to Dan now if he thought that with everything she'd been through she was still a journalist first. There were still things she wanted to know though. "The body, do you know who that was?" Gone was the friendly edge to her voice.

"That was Lynn Batchelor, poor girl. The coroner, Dr McAndrews is looking into the cause of her death now." He said. Alex remembered Tony McAndrews from last year, he was a kind man.

"So all of the missing girls are accounted for now then?"

"No there's still a couple of them missing but they're nothing to do with this case from what we can gather. We can't always find everybody and some people don't want to be found, they want to be left alone to make a new start somewhere else."

"Were they all helpers for June or did they have different stories? I mean, I was there but I didn't look after June."

"From the women we've interviewed they were all approached to help June." He said carefully, he knew he was giving out too much information but Alex had been through this too alongside the freed women, she deserved the truth. "I think, you were just in the wrong place at the wrong time."

"So what about June?" Alex was curious about her.

"Cathy told us she knew there had been others but the others knew nothing of each other, she had a letter on her that June had written, warning her about Shaun."

"So June knew then?" Alex was shocked.

"I don't think she knew what he was doing but she was under the impression that they were leaving because of him."

"So she'll give a statement too?"

"Yes, we hope so and now we have Shaun I think it'll be a straight forward case, he'll be going inside for a long time. In fact by the time this is finished I don't think he'll ever see the light of day again."

"I really hope that's the case. Will you let me know how Karen is, I can't bring myself to go back to the hospital at the moment, it's all still too raw, it's the last place I want to go but I want her to know I'm thinking of her."

"Of course I can." He was relieved, it felt like Alex was calming down again. "Can you come to the station tomorrow?" He asked pensively. He hadn't been looking forward to asking her this.

"Yes, why?"

"The TV people want to visit and get a reaction from Matt's family and friends, we've managed to keep them away until now but they want the story." He shuffled his feet.

"They have a job to do, the same job as me. Of course I'll be there. You've done a great job keeping them away from me up until now, I haven't even had a phone call. Now is the time we should tell them what happened."

"Thanks, I know it won't be easy. For the record it was Charlie at the paper that kept the press away from you, he must be very highly thought of because from what I heard not one journalist from anywhere argued with him.

"I'll thank him. He's one of the good guys in the industry. So what have you got planned for today?" She abruptly changed the subject.

"You know I can't tell you that Alex. We will however be keeping an eye out to keep everyone safe, you can be sure of that." He smiled at her. Alex wondered if all police officers gave things away by simply opening their mouths, she smiled back at him. So Jack would be fine because the police would be monitoring his every move, Tom wouldn't get away with this or at least that was what she hoped, unless he had a diversion planned.

Mary appeared next to Alex, putting her arm around her. "Are you alright love?"

"Yes, I think so, how are you feeling?"

"Nervous." She said quietly.

"What time are you going to the bank?" Alex asked.

"In about half an hour, do you want to come with us?"

"No I think I might go home for a while, I need to get used to being alone in the house." Alex said. Her Nan looked at her with a questioning look in her eye, but said nothing in front of Dan, Alex was up to something, she just hoped it wasn't something that would stop Tom handing over Lily. They had everything planned Mary wouldn't allow a slip up at this stage.

"Are you sure Alex?" Was all she could think of to say.

"Yes, they have caught Shaun, the women seem to be okay and everything is organised to get Lily back, you don't need me there now. You just need to get Lily. Have you seen Summer and Mark?"

"Yes they're just waiting now, there's nothing they can do either and Summer is still too fragile to be involved."

"Don't you think she should be there? She'd want to be the first to see Lily when she gets picked up."

"We don't think she's up to it love." Her Nan said, Alex just didn't understand, she knew Summer would want to be there and make sure her little girl was okay.

"Hasn't anyone told her what's going on?"

"Not yet, as I said she's just not up to it."

"Nan!" Alex shouted, she stood up and went for the door.

"Alex, let us sort this out, then we'll take Lily home, Angie and Steve will be there, Summer doesn't need to be. Alex heard what her Nan said but she was appalled that anyone would make that decision for Summer, she knew they were only trying to protect her but it felt wrong.

Alex drove straight to Summers flat, she knocked on the door and Mark answered. He looked better than he had two days previously, he showed her in. "She's in the lounge Alex, be gentle with her." Was all he said. She

216

nodded and walked through the hall and into the lounge, then she saw Summer and immediately understood what her Nan had meant. Summer was broken. She sat on the settee looking out of the window with a completely blank expression, she didn't even acknowledge Alex. Mark stepped in between them and sat down next to Summer, he took her hand and stroked the spot where the triquetra tattoo was. Alex watched, shocked. "Come on Summ, Alex has come to see you." He was so tender with her that Alex was touched, he was a good man. She squatted down in front of Summer and took her other hand, it was hot and limp. "Hey sweetheart are you okay?" It sounded like a stupid question even to her ears but she had to start somewhere. "Summer, we know who has Lily, we're going to get her back, today." Summer looked at Alex and smiled very slightly.

"She's a good girl, take care of her." Her voice little more than a whisper.

"Summer don't you understand, we're going to bring her home."

"Hmmm…" Summer replied. Mark looked at Alex and nodded his head towards the door. She got up and made her way to the kitchen and waited for Mark to join her. A minute later he was standing next to her and he explained. "We have had to dope her up Alex, when Matt died on top of everything else it was too much for her." Then he suddenly realised how Alex must be feeling. "I'm sorry Alex I didn't mean anything by that, I just meant…"

"Shhh Mark I understand what you meant, no one should have to put up with all of the things our families have gone through in the last nine days, I've realised that life isn't kind like that and we don't get to choose what happens and when. So she doesn't have any idea what's going on now?" She asked gently although inside she felt anything but gentle.

"I don't think she has a clue, I've tried to explain things to her but she just sits in there looking out of the window, I'm not sure she even knows where she is." He looked down and added. "Or cares."

"Oh Mark I'm so sorry, I promise I'll bring Lily back here as soon as I can, you stay with Summer and keep her safe and try and get her in a better place for when we get back, Lily shouldn't see her like this.

"I'll try and if you need me you will call, won't you?"

"Of course I will but I think you'll be more use here with Summer, I don't suppose you've heard but the guy who's got her is Tom. That's who we're looking for now."

"Tom, the guy the community helped out! I'll fuckin' kill him if I get my hands on him." He started balling his hands into fists, the whites of his knuckles showing through. Alex thought she may have made a mistake telling him but it was the truth and he had the right to know.

"Don't get yourself wound up Mark, he won't get away with this, I don't see how he can, there'll be police everywhere, they won't leave him with anywhere to run." She leaned forward and gave Mark a hug, it was as much to reassure herself as it was to comfort Mark, whatever the reason, the human contact seemed to calm him down a little bit.

Alex left them, drove into town and went to find a seat in the café by the side of the park, "The Breakfast Bap', it was a great vantage point to watch the park from.

Chapter Fifty One

The park looked as it did every other day, it was serene, there were people walking their dogs, throwing sticks for them and children playing on the swings, mothers chatting to each other and watching their offspring from a safe distance. Flowers and colourfully painted fences nestled in front of the river. It looked like the kind of place that nothing bad could ever happen, but looks could be deceiving, she knew from experience. This park had seen its fair share of traumas over the years, she had met Matt because of a woman's body being found in the park a couple of years ago, so much had changed in her life since that had happened.

Alex chose a seat at the bar in the window, looking outwards, she was sipping her steaming coffee and watching as people went about their lazy Sunday morning, totally unaware of what was about to unfold around them, she did wonder why Tom would choose a Sunday to do this, surely he must have known that there would be more people around, maybe it was just as simple as that, maybe he thought more people would mean he could get away without being followed so easily. Alex had no idea what made some people tick, she had given up trying to work it out. She was tired now, just wanting all of this to be over, she didn't like the waiting around, the uncertainty of what was to come. She noted that a number of unmarked police cars had driven past her at fairly regular intervals, she recognised some of the officers, they must have been getting into place each of them covering a different area, she hoped they picked Tom up before he made it to the park. She couldn't see how he was going to make this work, she thought he'd left it too long, given everyone too much time to prepare. She glanced down at her phone it was just after eleven o'clock, just one hour and it would all be over one way or another. She ordered another coffee, she had a good view from here and she wasn't ready to give this spot up yet.

Her phone rang whilst she drank her coffee, she glanced down at it, it was her Nan, she chose not to answer it, this wasn't the time to be answering a lot of questions about where she was and what she thought she was up to, she could hear how that conversation would play out in her own head already. Alex assumed they had the money and were heading out towards the park now. She kept watch, sipping at her coffee, she looked on as Dan pulled his car into the car park, he was with Tina and neither of them was in uniform. Alex couldn't believe they thought that Tom might just drive up into the car park and walk along the path to the bridge, surely they couldn't be that naïve. Her phone pinged, notifying her of a text message, she glanced down at it, it was her Nan telling her not to do anything stupid, she swiped it and made it disappear. She returned to watching the car park, the next car that pulled in several minutes later was a taxi which deposited her Nan and Jack inside the park gates and drove away again. Her Nan looked around, Alex felt an instinct to cower down in case she was spotted, although it would be almost impossible for her to be spotted from this distance. Alex watched them, Jack had a duffle bag slung over his shoulder. They walked a few steps as her Nan chose a bench and sat down, Jack bent down and kissed her, he spoke to her for a minute then turned and walked away.

Alex drained her coffee mug and left the café, she walked quickly along the road as far as the bridge, there were a few steps from the road leading down and a patch of grass to walk across that would bring you to the underside of the bridge. She walked down and sat on the bottom step, tucking herself tight against the wall to minimise being seen and she waited. She looked around trying to take in everything that was going on around her, there was a couple walking a dog and a woman sitting on a bench talking into her mobile phone, another woman walking along the path towards where Jack was. She could hear children playing and laughing but couldn't see them, they must be on the other side of the bridge. Everything was incredibly normal, just a pleasant Sunday morning in the park, there weren't even any of the homeless crew hanging about, it could be that they'd seen some police around and moved off to another area. In the distance she could see Jack, he was walking slowly along the path, he was early, there was still a good ten minutes before anything would happen, if you believed Tom. Alex could feel the tension building inside her, she didn't take her eyes off Jack for a moment. To look at him you would think he was just out for a Sunday stroll although he had a heavy coat on which was the only thing odd about the scene, the weather was nice, not warm but pleasant, maybe jumper weather, but not coat weather and Jack was used to the cold, he had lived in a cold place through many harsh winters, even in the summer the tunnels were cold. The seconds ticked by, Alex was ready, she didn't yet understand what for, but every inch of her felt ready to explode, adrenaline was coursing through her, she just needed a reason to move, but she couldn't afford to get it wrong, she stayed still. Jack kept ambling along the path towards her, she could almost see his face now, he looked thoughtful, as if he was a world away from Charmsbury Park. Alex could only imagine what was going through his mind, this park was where he had put the body of one of his dearest friends to be found and then last year where a body had washed up and caused an uproar when it was thought to have been a famous art dealer. Was it just her or was everyone thinking that this year it could be Jack or Lily. Alex squeezed her eyes closed for a moment and shook her head to dispel the idea, which brought with it thoughts of Matt, if it was down to her nothing more than handing over money and getting Lily back would happen here today.

Chapter Fifty Two

Alex opened her eyes after managing to move the devastating thoughts away, she had refocused herself and immediately saw that the woman on the bench was putting her phone away and was starting to get up. Everything around her seemed to be happening in slow motion. Alex pushed herself off the stone steps propelling herself forward, the woman was moving quickly towards Jack now. Alex was aware that Jack had seen the woman and he was moving quicker, but not quickly enough, the woman sprang at him and grabbed the bag from his grasp, sliding it off his shoulder in one smooth movement as she pushed him away. "No." Was all Alex caught him shout out as he stumbled down the bank, Alex was moving fast and almost got to her as it all happened but as she made a grab for the woman she was left with no more than a handful of fresh air, the woman was too fast for her. Alex heard the splash and saw Jack as he disappeared below the surface of the water, she instantly recalled the big coat he had been wearing, even if he was a good swimmer that coat would drag him down. Alex could hear shouts coming from further down the path. She didn't think about anything else, she dived into the cold water after Jack, gasping for breath as she lunged forward her mouth and nose filling with ice cold water, her feet in the air, pushing, as her body was propelled downwards to find Jack. The water was murky and dark but she caught a glimpse of dark material swaying ahead of her, she powered towards it, grabbing at it and swimming to the surface pulling it behind her. As her head broke the surface of the water and she gasped for breath she turned to look behind her and was relieved to see Jack's head come to the surface. She struggled trying to get the coat off Jack, it was heavy, she couldn't release him from it, so she dragged him with every ounce of strength left in her body. Holding his head out of the water she made slow progress towards the bank. "Kick Jack, help me...come on." She shouted. "Come on Jack!" She could feel the water trying to pull her in the opposite direction. It wasn't that far to drag him but it felt like a country mile, every sinew in her body screamed for release but she powered on, praying inwardly that he would be alright. Then it seemed like suddenly out of nowhere there were arms grasping at her, pulling her and Jack out of the water onto the grassy bank, she looked up and saw Dan looking down at her. He was holding her jacket, she must have thrown it off before she leapt in after Jack. Alex looked around to see two paramedics standing over Jack. "Is he okay?" She asked still panting for breath, as her Nan appeared at the side of him.

"He'll be fine, we just need to get him dry and warm. We're taking him in."

"No." Alex looked at Dan, pleading. "Don't let them take him in. Take him home if he's okay, we'll look after him." Alex didn't want anything to do with the hospital. The last person she loved that went in hadn't come out.

"I'll talk to them." Dan said as he walked towards the group gathered around Jack. She could hear him talking to the paramedic. He wandered back. "They have to check him over, but they won't keep him in. Okay?" He handed her a towel.

"Sure." Alex reluctantly agreed, rubbing her wet hair. "Did you get the woman? Where's Lily? Why on earth was he wearing that coat?" The questions tumbled out as she wrapped her jacket around herself to keep warm.

"Yes, the woman ran straight into Tina's arms, we're going to talk to her now. Lily isn't here." His words were interrupted by Alex's phone ringing in her jacket pocket. She fished it out and looked at the screen, it was Charlie. She answered it.

"You've got what?" Alex said. "I'm on my way." She disconnected the call and dropped the phone back into her pocket. "Lily's at the newspaper office, Charlie's got her, she's safe." Alex crumpled. The paramedic came to take a look at her and gave her the go ahead, she could leave. Slowly she picked herself up, checked on Jack as he was moved to the ambulance and gave her Nan a hug, she had been crying. "Alex you saved his life." She hugged Alex close.

"Nan, I have to go and get Lily, just look after Jack, he's going to be fine but he'll need lots of attention." Alex smiled.

"But Alex you're soaking wet." Mary said, but Alex was already running to her car, she was wet but she no longer cared, Lily was safe and that was all that mattered now.

She pulled up at the newspaper office and ran inside, the office was half full but no one stopped her as she ran towards Charlie's office, and there, sitting in the editors chair was Lily, smiling as Alex plunged through the door. She ran over to Lily and hugged her like she would never let her go again. Lily seemed fine and was unaware of everything else that had been going on whilst she'd been away. Charlie handed Alex a photograph. "It's the car that dropped Lily off, security weren't quick enough to catch him but there's his registration, it was Nick's quick actions that got it, the rest of us were useless."

"Useless? Charlie you were in the office on a Sunday, that's amazing in itself." She smiled up at him.

"Are you okay Alex? You look a mess and you're wet."

"It's been quite a week Charlie, I'll write it up for you one day." With that she put her arm around Lily and led her out of the building, smiling at Nick on the way past his desk and mouthing the words 'thank you'. They got in the car. "Did he hurt you, sweetheart?" Alex gently asked as she reached across and clicked Lily's seatbelt into place.

"No, the needle marks are itching though." She replied in a matter of fact tone.

"Needle marks!" Alex was shocked.

"They kept me asleep. Don't worry I'm okay." Alex had to smile, it seemed like she was taking it in her stride. "Is Mum okay?"

"She will be, when she sees you." Alex smiled at her, that was the moment she realised that she should have waited for Dan but after witnessing the state of Summer she just wanted to get Lily back to her, everything else paled into insignificance. The last few days had been too traumatic, Alex was happy to face the consequences for her decision, she just wanted there to be a happy ending for at least one of them.

Alex took Lily home to see Summer and Mark, she would ring everyone else when they got there, she wanted an update on everything else that had gone on that day too but for now getting Lily home was the most important thing in the world, she just wanted to see Summer's face.

Mark opened the door and let out a shout. "Summ! Come here." He bundled Alex and Lily inside, hugging Lily as he did so, it was almost like he couldn't believe his eyes. Summer didn't appear so they went through to the lounge, Lily went first then they heard the excited squeal, a second later they witnessed Summer beaming at her little girl and holding her tight with tears streaming down her face, they were all crying and smiling.

Alex disappeared into the kitchen and phoned Angie and Steve first, swiftly followed by her Nan and the police then the long list of everyone one else. It turned out that Charlie had already rung the police and told them about Lily appearing at the newspaper offices. They weren't particularly pleased about Alex taking her home but they were prepared to let that slide with the circumstances as they were and were pleased that she had given them the registration on the car that dropped Lily off. Within half an hour it seemed that everyone had turned up to see Lily and make sure she was alright, Lily was adamant that she was fine but Mark insisted that she went to the doctors the next morning to get checked over, Dan had demanded that of them. She could tell her story to the police then too, she needed time with her family now and she was going to get plenty of love and attention.

Chapter Fifty Three

Dan entered the car registration into the police computer, almost immediately a name and address came up, Mr Thomas Jacobs of Sheffield. He called his opposite number, PC Davis at the South Yorkshire police station and gave him all the details. It was too far for him to journey on the off chance that Tom had gone home. At least the phone call to Yorkshire that the phone company had come up with made a bit more sense now. They had the woman in custody, so far she wouldn't give them any information about herself or what she was doing in the park but he was sure they would get something out of her soon, there was no rush, she had been caught red handed, the money would be returned to Jack tomorrow. He was interested in finding out how all of this was linked now, but for tonight he just wanted to go home and relax, before he did he would drop in on Alex and make sure she was coping, it had been a hell of a week for her and he wanted to be sure she was okay. The traffic police were on the lookout for Tom's car, it would only be a matter of time before he was brought in. Dan walked into Matt's office and picked up a box of things from his desk, it was all of the items that he had sorted out on Alex's behalf, he hadn't wanted her to have to do this by herself.

Twenty minutes later he arrived at what was now just Alex's house and was pleased to see the car outside, finally he hoped she was getting this case out of her system and was trying to get back on track herself. He couldn't have been more wrong, he found Alex tapping away at her computer. "Hey, how are you feeling?"

"Hi Dan, I didn't hear you come in. Any news on Tom?"

"Nothing yet... I shouted through but you were absorbed in your work."

"Yes, well, it keeps my mind busy, without writing I think I might go a little mad. Do you want a coffee?"

"No thanks, I just wanted to drop this stuff over to you you'll know what to do with it all." He felt awkward, almost as if he was reminding her all over again.

"Don't look so worried, I won't go to pieces over a box of stuff, not whilst you're here anyway." She managed a smile but felt like she was dying inside, she'd just managed to distract her mind onto something else and now Dan opened the wound again. It was something she would have to get used to from now on, people stumbling over her memories and trying to be kind. It would never stop.

"So long as you're okay, do you need anything?"

"No Thanks."

"You will ring me if there's anything I can do won't you Alex?"

"I promise I will, if you promise to stop tiptoeing around me, I'll be okay Dan and I appreciate your concern but I need to move on and get through the process, there's not going to be any shortcuts, so please stop looking at me like I'm going to break. I'll be okay and if I'm not, you'll be the first to know." She looked up at Dan with as much confidence as she could muster.

"Okay, okay. I'll stop going on at you." He looked at her carefully but knew he had to resign himself to taking a step back. He pushed the cardboard box towards her and smiled. "I'll just leave this with you then. Can you make sure that Lily gets to the hospital tomorrow, she needs to be checked over. It's important."

"Sure, any idea who the woman is yet?"

"No she's not talking yet, but there's no rush, I'll get onto it tomorrow, tonight I just wanted to get home, it's been a tough day. I'll let you know when we pick up Tom." They said their goodbyes and Dan left, leaving Alex looking at a cardboard box full of Matt's personal belongings, part of her wanted to dive in and look through it but a bigger part of her couldn't face it, not yet. There was nothing in there that couldn't wait.

She kept herself busy doing some housework and took phone calls from her Nan, who told her that Jack was feeling much better now, if still a little shaken, Alex was pleased he was back at home with her Nan, he would be spoilt rotten. Then from Angie, who seemed to be doing a lot of crying and thanking her, she was glad the day had ended far better than it had started. That was when she saw a balled up piece of paper sitting on the floor by the side of the waste paper basket, she didn't need to retrieve it, she knew what it was and now she had no reason not to think seriously about taking the job in London, it might be just what she needed, a fresh start. The phone rang and cut through her thoughts, she picked it up without looking at it. "Hello."

"Alex?" It was a woman's voice.

"Yes, who is this?"

"Cathy… from the… warehouse." Her voice sounded nervous.

"Cathy! Are you okay?" Alex forgot about the job offer instantly. "Where are you?"

"The police have put me up in a flat, I had nowhere else to go but one of them gave me your phone number after I begged them for it. Don't be angry at them."

"Ah, that will have been Dan. I'm glad to hear from you." Alex smiled.

"Are you okay? I heard the news, I'm so sorry. Your husband seemed like a good man."

"He wasn't my... Yes, he was a good man." Alex felt the lump in her throat rise and threaten to give her emotions away.

"I'm sorry, Alex. After all you both did for us. I hope Shaun goes to prison for a very long time."

"Me too Cathy." Alex stopped in thought for a moment. "What can I do for you?" Cathy must have wanted something to brave the streets and find a phone box to call her.

"You're a journalist aren't you? That's what the police officer said."

"Yes."

"Will you tell our story?"

"I can't yet Cathy, it has to go to court and I've been told to leave the case alone."

"What about after the court case?" Cathy asked.

"How about we talk about it over coffee tomorrow afternoon?"

"Yes I'd like that, thank you." They discussed where they would meet and said their goodbyes.

Alex relaxed it seemed like everyone's lives were returning to normal, it felt like it was only hers that seemed irrevocably scarred.

Chapter Fifty Four

Alex woke up in her own bed wondering how she would get through the day, today would be tough, she had so much to get through but all she really wanted to do was to stay curled up within the safety of her duvet. With great effort she finally dragged herself out of bed and got ready to face the day, moving reverently around the cardboard box that was still on the table where Dan had left it, it was like the elephant in the room, she couldn't ignore it but she didn't feel ready to deal with it either. She drank coffee and showered much the same as every morning, only she knew it was all very different now, even though she was still going through the motions. She went into the lounge, smiled up at her 'Buddha Mountain' painting and below it on the mantelpiece the photograph of her and Matt standing in front of the mountain, not quite a year ago. Everything seemed so bitter sweet now, she hoped she could get through all of this raw emotion.

An hour later she drove to Summers flat to collect everyone and take Lily to the hospital, they were all in good spirits, the laughter sounded good, in no time at all they had arrived. Alex was feeling uncomfortable being there but she put on her business face and asked for Patty, within five minutes the ray of sunshine that was the medicine they all needed strode into the waiting room with a broad grin on her face. Alex pulled her to one side, "Patty will you examine Lily, the police say she has to be examined but I want you to do it." Alex hoped Patty would agree.

"I can't do that." Patty said shaking her head. "The police have designated doctors for those jobs."

"Can you at least be with her, please Patty. Lily's been through enough, she needs a friendly face, someone she can trust." Alex pleaded. Patty went off to talk to someone and immediately returned, smiling and nodding.

"The boss says yes." Patty took Lily's hand and skipped down the length of the corridor with her, both of them laughing as they went.

Almost an hour went by before Summer and Angie were called into the doctors room, Lily and Patty were waiting patiently for them. It seemed that Lily was fine and there was nothing physically wrong with her and no cause for concern. There was no reason for them to stay there any longer. The doctor had only one concern and went on to explain. "We found needle marks on her arm, from what Lily has told us it seems that she was given drugs to make her sleep, we can't be sure what was administered to her at the moment but we want you to keep a watch, just in case you notice anything unusual. We don't know if there may be any drug withdrawals or side effects and won't know what to expect until we know the drug that was used on her." Everyone nodded, the relief that there was nothing wrong with her was palpable. "That said she is a healthy girl with no signs of any problems, you can take her home now. I will just prescribe lots of cuddles." The women in the room were all so relieved they wanted to hug the doctor but they restrained themselves and settled for hugging Patty instead when they had all left the room.

As they all walked down the corridor to leave the hospital, Patty reached out for Alex's hand and pulled her to one side, allowing the others to keep moving towards the exit. "How are you bearing up, sweet girl?" She asked in true Patty style.

"I'll be okay, I guess." Alex honestly answered.

"You know where I am, if you need me, anytime Alex…I mean it." Alex could tell from her face she really did mean it, she was grateful for that, Patty was so easy to talk to and had a knack for getting things done. They hugged and Alex went after the others, she found them waiting at the car, chatting about how relieved they all were. Summer was quiet. "Are you okay Summer?" Alex asked. Summer just nodded. She had been through a lot and Alex thought that maybe she was simply recovering from the trauma of it all.

They took Lily back to Angie and Steve's house where Steve had been setting up a small family party for Lily's return whilst they had been away. Lily's eyes lit up when she saw the balloons and the cakes, it seemed all of her trauma was secondary to a party, it was good to see her get back to her old self so quickly, although Alex was sure there would be repercussions at some stage, hopefully easily coped with ones, if she was lucky. The group walked towards the house, Summer pulled Alex to one side. "Do you think Angie will stop me from seeing Lily?" Alex now understood why she had gone quiet on the journey home.

"Why would she?"

"She went missing when she was with me, then I went to pieces, she'd have every right not to trust me anymore… but I don't want her to take my baby away."

"Oh Summ, I don't think for a minute that Angie or Steve are thinking like that, why don't you go and talk to them, tell them what you're worried about. I'm not sure Lily would let them anyway, that little girl loves her mum."

"Yes but…"

"Do you remember what everyone went through to reunite you with Lily?" Alex interrupted her. "Summer

234

don't worry, it's fine." She looked at Summer and finally a smile dawned on her face.

"You're right Alex, come on then, there's a party in there." They linked arms and went into the house, everyone was there, Steve had done a great job arranging things.

Alex stayed long enough to speak to Mel, who was still wrapped up in her new boyfriend, she left when she had heard enough of how wonderful he was, she wasn't in the mood to hear Mel's love stories and thought it best to leave everyone to celebrate Lily's return, she didn't want to bring the party down, much as Summer tried to beg her to stay.

She sat in her car and phoned Dan. "Any news on the woman yet?" She asked.

"Actually yes, we sent a photograph of her to the Northern General Hospital in Yorkshire, they recognised her immediately as Mrs Patricia Jacobs, Tom's wife. She's worked for them for years. She's been absent from work for a week."

"So was it her that administered the drugs to Lily? Can you get her to tell you what she used?"

"She's still not talking but she will soon, she can't stay silent forever. I'll try to find out for you. Shaun is being interviewed again today too, the women have all done their statements."

"You have had a busy day then. Let me know if you find out anything. Any news on Tom?"

"Nothing yet. How are you?" He asked.

"Okay, just not up to partying with Lily quite yet. Thanks Dan." She said as she ended the call. She was hoping this would be all over soon and she could slip away and lick her wounds in peace.

Chapter Fifty Five

An hour later Alex was sitting at a table at the Red Bean café waiting for Cathy. As soon as she had walked in she knew it had been a mistake, all of the staff knew both her and Matt well and they had all been so kind to her that she began to feel like she would never be able to get away from the sympathy. She knew they were just being kind and concerned but it was too difficult for her to face up to. They were asking about the funeral and she knew she would have to sort it out soon, in fact she was supposed to do it today, she had been putting that phone call off, somewhere in the back of her head it made sense to her that if they didn't bury him then he was still alive, she knew it was stupid but it was how she felt. She had chosen a table as far from the counter as she could but she could still feel their eyes on her and imagine their pitying looks. She thought she could possibly add paranoia to her list of things that were wrong. She considered leaving the café, just at the moment Cathy entered, smiling, and took a seat next to her, she looked well. A waitress rushed over and took Cathy's order and went off to make her coffee.

Alex smiled at Cathy. "How are you? You look better than the last time I saw you." She said trying to be light hearted about everything. Cathy smiled but didn't immediately reply. "Have you seen the others?" Alex asked.

"Yes we got together and swapped notes, we're all worried about you."

"I'm fine, has Karen got her eye seen to?"

"Yes it's healing well, she needed stitches and it needed to be cleaned up, she's out of hospital now and she's going to be fine."

"And Beth?"

"Beth will take a bit longer but she wants to see you, she really trusted you. She keeps asking if you will go and visit her?"

"Is she still at the hospital? If she is, I really don't want to go there again for a while. The place holds too much pain for me right now."

"She'll be out soon, I'll tell her, she'll understand, maybe I could bring her to meet you here one day."

"Yes, I'd really like that. So everyone's going to be okay then. Have the police finished with you all?"

"No. I think that'll go on for a while longer but we've done the statements and most of our stories were the same except for Beth's."

"Oh." Alex was all ears now.

"We all went to help June initially, a few of us want to go and see her when this is all over, none of us can believe she was involved in this and she'll still need someone around to help her, we've talked about a rota to help her out, if it's going to be possible. Anyway, one way or another we all managed to annoy Shaun and we all ended up at the warehouse none of us knew how he came to use the place. In fact none of us knew very much at all, he kept most of us apart as you know. Apparently Jane and Karen remember him working on the rooms that he kept us in, he secured them so we couldn't get out and once we were in the only contact we would have was with him."

"Did he ever try anything?" Alex asked. At that moment the waitress brought over a tray with coffee and cakes and laid them out on the table. When she had finished Cathy continued.

"No, he didn't touch any of us, if that's what you mean, he wasn't sleazy. Nasty, yes, but we all had the impression he only had eyes for June. I'm not sure it ever crossed his mind to be that way." Cathy ran her fingers through her hair whilst she was thinking about what to say next. "He stopped at the warehouse every day to bring us food and he tried in his own way to look after us, as long as we were respectful to him he didn't hurt any of us, but if we weren't he could work himself up into a temper very easily. That was how Karen got hurt, he was sorry afterwards and took her some creams and lotions to keep the wound clean, only as you saw, it was badly infected, he just got either the wrong things or left it too long."

"Have you heard anything about him since he's been arrested?" Alex was curious.

"No, the police haven't mentioned him to us apart from in relation to what he did to us."

"So what was so different about Beth? What did he do to her that made her so terrified?"

"Beth had a bad experience and Shaun didn't help her, she had to deal with it herself."

"What sort of bad experience?" Alex picked up her coffee and looked at Cathy who was picking at a walnut on top of a piece of cake.

"You should probably talk to Beth, she'll tell you everything, she said you were really kind to her."

"I couldn't get her to talk much, she told me that June thought she was lazy and that she hated being alone in that room but that was about all. Is there something else?" Alex said.

"Yes there's a lot more, it's not my story to tell, it's hers. Go and see her Alex, she would love to see you."

"I can't Cathy, I can't go back to that hospital again, I went with Lily for her check-up and that was difficult enough. It was the last place I saw Matt." A lone tear ran down her cheek.

"Okay, I get it. I'm sorry." Cathy reached out to comfort Alex, but Alex dried her eyes quickly and ignored the sympathy.

"If you can't tell me, well that's okay. What do you plan to do now, will you go back to your family?"

"No, they didn't want me then, they don't deserve me now, I'll let them know I'm okay and maybe jump on a bus and start a new life somewhere else."

"Oh, you're not going to stay around?" Alex was surprised.

"The police have put us all up in a flat but that won't be forever and I need to get back on my feet. I'll find something to do with my life. I've always got by before."

"That's a shame, I'm sure I could find you some work around here, if that's what you wanted?"

"I'll think about it." They both smiled, Alex liked Cathy, she was smart.

"So are you going to tell me about Beth or are you really going to make me wait until she's out of hospital?"

"Will you at least ring her, she would really like to speak to you?" Cathy pleaded.

"Yes, I will. I'll ring her later. I promise." She meant it.

"Okay, well I'll give you the low down on her story then, or as much as I know. Beth was one of the few of us that wasn't alone in the warehouse, she'd been there a while, only the second to be incarcerated there and I guess she was frightened to be in a room on her own, so when he brought Lynn in he put them together. I think Lynn already must have had some sort of problems of her own, but he was good at picking people that in one way or another would end up dependent on him, he definitely

239

liked to pull people's strings. Beth had been okay, she just couldn't cope with being alone, Lynn's problems must have run much deeper and she wasn't coping well." Cathy continued to pick at the cake in front of her, leaving her coffee untouched. She fell into a thoughtful silence for a moment. "Things were difficult for both of them one way or another but one night Lynn had barely spoken to her and she was worried, she tried to shout out to someone, she needed to hear someone's voice because Lynn had just completely stopped talking, Beth shouted out to Jane but as you know conversation was difficult, eventually she gave up and curled up in the corner and went to sleep." Cathy stopped and took a drink of her coffee, she looked as if she was finding it hard to re-tell this story. Alex didn't interrupt; she wanted it to be told at Cathy's own pace. "When she woke up the following morning she went into the little bathroom, flicked the light on but nothing happened, it was early so the light was only dull, it took a few seconds for her eyes to focus, that was when she saw Lynn on the floor, there was blood everywhere, cold and congealed, splatters on the walls and pools on the floor. She says she remembers screaming, being sick and screaming again, there was nothing else she could do, Lynn was dead, Beth was terrified, she'd never even seen a dead body before that day. She didn't know what to do." Cathy took a deep breath and finished her coffee, not once meeting Alex's eye. "Beth couldn't believe she hadn't heard anything, she still blames herself for sleeping through it all. It turned out that Lynn had stuffed her own mouth full of ripped up sheet, presumably to stop herself from crying out when she… well, you know. I tried to tell Beth there would have been nothing that she could have done if Lynn was so determined, but Beth still blames herself."

"Poor girl." Alex almost whispered.

"Shaun turned up, Beth got a good look at the scene because it had been light by then, Lynn had smashed the light bulb and used the jagged edges to tear her arms open from the wrist to the elbow, the left arm had been opened wide the right arm looked like a jumble of criss cross cuts, she had just bled out, there, on the bathroom floor. He took her body away, Beth didn't know anything else, just that Shaun returned and cleaned everything up sometime later and brought her a book to keep her mind off what had happened."

"Yes the book she was so protective over. She told me it was so she didn't feel lonely and Shaun knew she liked to read. I wish she'd felt she could have told me."

"She wanted to, but everything happened so quickly in the end and then you had your own problems to deal with."

"I can't believe Shaun would think a book was consolation for what had happened, I hope the doctors can help her, she must be badly traumatised." Alex added.

"She's tougher than she looks." Cathy said and smiled, with the story told she was now looking Alex in the eye.

They chatted for a while longer about their lives and Cathy wanted to know all about Matt, Alex was happy to talk about him, she felt better for telling Cathy some of the wonderful things they had got up to since they met. It was good for her to re-live some happy times.

It had done both the women good to talk and get to know each other better. Before they left the café they promised to do it again really soon. Alex had started to feel human again, the talk and the coffee had done her good.

Chapter Fifty Six

As they left the café, Alex with a pack of her favourite ground coffee in her hand, Cathy began to walk off in the direction of the bus stop "Cathy, come and meet my Nan, I'll drop you home later." Alex shouted after her. Cathy turned and smiled.

"Maybe next time Alex, I'm going to the hospital to see Beth first, don't forget to phone her." With that she raised her hand, waved and continued down the road.

Alex watched Cathy until she reached the bus stop, then she turned towards her Nan's house, it wasn't far to walk, she glanced over at Matt's car, it would be fine where it was and she thought the walk might do her good, fresh air and a bit of time to reflect, alone.

As she approached the house, she could see the car was missing, they must have gone out somewhere. She had thought that after yesterday, her Nan would be keeping Jack at home and feeding him up to make sure he was okay. She knew where to find the key and she slipped around the back of the house to retrieve it and let herself in, there was no point in even trying the front door if they were out. She was hoping there might be a tin full of freshly baked brownies in the kitchen. She would happily sit and eat them whilst she waited for them to return. She reached over the gate and unlatched it, which was easier said than done for someone of her height, she went to the shed and found the key, under the workboxes and let herself into the kitchen. "Hello, anyone home?" She shouted.

"In the lounge Alex." Jack's voice made her jump, she hadn't expected a reply. She walked through to the lounge.

"I thought you were out, I didn't even think to try the front door. How are you feeling today?"

"A bit achy but okay, I wish I had learnt to swim, then you wouldn't have had to drag me out of the water. I'm glad you did though, thank you." He smiled.

"I'm sure you could have got yourself out if you hadn't been wearing that massive coat. It weighed a ton once it was wet."

"It weighed a ton when it was dry too but they had put an anti-stab vest on me and they wanted it covered up, so that was what they gave me."

"Now it makes sense." Alex added. "Where's Nan?"

"She's just gone down to the shops, she won't be long. Are you feeling okay today?"

"Yes I think so. I've been thinking, I need to make a few phone calls and get the funeral sorted out, it's too easy to just ignore it and hope it'll all go away. I miss him so much Jack." She stopped there, otherwise she knew she would end up in tears again. Jack nodded, there was nothing he could say, everyone was missing Matt and he understood what it was like coming to terms with losing someone close to you. It brought back memories of Ruby, she'd been a good friend to him in his days at the community and her loss had hit him hard.

Alex wandered off into the kitchen to make coffee and have a few minutes to swallow her tears without Jack seeing. Whilst she waited for the percolator to finish dripping into the jug she took out her phone and called Dan, he had all of the details of the undertaker, she needed to be sure she was speaking to the right person straight away, she didn't think she could go through doing this more than once. Dan had set things in motion for her and contacted a funeral director, for which she was grateful, now she needed to make the arrangements.

The phone rang out in some impersonal room somewhere in the Charmsbury Funeral Home. There was a click and a friendly hello, she found herself speaking to one Mrs Cooper, Alex had never thought of it as being a job that women did but in all honesty she had to admit she hadn't thought about it much at all, she hadn't expected to be thinking of it now either. Mrs Cooper was patient, thoughtful and she didn't try to push her into making any decisions she wasn't ready to make, Alex made an appointment to see her the next day, it was time to face up to her circumstances. The call ended and Alex took a deep breath, Mrs Cooper had been extremely kind.

She made her way to the lounge to tell Jack the outcome of her phone calls. Before she made it into the room she heard a man's voice that didn't belong to Jack, she hadn't heard anyone come in, she pushed her ear up against the door to try to hear who it was without interrupting them, she wasn't in the mood to be sociable unless it was with her Nan or Jack.

"Who are you?" She heard Jack ask firmly.

"Your worst nightmare Jack." The voice replied. "You got Lily back didn't you?"

"Oh, you're Tom, I recognise you now, so you're finally brave enough to show your face then, it was you that has caused all of the trouble, you have my money now so why don't you just get lost." Jack was bluffing, Alex wondered if he knew the money had been returned yet.

"Oh no Jack, I want much more than your money, I want the same in return as you took from me, I thought I could walk away but I need to finish this." He said.

"I don't know what you're talking about, I've not taken anything from you, I don't even know you."

Alex stayed behind the door, from the sound of Jack's voice he had it all under control, but she wanted to be sure, if it was Tom, the police needed to know, she reached into her pocket for her phone, she couldn't risk making a call but she tapped out a text message and sent it to Dan, flicked her phone to silent and slid it back in her pocket. She turned her ear back to the door and just caught Jack saying something about recognising Tom from the tunnel; that made Tom laugh. "Yes your precious community. They do look up to you there don't they…" He paused. "But they don't know what you're really like do they Jack!" He spat the last of the words out.

"I'm sorry to disappoint you Tom, but I don't have a clue what you're talking about or why you have this opinion of me. If you don't leave now I'll call the police. Now get lost!" Jack was suddenly sounding under pressure, Alex didn't know if she should intervene but she hesitated and held back, it seemed that Tom hadn't finished telling Jack what he thought of him yet. Her phone vibrated in her pocket she pulled it out and glanced down at it, Dan, she couldn't answer it but at least she knew he had received her message.

"Did losing Lily on your wedding day hurt, Jack?"

"Of course it did, why would you do that?"

"She's a good girl isn't she." The way he said it made Alex's skin crawl. "I wanted to hurt you Jack, really hurt you just the way you hurt me. I've lost my wife and family now but at least I made you suffer. I'd have liked to make you suffer a lot more too." Alex wondered if he was mentally stable, he sounded like he was beginning to rant.

"Seriousiy! Is that what all of this is about, you just wanted to hurt me?" Silence. "What did I ever do to you to make you feel like this Tom?" Jack sounded like he was back in control again.

"You really don't know who I am do you?"

"Sorry Tom, not a clue. Now I think you should leave, just go!"

"Think back Jack, think back to 1979, do you remember a party you had to travel to, as I recall you didn't get out very often so I should imagine it would be easy for you to remember that occasion. The journey alone would have been memorable." Tom's voice sounded almost smug. It was followed by nothing, the silence drew out for so long that Alex thought she should go into the lounge just to check that everything was okay, but she wanted to understand, to know, what was going on. Then Jack's voice cut into the quiet. "Thomas... that Thomas... but you were just a child... I think I'm beginning to understand." There was another pause, Alex wished she understood because she still had no idea what was going on. "You were in the car when your Dad drove us up to York. You do know that what happened to your Dad was of his own doing, he made me believe it was my fault but he was trying to control me, he brought it all on himself Tom."

"That's lies and you know it! He always used to disappear off to see you and leave us alone." Tom was beginning to sound angry now.

"No Tom I'm not lying, he was responsible, although I was sorry that he died the way he did... he wanted a life like mine, he could have had it too, but he chose not to. He was jealous of the way I lived because he hadn't been brave enough to stay with the community. Your Dad was like a brother to me Tom, we had been friends since before I first left home. I never wanted to believe that Peter would try to control me, I thought he was the best friend in the world and do you know, I think at first he really was. Then he murdered my brother and let me believe it was me that had done it for all of those years. Peter used it to control me Tom." Jack paused. "I trusted him with my life, I believed that he only ever wanted the best for me. I always knew he had wanted to come and live in the tunnels that we had discovered together but he chose a normal life, a life with love and a family... You were his choice. Only it was never enough for him."

"Tell it any way that makes you feel better Jack, he was my father and you took him from me, I hate you for that."

Alex was dumbfounded, then she heard a crash and breaking glass, she pushed the door open and went into the lounge at full speed. Tom was standing over Jack, who had fallen to the floor, knocking a vase of flowers over as he fell. Tom's hand went to his pocket and in a split second Alex saw the light glint off the blade that he was withdrawing from his pocket, she launched herself at him, taking him by surprise as she thudded into his back and made a grab for the knife. She missed, he moved too quickly, he spun around to face her and smiled. "Oh... the journalist... you really should have stayed out of this Alex." He was breathing heavily.

"Give me the knife!" She demanded. He raised the hand that wasn't holding the knife and swung his fist towards her, the force of the blow sent her reeling sideward as he caught the side of her face. She immediately regained her balance and flew back at him again, doing anything to keep him away from Jack, who was still lying on the floor. She lunged at the hand that was holding the knife and found it this time, grabbing him by the wrist and smashing it against the side of the table, the knife flew out of his hand. "If you've hurt him I'll..." Suddenly she was aware of being pulled backwards, she struggled, there were hands on her, holding her tight as Dan appeared into her vision and grabbed Tom in the same manner, she noted a lot of uniforms around her. Once he had a tight hold on Tom he looked over to Alex. "You're going to have a real shiner of a black eye tomorrow." He smiled at her, winked and she relaxed a little. There was already a paramedic attending to Jack, he was sitting up now, on the floor, with his back to the settee, there was a dribble of blood on his hand and thankfully apart from that he looked okay, just shaken.

Dan looked at the paramedic. "Can you look her over too, that eye looks nasty." The paramedic nodded and carried on seeing to Jack who was now refusing to go anywhere near the hospital, he bandaged Jack's hand and was happy to leave him to recover in peace. He looked at Alex's eye and smiled. "I think you'll live, wonder woman."

Just as all of this was happening her Nan chose that moment to return from her shopping trip and wondered what on earth had been going on, panicking she went immediately to Jack's side. Dan bagged the knife, cuffed Tom and took him away for questioning as soon as he was happy that everyone was okay. Mary was assured that Jack was going to be okay but she sat with him for a while before she was happy to go into the kitchen and put on a pot of coffee. Alex tidied the lounge and made sure everything was as it should be and threw away the broken vase. Jack sat in his chair, still a little stunned by what had gone on but very obviously relieved now it was all over. Mary appeared in the lounge a few minutes later with coffee and cake, they sat together and explained to her everything that had happened and who it was that had caused all the trauma.

Chapter Fifty Seven

After all the excitement of the day Alex was glad to get home, she had one thing left to do, a promise that she planned to keep. She poured herself a glass of wine from a chilled bottle in the fridge and settled herself on the settee as she picked up her phone and rang the hospital. They put her through to Beth straight away. She sounded a lot more cheerful than Alex thought she ever could, Alex admitted to knowing her story, adding that she had made Cathy tell her because she couldn't face being at the hospital, they chatted for a while and Beth seemed genuinely happy to have heard from her. She was hoping to be out of the hospital in a couple of days and they made plans to meet up. The call had cheered Alex up too, good things were starting to happen and right now she needed to focus on that. She drained her glass and decided to have just one more before she went to bed, she thought she deserved it after her tussle with Tom earlier. She turned the television on just so she would have some noise in the house, the hum of voices was soothing, it felt like company, it was far too quiet in the house when she was on her own. She stopped to look at the painting of Buddha mountain, that had ended up giving her some of the most memorable times she had had with Matt, she was glad they had shared that time together, it had been magical. It also reminded her that she still hadn't replied to the email from Pet about returning to Thailand, maybe it would be good for her to get away soon.

Many tears and another glass of wine later Alex made her way into the kitchen, the screwed up job offer sitting on the floor by the side of the bin was still calling to her, but for now she ignored the call of it, because the box on the table was calling her too, she had cried enough tonight already, the box would have to keep until tomorrow. She knew she was employing avoidance tactics but clearing the box would make it all too real and she wasn't ready for that yet. She finished her wine, leaving her glass on the kitchen counter she went to bed.

Alex slept fitfully and woke up with a headache, dreading the day ahead, there was too much to do and her face was sore this morning, all she wanted to achieve was getting through the day. Her thoughts were tumbling over each other and everything seemed daunting but she took a deep breath and swung herself out of bed, her feet landing on the sheepskin rug that her mum had bought for her many years previously, for a moment she marvelled that amongst all of the turmoil in her life how comforting it felt against her skin. Then a thought crashed in that everything felt the same but Matt would never feel that comfort again, ever. She looked across the bed to where he should have been, now there was nothing. She robotically got herself ready for the day ahead, checking her eye whilst she was in the bathroom, it was turning yellow, the bruise was starting, she didn't really care. Life would go on whether she was ready for it or not, so she may as well get on with it.

She was in the kitchen, tidying up and making coffee when there was a knock at the door, it was Dan, he must be checking up on her again. She opened the door and gestured for him to come in. "Good morning." He said carefully, as if he was testing the waters of her mood.

"Hmmm…" She murmured. "Coffee?"

250

"Please." He brightened. "Are you okay?" He asked as he followed Alex through into the kitchen, he noticed that the box was still in the same place as he had left it, untouched.

"Yes, I guess..." She stopped and thought for a moment. "I don't suppose you're free for the next couple of hours?"

"I can be, what do you need?"

"It's a big ask but I have an appointment at the funeral directors and I'm scared Dan, I have no idea what to expect or what to do."

"Of course I'll come with you, is there anyone else you want there too?"

"No, not if you'll come with me." She shuffled her feet, feeling embarrassed, she wasn't used to asking for help. Normally she was the strong one, the independent one, but she knew she needed help to get through today.

"Your eye looks sore, is it okay?" He asked, changing the subject as if realising that her asking for help was a big deal. "I told the media that they would have to just talk to us at the station yesterday, I didn't think you'd be up for the interview, especially after what you went through with Tom."

"Thanks Dan, I had honestly forgotten about it with everything else but I'm relieved I haven't got to stand in front of cameras and re-live it all. Sorry I've let you down though." She paused then changed the subject. "My eye's okay, I'll put some make up over it before we go." They sat in a companionable silence drinking coffee, lost in their own thoughts for a while before Alex went to sort her face out, Dan waited in the kitchen for her, wondering why she hadn't looked through Matt's things yet, he had expected her to have gone through everything immediately.

Alex came back into the room looking as good as she normally did, Dan smiled at her. "Feel better now?"

"A little, I'll be glad when this meeting is over though." They left the house and Dan drove her to the funeral directors.

Mrs Cooper was a small woman of around fifty years old with a gentle face and a soft voice, she showed them through into her office. Alex had expected old fashioned décor with formal furniture, she hadn't expected modern spotlights, glass coffee tables holding boxes of tissues and low red sofas. She relaxed feeling more comfortable than she would have ever thought. Mrs Cooper explained what would happen and asked Alex if she had any special requirements. Alex had no idea what special requirements anybody would want, she'd never been in a situation like this before. "I'm sorry I don't understand." She muttered.

"It's okay that's what I'm here for. I need instructions on whether Matt would have wanted to be buried or cremated and do you know where?"

"Cremated, I'd like to scatter his ashes myself, maybe keep them for a while, if that's allowed."

"Of course it is, it's up to you. I also need to know what sort of ceremony you would like."

"I don't know." It was all seeming too real now, Alex didn't know how much longer she could hold it together.

"Don't worry, I'll give you some information and you can let us know, also think about music that you would like played, something he would have loved himself."

"Okay. That's less difficult." Alex said in a small voice, Dan held her hand tight.

"You can have tributes and readings too if you would like?"

"I'll take care of the tributes, if you don't mind Alex?" Dan asked. Alex nodded in response she didn't know what else to say. Mrs Cooper smiled at her and reached over to gather some leaflets together, she handed them to Alex.

"It's all a bit overwhelming isn't it? Take a look at these and tell us what you want, we'll do our best to arrange whatever you need." She could see Alex was struggling so she brought the meeting to a close. Dan ushered Alex out of the office and back into the car.

Chapter Fifty Eight

Alex spent the rest of the day at home. After the shock of reality hitting her, she decided it was time she had to stop falling apart and start making some decisions. She ploughed through the paperwork that Mrs Cooper had given her, she knew she needed to toughen up and get things organised, nobody could do this for her. As she looked deeper into the information she started to form a picture of how things would pan out. She would do her very best to give Matt the final goodbye he deserved. She refused to call it a funeral but she could still make the decisions, the more she read the more she had a clear view in her mind of what Matt would have wanted. She phoned his Mum and talked things over then she rang round her own family to get some more input, as the day moved on she came close to having everything decided. Now she just had to put it all in motion and that was where Dan and Mrs Cooper would be a great help.

It was late afternoon when her phone rang, she looked at the caller ID, it was Cathy, Alex was glad of the distraction. She answered the call. "Hi Alex have you heard the news?"

"No, what's happened?"

"The woman is talking." Cathy said.

"Sorry, what woman?" She was momentarily confused and had no idea what Cathy was talking about, her head still full of funeral arrangements, then the penny dropped. "Oh, I'll have to ring Dan, how did you find out?"

"Tina came round a while ago just to check on all of us and let it slip whilst we were chatting."

"Well that's great news. How are you getting on at the flat?"

"I don't like it there but there are no alternatives at the moment."

"I'm sure it'll get better, come over here later if you need to get out for a while, I'd like the company." Alex said, immediately wishing she hadn't, not because she didn't want Cathy there, but she didn't want to inflict her sadness and moods onto anyone else.

"I'd love that." Cathy answered. Alex's heart sank, now she had to entertain. On the other hand she thought it might just do her good, she would have less time to wallow. Alex gave Cathy her address and they said their goodbyes.

Alex immediately phoned Dan to get the update on the woman who had collected the money and tried to drown Jack. "You know I can't tell you Alex." That was the standard reply she always expected, then he surprised her. "But I suppose after everything you've been through and you are Jack's family after all." He paused. "Her name is Patricia Jacobs, Tom's wife. She didn't have anything to do with the abduction but she got involved afterwards because, she says Tom didn't know what to do with the child. She's a nurse so had access to drugs that would keep Lily asleep, she said she used Propofol. She was careful and took care of Lily as well as she could. She picked the money up because she knew everyone would be waiting for Tom, no one would be expecting a woman. She was sorry that Jack got hurt, she genuinely didn't mean for that to happen. For what it's worth I believed her."

"Wow all that information from a police officer." Alex said smiling.

"Don't ask me to repeat it all, please." He was relieved that Alex finally sounded interested.

"Why didn't she just go to the police straight away, did they really think they could get away with it?"

"She wanted to help her husband. Not a great reason but understandable in some twisted way I suppose, she told us everything when she knew we had discovered her name and that we had Tom in custody too."

"So she really thought they could get away with it in the end then?"

"I guess she did."

"Were they in Blunsdon?"

"Yes, Tom had a flat there whilst he was checking out the tunnel here."

"So he didn't plan for things to happen this way then?" She mused.

"We don't think so but we need to talk to them both more yet, this won't be over for a while Alex."

"I understand and I'm grateful for you keeping me in the loop, Cathy's coming over later if you want to stop by, there'll be wine." She added.

"I might just do that..." He thought about asking if she'd sorted the box yet but then he thought better of it. "Yes, maybe I will."

There were plenty of phone calls throughout the evening checking on her, when Cathy turned up she had to turn her phone to silent for a while just so that they could talk, they got on well and Alex was shocked at some of the things that had happened to Cathy throughout her young life. Alex was also impressed that she had such a positive outlook on life. Cathy was a survivor.

Dan turned up a little while later and Mel came round to check on Alex because she hadn't been answering her phone. Together they had an easy comfortable evening telling stories about each other and sharing their memories of Matt. They all left at the same time, well after midnight and suddenly where there had been laughter and chatter Alex was now feeling the cold sting of loneliness.

This was the way Alex's life went for the next few days, gatherings of friends to keep her spirits up followed by times when she felt totally alone, she knew she needed to get life on a more even keel. She had found the strength to organise the celebration of Matt's life and Matt's mum, Jack and her Nan had taken over sorting all of the things out that she didn't feel strong enough to face up to. The days ticked by and still the box sat on the kitchen table untouched.

Cathy was becoming quite a feature in her life, she was tough and was good at cheering Alex up when no one else could, she accompanied Alex when she went to the funeral parlour to see Matt, Cathy had even stopped over a couple of nights in the spare room just so she wouldn't feel so alone. Alex had met up with the other women, she had also managed to go and visit Beth in hospital. Beth had hoped that she would have been out sooner but the hospital didn't think she was quite ready yet, but she was being well looked after and was looking so much healthier now.

Chapter Fifty Nine

Finally Alex turned her attention to the box, she had lived her life ignoring it for the past week and now everything was organised and there was nothing else to think about except for getting through Matt's day. However much she tried, the word funeral couldn't attach itself to her vocabulary. Now she felt like the time was right to tackle whatever the box held, she knew it would be work stuff but it still felt strange going through the things that only Matt would have handled and the few things he thought were important enough to have around him at work. She knew there wouldn't be much, Matt had always liked to work with no distractions, he had always said that was why he didn't have much personal stuff in his office. She pulled off a length of brown packing tape that held it closed and pulled the top open, on top was the photo he had taken from the house, it was of the day they had reunited Lily with her mum, happy smiling faces looked back at her. There were a couple of notebooks and a police awareness t-shirt that he would wear when he went around local schools to talk to the children. Alex picked it up and put it to her face trying to smell his fragrance but it was clean and fresh, there was no sign of Matt on it. There was more paperwork, that looked official, she would have to go through that later it looked like rules and regulations, underneath that was an envelope with her name on, not a formal letter it just said 'Alex' on the envelope. She picked it up and looked at it, her heart quickening, it was his handwriting. She placed it down next to the box and continued looking through what was left, there were a couple of photographs of her which she didn't even know he had. She put them next to the letter, which was just too much of a pull, she picked it up and turned it over in her hands, pushing the box away to give her some space on the table. She peeled it open, slid the paper out and read his last words to her.

Alex,

I hope you never read this letter but if you are holding it in your hands now then something serious has happened to me. There is always a chance of that in this job.
I imagine you sitting at the kitchen table reading this, looking solemn and having a cup of your favourite coffee to hand. Try not to be too sad, what we had was amazing, we were happy and most people never find that level of togetherness, please be glad for that Alex. I don't have the luxury of knowing if we had enough time to be married, if we're not I need you to know that it was the one thing I wanted more than anything, since the first day I met you in the station, when I kept you waiting because you were just another journalist taking up my time. I fell for you there and then and from the look in your eyes I'd like to believe you felt the same. We had a lot to thank Jack for, if he hadn't had his heart broken, the tunnel would never have been there and you may never have come to see me.
We got there though didn't we and had some great times, remember Thailand? You

*running over there to chase down Michael,
me not having a clue where you were, but I'm
a policeman, I tracked you down and it was a
good job I did, you were always getting into
scrapes. I hope you will always remember
those days when you look at your painting.
Then the time you came home in a Rolls
Royce, I was so impressed. They were some
of the best times Alex, we had some fun didn't
we? I was lucky to have met you and I hope I
made you happy too.*

*Don't worry about anything sweetheart,
everything will be taken care of for you, just
say goodbye and move on with your life, I
want you to be happy, with or without me. I
hope you find someone who loves you as
much as I did and that they treat you well.
Just give me a thought sometimes and smile,
I'll be watching over you and if there's a
way, I'll be making sure you stay safe. I love
you Alex, but gladly you knew that, didn't
you. Now I have the luxury of loving you for
eternity.*

*I love you
Forever.*

Matt.

Alex reached for her coffee, he knew her so well. There
were tears rolling down her cheeks but she was strangely
happy at the same time, Suddenly she felt like he was in
the room with her, she felt more peaceful than she had
since all of this had started.

Chapter Sixty

Alex picked up her phone, she wanted to talk to her Nan about the letter, it was the only person she wanted to share it with. As soon as she had mentioned a letter her Nan asked her to go over and see her, she didn't want to discuss it over the phone. Alex turned up at her Nan's to the welcoming smell of baking, it really did seem like life was getting back to normal for everyone. When she arrived Summer, Mark and Lily were already there too, Alex wasn't sure she was ready to discuss things with them but they were her friends and it was lovely that they wanted to support her. They sat around and chatted for a while, Alex got the impression she was missing something, just a feeling. "Where's Jack?" She asked.

"He had to pop into town, he'll be back in a minute." Her Nan replied. They all sat round drinking coffee and eating far too much cake. Alex often wondered how her Nan stayed in such good shape when she was constantly baking cakes, she'd never seen her exercising or mentioning that she was on a diet, Alex could only hope it was in the genes. Lily was looking well and no one would guess the ordeal she had been through, she was chattering away as if nothing had ever happened.

A short while later Jack returned from town, "Well I didn't expect a welcoming committee." He smiled obviously pleased to see the house full and people smiling. He sat down and began to tell them what he had been up to that morning. "Alex, after you phoned your

261

Nan this morning and told her about the letter, I knew I had a job to do today."

"You knew about the letter?" She asked.

"Kind of, but not what he wrote, but I knew some other things." He reached into his pocket and pulled out a small bag and handed it to her.

"What's this?"

"Just open it and take a look." Jack said.

She took the bag from him and pulled out a small purple velvet box from inside, she opened it and it held a beautiful diamond ring. "I don't understand, although thank you and it's so very beautiful."

"No, you don't understand do you?" He stared her in the eye. "Matt had it made for you, he was going to propose, he left it with the jeweller until the time was right. He designed it and chose the stone. He told me about it when he commissioned it earlier this year." He reached out and touched her hand. "Put it on, it was his personal gift to you."

Alex couldn't speak, the tears coursed down her cheeks, this time it was a mixture of happiness and painful memories but she slipped it onto her finger and it fitted perfectly. Matt was still surprising her even though he was no longer here, he truly was watching over her.

That was what got her through the next few days and the funeral, it was a difficult day, one she had been dreading but there were so many friends there that it all seemed alright by the end of the day. There had been a lot of heartfelt tributes which Alex was pleased about because she hadn't been able to speak herself, Matt's mum gave a wonderful insight into him as a boy and managed to make people smile at her memories. Once it was all over she noticed how much her diamond was sparkling as if he really was there with her, letting her know it would all be okay. She thought she was going mad when she caught herself thinking in those terms but it was strangely comforting.

The worst day of her life went by in a blur but her friends had carried her safely through it.

Chapter Sixty One

With the funeral behind her Alex managed to move on through her life, every day becoming a new way of living there was a new routine to adapt to. Matt's mum had returned home soon after the funeral and everyone else had begun to pick up their lives where they left off before Lily had gone missing. Alex knew it was time she returned to work, Charlie had been wonderful throughout the whole case and she wanted to pay him back by writing the story of the girls, she also wanted to talk to him about her job offer, the more she thought about it the more she thought it would be good for her. A fresh start, a new life where memories of Matt couldn't hijack her at every turn and remind her of what she had lost, she felt like she needed that, but by the same measure she wasn't sure she could move away from the comfort of his memories around her. Charlie would have some sensible advice. She finally picked up the screwed up letter and flattened it out, whether she took the job or not it would look great in her CV.

The good news was that Lily had not had any bad side effects from the drugs she had been given aside from wanting to sleep with a light on and she had slipped back into life as usual, she had handled it all so well even the adults couldn't believe her resilience, there had been a subtle change, she was starting to lose her childhood. She seemed a lot more grown up now but that was hardly a surprise after what she had been through.

Dan kept in touch regularly to keep her updated on Tom and Shaun who were both awaiting trial dates, he had assured her that Shaun would be going away for a very long time. Tom would be too but his wife was shattered by what he had put her through, they were hoping for a suspended sentence for her, for now she was in counselling. Alex was now feeling numb to all of them, she knew the system would deal with them.

She put the percolator on and flicked on the radio, the news was on, she was relieved that she was no longer the story that was being focused on, she had finally given the journalists an interview just to get them off her back. She poured herself a fresh cup of coffee as Coldplay came drifting out of the radio, she glanced down at the ring on her finger and was certain that Matt was watching over her.

Acknowledgements

Thank you to everyone who has taken the time to read my novels and get to know Alex. I know how precious your time is and I'm grateful that you have chosen to give me some of yours yet again.

I would also like to thank everyone who helped me along the road to 'After The Light, After The Love' and gave my other books such lovely reviews, making me want to take Alex on another adventure. As always, thank you to my husband who put up with me throughout the whole process, Kirsty Prince for her proofreading, Alysa Blackwood-Bevan for her unfailing support and Trish Cook for medical information. There are many more people involved and I am grateful to every one of you.

If you would like to contact me or leave a review you can use my Facebook page 'SC Richmond' (facebook.com/scrichmond3/)

Or visit my website at https://scrichmondauthor.wixsite.com/mysite

As always I'd love to hear from you.

'The Community'

S.C. Richmond

A mystery and love story that spans fifty years.

Jack still mourns his lost love but now he has more to worry about. His friend has died and Charmsbury's local journalist, Alexandra Price, is getting closer to discovering The Community.

Alex has no idea as to the identity of the woman's body that has been found in the park, but it leads her on a journey of discovering more about her home town than she could ever have imagined.

What connection could an unknown body, an abandoned baby, missing people and a triquetra have? She sets out to find some answers, unaware of how it will affect the people she loves the most.

Available now at all good bookstores.

Reviews included… Brilliant, enchanting, romantic, intriguing and enthralling.

'Pictures of Deceit'

S.C. Richmond

Internationally renowned art dealer, Michael Masters, returns home to Charmsbury with his long awaited 'Starlight' exhibition.

What should have been a relaxing evening turns into a nightmare for Alexandra Price, local journalist, when she appears to have been the last person to have seen Michael Masters before he vanished.

The boundaries of friendship will be pushed to the limits during Alex's foray into the art world. Has she been set up? Or could the body that washes up really be that of the famous art dealer?

Join Alex and her friends on an exciting and perilous chase across the globe to discover the truth.

Available now at all good bookstores.

Reviews include… brilliant, gripping, totally unexpected, intriguing.